MW00816544

# Coming Soon from Marissa Lupe

**STARS LIKE FIRE** -*Spring 2024*
**THE BONE INVENTORY** -*Winter 2024*
**STARS RAIN DOWN** -*Spring 2025*
**NEW SALEM IS COMING FOR YOU** -*Winter 2025*

# Stars Like Acid

MARISSA LUPE

Howlite Publishing LLC

Howlite Publishing LLC
Meeker, CO
United States
marissalupe.com

Stars Like Acid

First Edition, 2023
This is a work of fiction. Names, characters, business, events, and incidents are the products of the author's imagination. Any resemblance to actual persons, living or dead, or actual events is purely coincidental.
eBook ISBN: 978-1-960824-01-1

Paperbook ISBN: 978-1-960824-02-8

Hardback ISBN: 978-1-960824-00-4

Library of Congress Control Number: 2023905848

Fiction/Science Fiction/General
Formatting interior book design and cover art by

Howlite Publishing LLC

For Moms Who Write,
I see you,
You matter,
Keep writing.

To Julia, Amanda, Liahona, Kari...
Without you, I'd lose my words.

Always, my loves-my family, let's go to the place where we
can
see the stars.

# Contents

# Prologue Earth

The destruction of Earth had been centuries in the making, yet it all came down to this moment; this one choice, this one act of violence that would tip the scales too far to be righted.

The blackened streets were slick with rain that reflected against the dark night. The windshield wipers were turned to the highest setting, squeaking with each back and forth as if in protest, as though they would fly away at any moment from the effort. Yet still the car moved on, the streetlights streaking against the windshield like a twisted technicolor rainbow.

Two girls sat in the backseat, wrapped in the pleasant imagination of their minds. They were so close in age that they spoke their own language, one they had created as soon as their mouths could form the words. Inseparable. Seated next to them were their parents, wrapped in a lovers' embrace, the mother's head resting on her husband's chest. They were at peace.

"Madam President, there's a blockade in the road up ahead. We're going to have to turn around." The man in the driver's seat whispered into the cuff on his wrist, as if that could protect the numerous security measures that would ultimately fail them this night.

Their fine car hadn't even completed making its U-turn when a large black SUV slammed into its side. Thunderous clashes of metal against metal bore into the ears of the two girls and they screamed. Roll after roll sent more glass flying, slashing small cuts into their tender flesh.

A large piece of metal hit the side of the older girl's head. Despite the blood gushing from her wound, it wasn't enough to render her unconscious, or to spare her seeing the cold emptiness of her mothers' eyes.

Casualties of war.

If she had lived, if the first female president had prevailed, perhaps humankind could have had a chance. But as the last breath of life escaped her crimson lips, so too died Earth's best hope.

Mercifully, the rapid blood loss finally allowed the older girl to forget this night as she slipped into a dreamlike state.

## Days Later

The heat of the day pressed down on her, an unrelenting and cruel force of power. Overcome with heavy and overwhelming drowsiness, Téa closed her dark brown eyes, attempting to block out the scorching sun. Something was missing, but when she tried to think, the pictures were all jumbled in her mind. Her heart knew that Jefferson Home for Girls was not where she was meant to be. But why couldn't she remember?

A rough shove from behind made her eyes suddenly fly open, pulling her from her thoughts. She fell hard, the sharp pain bringing tears to her eyes, as her knees smacked the ground loudly.

"Mama!" she cried out in fear.

A boy with dark hair and ebony skin laughed at her torment from the other side of the yard, watching as her attacker stepped down hard on her fingers. Téa yelped again in agony. She didn't understand why the home for boys and the home for girls had to share outdoor time. At least the other girls left her alone.

Téa looked up, only able to see the cruel smile in Donny's blue eyes and fair skin as he laughed at her suffering. The blinding sun blocked everything else out. He stepped on her fingers once more before running away with his tow-headed friends.

Téa whimpered and cradled her hands as she stared at the other five-year-olds through bleary eyes. Sniffling, she struggled to stand.

Bartholomew, the boy from the other side of the yard, sidled up next to her and spat by her feet. "You don't belong here," he said meanly.

The playground was a bare concrete square slab outdoors, with no play equipment, not even a ball. Only two sets of bent and splintering picnic tables filled the space. At one table sat the light-skinned children. On the other, the dark-skinned children.

Téa, who was something in between with her light golden skin, had yet to make a single friend. She didn't belong and they reminded her of it every day.

*How many days had she been here?* She squinted her eyes as she looked around. *How did she get here? Where was her family?*

"Lunch break is over!" A voice boomed and crackled from the staticky speakers hanging from each corner of the brick walls.

Téa glanced down at her legs and saw blood running from the cuts. She whimpered but held back the rest of her tears, pushing away the half of her that showed weakness.

"Crybaby!" Donny yelled from across the way as she walked toward the door to line up.

Bartholomew breathed angrily in her face. "Go back where you came from, *rich princess.*"

Téa trembled, her little body shaking. *I want to go home.* But she didn't know where home was.

Her head hurt so much. She could not remember how long the sharp and intense pressure had been squeezing her brain and clouding her mind. When she'd told one of the adults, they reprimanded her for complaining.

The line of girls made their way inside the building, leaving the boys behind. They were brought to the learning room, where the desk chairs were uncomfortable and wobbly. Téa had no pencils or paper. The teacher at the front of the room wrote letters on the chalkboard while the thirty other children recited.

"A"

"B"

"C"

"D"

Téa already knew her alphabet. Somebody kind who smelled like lavender and brushed her fingers through Téa's dark curly hair had spoken them softly to her. The memory, so blurred and fleeting, she couldn't be sure if it was real.

"Téa!"

Her head snapped up. The teacher's nostrils flared as she yelled at Téa. "You will repeat the letters!"

The teacher walked down the aisle toward her, slapping a ruler rhythmically against her hand. She paused at Téa's desk and looked down at her. "Don't make me warn you again."

Téa nodded, her lip quivering.

As the teacher walked away, the little girl with red hair who sat next to Téa whispered, "It's okay," and passed Téa a small slice of bread. "I'm Juliette, what's your name?"

Téa shook her head and clasped her hands in her lap, terrified the teacher would catch her talking. A single tear ran down her nose and she wiped it away with her sleeve.

*Metal against metal clashed so loud it hurt her ears, the sound ricocheted off every surface. She was upside down and glass crunched underneath her. Bright white lights shone in her eyes, and she thought her head might split in half from the pain. Screaming, so much screaming—was it coming from her?*

Shrieking, Téa sat up in the small bed, her feet dangling off the end. The nightmare had her heart racing. She took deep, gasping breaths to try and stop the shaking. There were no nightlights in her room and no windows; so dark that she couldn't even see her hands in front of her face.

She thought of her familiar, warm, silky soft sheets decorated with purple butterflies that had always made her feel safe. Her sheets, her home...why wasn't she there now? The icky thin brown blankets in this place were scratchy against her skin and smelled funny. She clutched at the bedding, and realized it was wet. Her eyes widened and her heart began to race again. She had to clean it up before they found out—

Too late.

"Screaming again!" An adult's voice came along with footsteps that thumped loud against the hard floor, keys jangling against the locked bars. "You're going to wake the whole place!"

A hard white light flooded her small space.

The adult gasped and pulled her thin blanket down further. "You peed the bed again?"

The hard strike across her face stung so badly tears instantly sprang to her eyes.

"You spiteful little girl! You'll sleep in your filth!" the adult scolded as she started to leave. "Let's see if you learn your lesson," she hissed as she locked the bars.

Loneliness tore at Téa's insides.

In the morning, she was seated in the cafeteria about to eat her breakfast of bland oats when the speaker box crackled. "Téa Garcia, report to the Director's office immediately."

Téa stood from the table, heart pounding. She looked for a reason why she could be in trouble. She had been so good the past few days. Followed all the rules, or so she had thought.

Click.

Click.

Click.

Her little shoes tapped against the floor. She wanted to chew on her fingernails, but remembered that meant three hits with the ruler, so she clasped her hands behind her back as she walked. Téa paused in front of the Director's office, took a deep breath, and opened the door.

"Téa, welcome. Have a seat please." The Director's speck-led silver hair was gelled back like an impenetrable helmet of glue. His smile did not reach his dark gaze.

Téa placed a hand on each arm of the big chair and hopped up, wiggling side to side until she was seated firmly. She placed her hands in her lap, just so, and waited quietly.

"You are one lucky girl, Téa." The Director beamed at her with his lying eyes. "You have been selected to participate in a Dunamis outreach program. You have been adopted by Steppe Two. Congratulations."

Téa wanted to smile and shout for joy, but something held her back. Steppe Two did not sound like the name of a person. She knew it meant something that only grown-ups understood and failed to explain properly.

The Director glared at her, waiting for a response. Téa squeaked, "Thank you, Sir."

Pleased with her response, he grinned again before he spoke. "A member of Dunamis will arrive shortly to trans-port you. I expect your best behavior."

"Yes, sir." Téa wanted to cry, but she wasn't sure why, and knew she shouldn't. Instead, she chewed on her cheek to keep the tears away.

Moments of silence passed and then there was a knock at the door.

"Come in," the Director beckoned.

A tall, fit man with brown hair, and a black suit entered the small office. The Director stood to greet him. "Lieu-tenant Hillside, welcome. Can I get you anything?"

Hillside leaned over Téa to shake the Director's hand, and he smelled familiar, like home. She wondered if this man might be taking her to her mom or dad, and hope blossomed in her heart.

"I trust the girl is ready for transport?" Hillside asked.

"Yes, just as requested." Another false smile from the Director, who paused before asking, "I'm curious, why this girl specifically? We have many more *clean* girls that might be better suited."

The tall man in the suit glared at the Director. "Thank you for your assistance. We'll be leaving now."

The Director said nothing more but saluted the man in the suit.

"Come along, Téa." The tall man held out his hand, and she reached for him. Her small fingers fit entirely inside his palm. He was careful not to squeeze too hard when she jumped down from the chair.

He led her away from the prison-like building to where a big black car waited. Téa wanted to look outside during the drive, but the car had darkly tinted windows that were high up, and even stretching as far as she could, she could only peek.

The man in the suit smiled kindly and gave Téa gummy fruit snacks and water. She wanted to be alert so that she would not make any mistakes, but it was so easy to relax against the soft black seats.

He cleared his throat. "Téa. When we arrive at Steppe Two, I will only have a few moments to show you where your room is. Unfortunately, I think it'll be a long time before I see you again." He took a deep breath and Téa's eyes welled; she wanted to stay with the nice man.

He patted her knee gently and continued, "When your alarm clock goes off every morning, leave your room and you'll follow the soldiers to the mess hall. There, you'll eat breakfast and as soon as you finish, follow the hallway with windows to the classroom. When school is over, don't follow the other children, follow the soldiers, and you should be able to find your way back to your room." He took a deep breath and looked at her. "Do you think you can remember all that, Téa?"

She nodded silently.

The man's voice broke when he tried to speak again. He paused and looked away from her. After a few minutes, he glanced back at her with a sad smile. "I wish I could take you away from here."

He was quiet for a moment, then said, "Once you figure out where everything is, try to take your showers after everyone else has gone to sleep. You'll have the women's bathrooms all to yourself; there are no more female soldiers."

Téa did not understand why the man was telling her all of this. Wouldn't the adults tell her what to do? She fidgeted in her seat and had the urge to chew her fingernails again, so she sat on her hands.

They remained in silence for the rest of the trip. She noticed a blinking red light in the display up front, just like the cameras at Jefferson Home for Girls that the director watched, and she wondered if that was why the tall man didn't talk to her more or give her another snack when her tummy rumbled.

She looked up at the sky through the dark window. Occasionally the tops of trees passed swiftly by. Then she saw it.

A bird.

Hope soared in her heart along with it. Its wings gleamed in the sunlight as the bird floated along in the air, moving its glorious feathers up and down through the breeze. Téa smiled and closed her eyes. She imagined she was the bird, flying far, far away from here, as the wind lifted her wings towards the sky.

# Chapter One

# Earth

**Fifteen Years Later**

B ulky, smelly, and sleazy; most of the men on the military base were of similar caliber. The worst of them, Melton Farris, could not seem to leave her alone.

"Hey, where you off to, Nips?" Melton said as he thrust his hips and licked his lips. "Want to stop by the barracks later? I'll make it worth your while."

Téa's skin crawled as she glared at him. She hated that nickname, Nips. Only the most vulgar of the men used it.

Knowing she would never be as big and strong as some of her male counterparts, she had to fight smart. Téa 'borrowed' every book she could that would teach her different hand-to-hand combat techniques and replaced them before anyone noticed they were missing. She broke a soldier's nose in self-defense for the first time at age fourteen, and ribs at fifteen. Now, at twenty years old, she was formidable. Fit, strong, and more cunning than any of them realized. Most of the men had learned to leave her be. Still, there was the handful that kept at it.

"In your dreams, Farris." Face twisted into a snarl, Téa lunged towards him with such ferocity that his back smacked into the middle of the wall behind him. He tried to duck as she punched the air, stopping an inch from his face. "Don't you dare speak to me again." She spat.

Téa clenched her fists as she rounded the corner, wishing they would *all* back off. A quiet hum emanated from the fluorescent lighting. She lengthened her stride and rounded another corner before leaning against the cool white brick wall, took a deep breath, and resisted the impulse to clutch the silver chain around her neck. It hid underneath her shirt and held a simple glittering band.

Even worse than the disgusting men were the ones with a cold gaze and fair complexions who hated her dark curly hair, deep brown eyes, and golden skin. They were the ones who would leave cockroaches in her bed and spit in her food. Then there were the select few who thought they could have their way with her *because* of her defining features. As a result, Téa was always on the defensive, always on edge.

She often thought back to the day she left the orphanage. Too young to remember much of the man who brought her here, but enough to remember a general sense of being cared for. She had a small hope that somewhere, outside the walls of this military base, there were decent men. Men who might even treat her like she were a human worthy of kindness. If only she were allowed to leave, or knew where to go if she did get out.

She continued her way through the long, still corridors. A strong scent of bleach on the concrete floors assaulted her nose. She would give anything to smell a living piece of plant life, like those she had read about. Perhaps lavender or rose, anything fresh and full of life as opposed to the stench of the jail-like barracks.

A bolt of memory shocked her senses, wildflowers, warmth, and thoughts of running free. The image, so clear, as if she were actually there, smelling the sharpness of the grass and feeling the sun on her face. Then the hall lights buzzed her eardrums, and she was back. Shellshocked for only a moment at the impossible image.

The military base was the only home she had ever known. A place where the other occupants were a danger to her small frame. When she was young, jostled around and toes stepped on as she waited in line in the mess hall. Where she learned how to hide, how to sneak extra provisions and bribe the guards. At least those guards, if not kind, were neutral and useful. Too busy looking out for themselves to worry much about her.

Téa rounded the final corner of her walk, and when she arrived at her quarters, she spotted the formal-looking envelope taped to the door. Immediately she took it down and ripped open the flap. She read quickly; she had officially been recruited to Operation Luna. Set to report to Commander Hillside at zero four hundred, for her first assignment.

*Finally.*

She would be granted the official benefits and protection of Dunamis. Until now, she was uncategorized, floating along in an unstable in-between. Not a civilian and not a soldier.

Most new recruits reported to their commanders at zero six hundred. Téa was curious about the early hour being demanded of her. She felt untethered by the break in protocol, suspicious even. She shook off her doubts. This is what she's been waiting, wanting, and dreaming for: freedom.

With her hopes considerably higher than a few minutes ago, she made her way to dinner. Watery imitation beef stew was on the menu for tonight. Téa tried and failed to block out the stares coming from the soldiers. A coldness in her chest wormed its way through her, tugging at all the dark corners of her isolated mind. She swallowed without chewing, trying not to taste the foam-like cubes. If only she could store up enough provisions to avoid the mess hall entirely. Unfortunately, even what she stole was only ever enough to stave off the hunger that clawed at her insides, never extra.

At zero three hundred, the alarm clock sounded to start her day. She pulled on her fatigues, grabbed her toiletry bag, and made her way to the kitchen. Dark and empty, it would be hours before the sun would rise. Only a faint red glow from the emergency lighting accompanied her. Each step echoed on the tile as she walked through the mess hall, the steel and glass food holders were long vacant. She was fortunate to find a couple of packaged saltines next to an empty soup station.

Téa ate the meager ration as she made her way to the washroom. She brushed her teeth, splashed some water on her face, pulled her thick tresses back into a simple bundle, and secured it.

Rested, fed, and ready to go a full thirty minutes before she was set to arrive at headquarters. Téa took her time walking the halls. She was accustomed to being the only soul awake before dawn. The only time she could be at peace. The only way she could avoid the hungry stares that craved more than food.

The base was connected by walkways, designed so its occupants never had to step outside. Leaving the barracks, the building became more sophisticated. The higher-ups dictated more luxury. Marble flooring replaced concrete. Light cedar walls instead of brick. Even soft white lighting poured out from the baseboards illuminating the way, instead of harsh beams falling from above.

Téa stopped in front of double glass doors, frosted for privacy. One guard posted on each side of the entrance, both stood to attention.

*Operation Luna Mission Control*

The words were etched into the wood above the glass entrance.

"Téa Garcia, reporting to Commander Hillside," she spoke.

Being the only female on base was her form of identification, never honored with an actual badge. Silently and stiffly the guard on the left saluted, turned on a heel, and opened one side.

She walked in and almost forgot to hold her composure. She had never been granted access to this room before. An expansive flat rectangle space reached out in front of her, shiny and black. Heavy metal doors lined the sides, which led to unknown places. Above that, stadium-style seating rose all around her.

Dozens of people filled the towering spaces. Each stared at a holographic display directly in front of them, which cast an eerie blue glow against their faces, a stark difference to the shadows that spread into every crevasse.

It reminded her of Mrs. Riss, her holographic teacher. When she was younger, she was deemed 'too dangerous' to be around the other children; they isolated her in a classroom with a clear view of the playground where she could see the other children laughing and playing. Her heart ached as she wished for a friend.

Suddenly, she wasn't so sure if they *were* people. Their movements, or lack thereof, were too robotic. They talked into invisible earpieces, seemingly unaware of her solitary presence. Somehow their voices did not carry, as though their words were being absorbed into whatever device they were speaking. It was unnerving watching so many mouths move without sound, their bodies locked in place apart from the moving wet holes where noise should leave.

She had scarcely walked ten paces when she heard a strong, kind voice come up behind her.

"Téa. Welcome to Operation Luna Mission Control."

The voice sounded familiar, but she could not place it. She turned to find that Commander Hillside had surprisingly friendly eyes. He did not greet her military-style but held his hand out for her to shake, smiling, outfitted in his custom-tailored dress uniform.

She took his hand, feeling the soft yet firm grasp. Téa narrowed her eyes in thought, she wondered if she had met him before.

"Happy to be here, Sir."

"Please, call me Hue."

"Sir?" This was unheard of. No one knew their commanding officers' first name. She looked around her, waiting for an ambush.

"At ease, Ms. Garcia. You have been assigned a unique task, one that can allow lax formalities, if only for a moment." She dropped her shoulders and took a breath. "Now, Ms. Garcia, how much do you know of Operation Luna?"

"Sir! Er... Hue. Operation Luna started twenty years ago. The active build and improvement of a space station adjacent to the moon. Meant to be a small-scale replica of our Earth and the last hope for Mankind. Where we are now is what remains of the state of Virginia. Main base, Sir, codename 'Steppe Two'. Where all duties assigned directly benefit the progress of life on Space Station Luna. Operation Luna is military knowledge only."

"Very good Ms. Garcia. And what of the Connex-A gene?" Hillside narrowed his gaze and tilted his head, waiting expectantly.

"Sir, assuming it to be top-level security clearance. I have overheard the term only once in medical, and without details." Unease settled in her belly. Téa was not sure if she should have mentioned ever hearing the term. She shifted her weight back and forth on her feet before reminding herself to hold still.

Hue nodded, seemingly satisfied with her answer. "Very well, Ms. Garcia. You will never mention to anyone that I posed this question to you, understood?"

Doubt flashed through her mind, but now was not the time to question authority. "Understood sir, Hue." Téa stood in uncomfortable silence for a beat before she asked. "What happens now?"

She watched him as he shuffled his feet and wrung his hands, as though he was unsure of how much to say. Odd for a man of his rank.

"You are aware Ms. Garcia, of the Worldwide Re-population Act, yes?" he asked.

The law was enacted the same year as Operation Luna and applied to all civilians. With diminished planet-wide resources, the population had to be kept to strict minimums. Mankind also needed to thrive.

"I am aware Sir; I haven't given it much thought as I do not plan on having children."

The humans blessed with the healthiest genes were selected to be allowed one child. Research began to isolate the most desired genetic traits and matched opposite-sex partners by way of the Worldwide Re-population Act. Uncontrolled partnering and breeding were outlawed. Same-sex couples were punishable by death, a Dunamis precaution in case the individuals' genes were found to be of value. Dunamis could not risk allowing its assets to be consumed by disease or desire. All civilians were required to be tested, and if selected, forced into arranged marriages to produce their one child, using forceful IVF when necessary. After the enactment of the WWRPA, suicides rates soared. Civilians who refused to cooperate with the Act were considered a risk for self-harm and were imprisoned and confined until it was time to procreate.

Soldiers were exempt. However, they could choose to be tested and matched. Even in her isolation, Téa knew the laws of Dunamis better than most. She was terrified of making any error, for fear of being imprisoned or sent to the outside with no resources.

There was a sadness in Commander Hillside's eyes. "Unfortunately, Ms. Garcia, you have already been tested during your last physical and matched with a fellow soldier. Your status as an orphan, adopted by the state, has left you without exempt status."

# Chapter Two

## Earth

The air in Téa's lungs seized. A chill ran from the tip of her forehead to the bottom of her toes. The room spun. She grappled for something to hold onto.

"I've got you... Téa." Hue whispered, "I understand what this must mean to you. I opposed this decision as much as I was able, but I was overruled."

She could hardly hear the words coming from this stranger holding her. Why had he advocated for her? None of it made sense. She would not be forced into marriage. Not after all these years fighting for herself. How could they take what little freedom she had, away so easily? Nauseated, and stomach-turning, she wobbled. Téa started lowering herself to the ground, but Hue pulled her back to her feet.

"Listen, Téa," he said firmly. "I know this is a lot to handle. But this will be our one and only visit to speak freely. It is imperative to your survival that you accept this. Your match is a man only two years your senior. He is a high-ranking officer, the son of a General. This is the best possible match you could have ever hoped for. You will be allowed one year to train together."

The world tilted. Hue grabbed Téa tighter and spoke more urgently in her ear.

"During this time, you will be preparing for a top-secret mission, assigned to you alone. You will not be informed of this mission until your one-year training is complete. You will not speak of this mission to anyone. Only after the successful completion will you then be forced to marry and have your child. Do you understand everything I have just told you?"

She thought she understood, but most of the words were like water slipping across stone, a blur.

"Miss Garcia, your match will be here in less than fifteen minutes to be introduced to you. It took a great deal of planning for me to have this time with you beforehand. Surely you noticed the unorthodox hour. I'll say again, do you understand everything I have told you?"

Slowly she nodded. She looked him in his eyes. How odd to still see kindness and now sympathy from the man who just executed her death.

"Yes, Hue, I understand," she said somberly.

Hue Hillside took a deep breath, relaxed his grip on her arms and held her shoulders a bit more gently. "I am sorry Téa, but this was the only way. You will at least have your

22

year to prepare. When Lieutenant Strauss arrives, you will resume to address me as Sir, is that understood?"

"Yes, I understand."

"And you will not disclose the nature of our conversation today. Only that I introduced myself, and that I had the great privilege of informing you of being matched. Is that also understood?"

Téa nodded, acknowledging that she understood. Sludge held her jaw closed; so many questions caught behind her teeth. Her brain had forgotten how to speak. Sensing the importance of what Commander Hillside was trying to impart on her, she tried to pull herself together.

How long had she been here? There couldn't be much time left. "Sir... why me?" She knew it was wrong to say out loud, but something told her Hue would not reprimand her for asking defiant questions.

He shook his head and released a defeated sigh. "In short, because you are female." He looked trapped. Like a well that wanted to overflow but someone kept digging out the bottom.

She risked one last question. "Why are you being so kind? Why try to prepare me for the inevitable?"

Hue sighed and smiled. "Miss Garcia, I am aware that you have known little grace in your life. If you learn anything from this, learn that there is still good to be found in this world."

Hue's demeanor changed and he straightened. "I am assigned to be your mentor. Your arranged marriage match will be your training partner, Lieutenant Strauss. You will have monthly one-hour sessions with me. *Documented.*

During these sessions, we will go over your progress and discuss any troubles you may be having."

Téa made a mental note that Hue pointed out the sessions would be documented. She must not show Dunamis any sign of weakness. She knew the soldiers who failed their training did not go home.

It was mere seconds, too soon, when she heard distinct heavy footfalls echo from the far end opposite them. Hue took a step away and stood to attention.

The man that walked towards them was different from the comrades familiar to her. He was muscular without the bulk. Tall, but not so much that she felt small. Strong lines shaped his clean face. Dark gray eyes that had her gravitating towards him. She had never seen this man on base before. She would have remembered. He wore a light brown vest with a midnight blue tie, and underneath that was a stark-white collared button-down that hugged his solid arms.

"Commander Hillside. At ease," said the Lieutenant-General. "Thank you for greeting Ms. Garcia this morning. I trust you had enough time to explain your mentorship, as per your request?" His voice was sure and clear.

"Yes, Lieutenant General Strauss."

Hillside was at least two decades older, yet Strauss held himself in a refined manner that made it obvious Hue was the beta of the two, in more than just rank. Strauss was not even in uniform, and he exuded respect. "I'll take it from here then, Commander. Dismissed."

Hue saluted the younger man and exited the space.

"Shall we, Ms. Garcia?" He offered her his right arm with his elbow bent. She instinctively moved her hand under his arm and let him lead the way, all the while trying not to shake.

They walked half the length of the long black floor when Strauss faced left and stopped. It was the largest metal door in the room. He punched six numbers on a keypad to the right. A green light appeared overhead with a beep and click. The heavy plate swung out accompanied by a sucking noise, letting out a gust of moist air.

Blinding white light enveloped Téa as they entered. She no longer stood on a firm floor; it was spongy underfoot. Téa struggled to adjust. When the room came into focus... she was sure the Lieutenant had brought her to a different planet entirely. She gasped.

"Welcome, Téa, to Genesis."

Green. It was all green. She had never seen so much life before. They were inside an atrium, at least sixty feet high and eighty feet across. Every inch filled with more vegetation than she could have ever hoped to see in her lifetime. She'd only ever read about atriums like the one she stood in, and to see it in person was just as breathtaking as she imagined.

"What do you think, Ms. Garcia?" he asked, smiling with a face full of perfect teeth.

She looked up, unsure what kind of trickery this was. When she realized he needed an answer, she replied truthfully. "I did not think places like this were still possible. Is it all real?"

He nodded and led her further into the space. "It is more real than you or I could ever wish to be. 'Genesis' is the most important room on this whole quarter of the continent." He was quiet for a moment before he continued. "If I may be honest with you, Téa. My desire was to make a good impression. I suspect Commander Hillside disclosed the purpose of our meeting today. He requested to inform you personally, presumably to ensure confidence during your future mentor sessions. I want you to know that, despite the circumstances of our arrangement, I do intend to be a good partner to you on and off the battlefield. I hope you will give me a chance to treat you well."

Téa had never experienced so much heat and pressure moving through her body. This morning was not going at all how she had prepared for.

"Sir, may I please sit down?" She did not know how much longer her legs would hold her up.

"Of course. And please, call me, Zephyr. No matter who is present, you and I are the most important people to each other now. Do you understand?" His tone of voice was kind, but still, he was giving her a command.

"Yes, Zephyr, I understand." She sat on a black curved bench that he guided her to, as she tried not to fall over. After taking a few breaths she spoke without looking at him. "Commander Hillside did inform me that you and I have been matched. That he would be my mentor."

Finally, the pressure eased, and she raised her shoulders to look at him. Zephyr had moved to sit beside her, and she realized he was holding both her hands. A tingling sensation spread through her limbs and she tried not to look away when he addressed her.

"Yes, you are my match Téa... Do you know who I am, outside of my name and rank?"

She shook her head once, and he explained almost direly. "I am the son of General Thomas Strauss. He is in control of the North American Continent."

He paused again, waiting for a reaction. She wasn't sure how she was supposed to take this news. Did he expect her to be happy about being forced into a powerful family? She had heard rumors about the General that had kept her up at night. Was he trying to intimidate her? She held her tongue and listened as he continued.

"When the military took control from the heads of state; Steppe Two became central command. As the world died, the center of the continent lost its natural vegetation. Flooding waters receded; the coastlines were re-formed. The Far South, and the Greater North are diminished but still habitable. Dunamis preserved this space and it's the only reason the immediate surrounding area can survive. We are the remaining majority of what was once The United States of America with the North and South parts of this continent now one nation known simply as, 'Dunamis'. Other continents did not fare nearly as well. We are the greatest hope humanity has left."

She was so young when the Decline was happening. She didn't know firsthand about what used to be. Her education was isolated, and her world experience non-existent. What he was saying to her did not have the impact she sensed he was expecting. He watched her and understanding seemed to dawn on him. Slowly he continued.

"Téa, I am second in command to my father. He has determined that it is time for our family legacy to expand. As such you and I will be married and produce a child. I am to take his place someday." He nodded pointedly towards her waiting for some type of response, but Téa was frozen.

It didn't matter if her future husband was going to be a leader of a nation someday. Téa knew once a woman was married, she became property and the wives of the upper military were for show, like dogs paraded around an arena. Not to speak or have an opinion, but to stand by her husbands' side, invariably the picture of perfection. She despised the idea of being cookie cutter perfect, traipsing around the world, following this man like an obedient puppy. She would rather not be married at all. But, considering she did not have a choice, staying home, out of the limelight, sounded like a much better option. She wanted to ask, 'Why me?' Surely there was a daughter of some other lieutenant out there who has experience in this bureaucracy? Someone else with desired genetic traits.

But she knew she could be shot on site by this stranger for questioning. This person of power, who no matter their compatibility, would consider her expendable, and it didn't matter if he held himself in a welcoming and gentle manner, she'd heard what happened to women who assumed their husbands were understanding underneath their façade.

Téa gathered what bravery she could muster; this might be her only chance to ask questions. She took a deep breath and said, "I understand, but is it not typically the wife's duty to take care of the home?" Hoping maybe he would change his mind about having her glued to him.

He smiled when he looked at her, "Téa, I wish for us to be more than the traditional husband and wife. Allies even. I want to know you, and for you to know me. I wish for us to be equals. I have read your file, and your world experience due to no fault of your own, is lacking. However, your combat results have exceeded expectations, and your self-defense testing is impressive. You are smart, Téa, and together we will be more powerful than any one human has ever been. We can ensure Operation Luna succeeds, and that the world survives."

She knew she should say something, but her throat did not seem to have any air left and her jaw was locked in place. Téa also noticed he did not say anything about a top-secret mission, and no mention of a Connex-A gene. She was sure it had something to do with why she was being assigned to such an important man, but Zephyr did not hint at anything deeper in their connection other than desirable DNA compatibility.

Zephyr released her hands, placed his palm on her back, and helped her to stand upright. "Why don't we go get you settled into your new home? Are there any belongings you would like to retrieve?"

She shook her head and managed to croak out a few words, "No, there's nothing."

# Chapter Three

# Space Station Luna

Annabelle's heart raced as she ran through the stark white corridors. Each footstep was quick and light as she hurried along the clear floors, graceful machinery like the inner workings of a clock hummed below the transparent polycarbonate keeping all three-hundred and forty-two souls that lived on board alive. Her digital watch continued to flash red, urging her to move faster. She rounded the last corner, a hand on the wall for stability, as she spun herself into the plant nursery, her straight black hair cascaded around her shoulders as she came to a sudden halt.

The sound of her own breathing was heavy in her ears as she looked around the room for the source of distress. There. A pulsating red light above one of the many glass boxes containing growing greenery. She rushed to the source of trouble and reset the soundless alarm, then began her diagnosis.

"What's the problem here, Stanley?" Annabelle muttered to herself as she spoke to the ginger plant growing there. Ian always made fun of her for naming the various plants, but they were her babies. She grew them from seed, nurturing and protecting them. Besides, the more she loved the flora the better they grew, and that benefited everyone.

"You can't die on me now, Stanley. You've got three pregnant ladies counting on you to help their nausea." She whispered again as her dark brown eyes and slender fingers continued to hunt for the source of the problem. "Ah, here we are, you've lost your water supply." She spoke to herself as she reconnected a small plastic tube that funneled water to the foliage.

"There, all better." She said to herself as she smiled and placed her hands on her hips. A knock on the doorway behind her drew her attention.

"Everything okay in here?" Ian's tall muscular frame and bright eyes crinkled at the corner as he smiled at her.

"Of course." Annabelle spoke, "Nothing I can't handle." She winked and grinned.

Ian's voice was deep but clear, "So, what's on the agenda for today?" He asked as he shoved his hands in his pockets and followed Annabelle away from the greenhouse.

"Sorry, Ian-" She half twirled towards him as they walked while clasping her hands behind her back with a mischievous smile curled on her lips. "I have a date."

Ian raised one eyebrow, "Oh really?" He tilted his head towards her, "Does she have a friend? Maybe we can double?"

Annabelle squinted her eyes at him and grinned. "You would seriously date any adult human, wouldn't you?"

Ian placed two fingers over his heart, "I refuse to acknowledge that." He laughed, "Besides, I can't help it, I like people." He shrugged.

Annabelle chuckled, "Well sorry, *bruh*. This is a solo mission."

"I really hate it when you call me that." He shook his head, "You see one 90's movie and suddenly it's all, *bruh* this, and *aiight* that." He sighed, "Just call me your brother and say alright.

Annabelle's smile dropped slightly, suddenly thinking of the dreams she had nearly every night. About the family that she was not sure even existed. She could never see their faces, but she felt their love. She wished more than anything that they were real. A majority of the second generation were orphans and there were so many who could understand her longings, yet she could never bring herself to confide in her friends or the people who raised her. Something about her dream family seemed like found treasure, something worthy of protecting, something that was only hers.

She shook her head free of her thoughts and spoke just above a whisper with her eyes downcast. "But you're not my brother, Ian."

Ian stopped, gently but firmly grabbed hold of Annabelle's shoulders, and looked her in the eyes, "Hey, since when has blood ever mattered between us?" He let go of her and asked softly, "What's up, Belle?"

She shook off the faint cloud that had dropped on her and smiled warmly, "Nothing. You're totally right, *bruh*." Annabelle said as she laughed and nudged his shoulder with hers. Ian shook his head and chuckled.

Annabelle groaned in frustration as she tossed the fourth ensemble to the floor of her living quarters. It didn't seem to matter how many clothes she tried on, nothing felt right. She flung herself onto her bed with a defeated sigh. *Ugh, why is fashion so hard?*

A knock on her door sent Annabelle scrambling, "Who is it?" She hollered as she hurriedly scooped up handfuls of garments off the ground.

"It's me, Sawyer. Are we still on for tonight?" A questioning voice drifted through the closed door.

Annabelle shoved an armful of clothes into her closet and slid it shut. Sure, the General could hardly send up the estrogen pills, fever reducers, and morphine that Luna so desperately needed, but clothes, there was an abundance. When over half the world's population depleted so quickly all those years ago, single use items became hard to find and produce, but *stuff*, they were swimming in it. She paused and looked down. *Pick something already.* She was only wearing her bra and undies.

"Ah, yeah, of course, absolutely! Just one second." She shouted in response as she frantically looked around for something to wear. She shoved on a fuzzy blue sweater hanging on the back of her desk chair and a pair of black skinny jeans from underneath her bed, quickly tied her hair up into a ponytail, and shoved her bare feet into a pair of tan ankle-high boots.

Annabelle brushed a stray lock of hair behind her ear, took a deep breath, then smiled as she opened the door.

"HI!" Annabelle said, a little too loudly and enthusiastically, pink flooded her cheeks.

"Hey," Sawyer said coolly as she leaned against the door frame, arms crossed and smiling. "Are you ready?"

"Yep!" Annabelle let out a nervous laugh, "Absolutely." Smiling as she closed the door behind her.

Annabelle followed Sawyer in silence through the white hallways before finally asking, "So where are we going?"

"It's a surprise," Sawyer said with a sly smile.

"Oh, I love surprises!" Annabelle said with a skip in her step.

Sawyer led Annabelle to an empty observation deck, where a single round table and two chairs stood. The table had been covered in shimmery gray linen and a single lit candle was placed in the center. Two silver plates with artistically placed food were still steaming.

"I know how much you love this spot, so I thought we could have dinner with a view." Sawyer gestured to the great expanse of stars before them, where they could view the Earth and the Moon equally, something Annabelle would never tire of. The twinkling noiseless song of glitter light danced against the blackness for their eyes to drink in. Sawyer pulled out a seat for Annabelle and she sat down.

Annabelle's heart beat rapidly as she waited for Sawyer to sit down, and she wondered if Sawyer could hear her racing pulse. She could smell the aloe vera lotion on Sawyer's skin as she leaned over to help scoot Annabelle's chair in. She could see the gleam in Sawyer's eye as Sawyer looked at her so lovingly.

This was only their third date and it seemed so... *intimate.* Annabelle was definitely attracted to Sawyer, but she wondered if things were moving too fast. Annabelle was very much a spur-of-the-moment type of person, and this date seemed so *planned,* so *adult.* Although, she supposed she was an adult now, even if she didn't always feel it. Their very small age gap suddenly seemed so big.

"Hello?" Sawyer quietly said as she slowly waved a hand in front of Annabelle's face with a chuckle and a smile. "You still with me?"

Annabelle forced herself to focus on Sawyer instead of her drifting thoughts, "Uh, yeah-yes! It's beautiful, I love it." She grinned and reached for Sawyer's hand across the table.

"I hope you like peppers," Sawyer spoke. "I made a spicy cauliflower hash with smoked salmon." She smiled and scooped up a forkful of food.

"I do!" Annabelle said excitedly, then looked at her plate and tried to keep her face from betraying her. "It smells delicious," Annabelle lied as she grinned. Annabelle wondered if Sawyer would notice if she picked around the peppers. The only peppers she liked had heat, like jalapenos. Green, red, yellow, orange, no matter the color, bell peppers with no spice, no heat, seemed like a waste to Annabelle.

*Why didn't you just tell her the truth?* Annabelle wondered to herself as she chewed. *It's not like we are supposed to know everything about each other right away.* Annabelle looked up into Sawyer's dazzling green eyes and short red hair, and her stomach did a somersault. *Ah, right, that's why.* Annabelle's face flushed again and she gulped down some water.

"So, how's the greenhouse doing?" Sawyer asked.

Annabelle perked up in excitement. *Plants I can do.* "Oh, it's awesome! I finally got some cross germination to happen between a subspecies of calendula and daisy, I think it might help with-"

"Skin inflammation." They both said at the same time.

They smiled at each other. *I love that about her.* The way Annabelle's interest in breeding medicinal plants, blended with Sawyer's medical knowledge, made Annabelle feel all warm and tingly on the inside.

"And I have a new batch of ginger root for-"

"Nausea." They said, again at the same time.

"Yes!" Annabelle said excitedly.

"Edward, you know the ob-gyn, is going to be thrilled."

Annabelle grinned again before saying, "And the elder-flowers and yarrow are thriving, it'll help so much with our fever reducer supply. I know the last delivery had almost no acetaminophen."

Sawyer glanced up from her plate. "How'd you know about that?"

Annabelle swallowed a bite of food and shrugged. "Heard it in passing."

"Hmm." Was Sawyer's only reply as she continued to eat her food.

*Careful, Annabelle, too much too soon.* Annabelle had been sneaking into the surveillance room a bit too often lately, she was sure to be caught if she wasn't more careful. But any chance to see life on earth pulled at her. It was addicting watching how the other half lived. So unaware as they went on with their day-to-day routines, succumbing to the hands they had been dealt.

Plus, there was *her*. Annabelle couldn't help but take any chance to watch her. To witness her strength, her resilience. Annabelle would give anything to be just like her. To meet her. To save her. To save them all.

"Hey, did I lose you again?" Sawyer interrupted Annabelle's wandering mind.

Annabelle cleared her throat and smiled, "No, sorry, just a long day. Where were we?" She said before taking another bite, carefully avoiding the peppers.

"Elderflowers and yarrow, and their uses for reducing fever."

And just like that, her mind was pulled right back to the conversation before her. To her happy place, the greenhouse, full of growing and living things with so many uses. Being with Sawyer became natural again, easy. The way their conversation ebbed and flowed always overpowered the nervous attraction of new butterflies. The electricity between them sizzled, their looks became deep and long-ing.

After dinner, Annabelle walked Sawyer to her room and it took every ounce of strength she had to say, 'no', when she was invited inside. But it was too soon. She wasn't ready. They parted with a brief gentle kiss, soft with the hint of cherries on Sawyer's lips. Her heart began to race again, Sawyer's touch left her woozy.

"Goodnight, thank you for dinner, it was lovely," Annabelle said with a smile.

"I'd cook you dinner anytime, anywhere," Sawyer said with a wink. Then brushed the back of her hand gently across Annabelle's cheek. "Goodnight."

Annabelle walked on air smiling ear to ear as she moved down the corridor. But as her thoughts traveled again, the surveillance room called to her. The pull was undeniable. She changed course, and slunk through the halls, dodging the few people still awake at the late hour, and when she reached the correct door, she tapped the touch screen lock pad, entered the stolen passcode, and quietly slipped inside. At the front of the room was a solid wall with coat hooks. Annabelle slowly peeked around the wall and saw that the room was empty.

She hurried to her normal spot at the back corner of the room, pulled off the ventilation cover behind her in case she had to slip inside the air duct to hide quickly, and took her seat. The familiar hum of the computers as they booted up in the dark, sent the warmth of anticipation through Annabelle's fingertips. Heat traveled up her arm, and it crawled down through to her toes. The combination of not knowing what she would see on the screens, and getting caught doing something she knew she shouldn't be doing, thrilled Annabelle.

The monitors finally lit up, temporarily burning her eyes while she adjusted to the brightness. Annabelle clicked through each view until she found the one she was looking for. There she was, her idol, the woman she looked up to. How she wished to speak with her, befriend her.

Annabelle reluctantly pulled her eyes away and searched for the General. When she found him, bile rose in her throat, and the sting of sick threatened to overwhelm her. He needed to be stopped. The things that she had seen him do were despicable. Beatings, killing soldiers when they didn't follow a simple command, and then of course there were the rooms that didn't have cameras. Those rooms terrified her the most, boys and men both were dragged into them kicking and screaming and they rarely came back out.

Suddenly, a flash of anger surged through her at the memory of her defeated proposition to the community. Her idea to shut down Operation Luna and return to Earth was met with incredulous disbelief. They all still trusted that the research they were doing on Luna mattered, and Annabelle couldn't come up with a sound rebuttal without admitting that she was breaking the only rule Luna had. The supposed records room was off-limits.

It was that moment when the community so swiftly shut down her plan that Annabelle realized no one would believe her. But Annabelle didn't let go of her hope. She knew deep down that the salvation of humankind resided on Earth, within the soil that she knew in her heart could still hold life. If only she could find the proof to get the others to understand.

After an hour of watching, when her eyes were so heavy she could have fallen asleep right on the desk, Annabelle shut down the computers, put the vent cover back, and dragged herself back to her room. She couldn't risk infusing the air with her troubled feelings, so when she got to her room, she rolled out her yoga mat, breathed deeply, and meditated until her core was at ease once again.

# Chapter Four

## Earth

Outside base, the dry hot air flung sand across her face, scratching at her skin as they made their way to a black SUV parked only a few feet from the exit. A man in a dark suit held a back door open. Téa climbed in first and Zephyr shut them in.

They rode in silence. Zephyr held one of her hands again, his were warm and strong, the tendons visible as he gently squeezed, almost as though he was willing a connection between them. Téa tried to steady her pulse, scared of what might be ahead. She had never seen so much vastness. She was not sure what she expected to see beyond the perimeter, but it was not this. Sadness spread through her. Everything was parched and monotonous. Dilapidated houses scorched white from the sun. So much debris from a world long gone.

Cool air blew from the vents inside the car, calming the heat of her skin, and soft black leather covered the seats. In front of them was a small clear fridge with ice and a selection of drinks.

Seeing her eye the liquids, Zephyr asked, "Are you thirsty?"

Yes.

But she couldn't say it, a lump formed in her throat. She was exposed, vulnerable, trying her best to keep up with how quick the world was moving around her.

Finally, she nodded. He reached across her body and used a small pair of tongs to fill a cup with ice. He poured crystal clear water to the brim.

She took a sip. Pleasant shock covered her taste buds. She downed the rest. She had never had ice, and water on base had a brown tint.

Zephyr laughed, "Would you like some more?"

She nodded greedily, and he refilled the glass. This one she took her time with; still, it was gone in minutes. More healing than anything she had consumed before. Her throat was soothed, and her body cooled.

The pit in her stomach loosened. Her jaw relaxed. She shifted in her seat to look at him before she spoke. "Thank you."

The simple gesture seemed to spark a hopefulness in him. "Anything you need from here on out is yours. I want nothing more than to make you happy." He looked out the window and said, "We're here."

Eager, for perhaps the first time in her life, she turned to look out the window and only saw an empty dirt field. Her pulse quickened, and a fearful heat flashed through her chest. What had she been thinking? There was no arranged marriage or new home, just a pit destined for her body to be dropped in. She prepared to fight her way out of the car when he asked her...

"Have you ever seen a helicopter?"

*Never*, but she had read about them in one of the many manuals she scavenged. Still unsure what to admit or not, Téa decided to remain silent and shook her head.

"This is the quickest way to Sandstone Estate. It was abandoned thirteen years ago, and my father acquired it for our private family residence, planning for a better future. For now, it is much too large and utilizes many resources. Only around fifty percent of the estate is upkept. It's two hours by helicopter. Father comes home on the weekends. It has everything we need to work, train, and learn together. Most of our time will be spent there."

A flash of spinning metal appeared outside the window.

"Are you ready?" he asked.

She nodded and squeezed his hand.

He leaned in and whispered in her ear. "I have you, I won't let go."

As soon as he opened the door an enormous gust of wind blew against her. It robbed her of breath as the powerful machinery overwhelmed her. She reeled away from the wind that the giant beast generated, covering her face, but Zephyr pulled on her and she ran with him. He boosted her into the belly of the great metal animal. Inside the helicopter, he positioned a pair of headphones over Téa's head and then his own. Zephyr's voice came from the fabric over her ears.

"You made it! Are you okay?"

She could only manage a quick nod, body shaking as she gripped her knees.

They rocked around the fuselage as they lifted upwards. Flying over the desecrated landscape she felt a kind of sadness. There was nothing left. She had not expected to mourn something she had never really known. The time she spent isolated in the classroom from the other children was filled with hours upon hours of reading. Téa craved the knowledge stored within the dry pages and hardcovers of every book they allowed her to devour. But reading about the world before, and experiencing the after, filled her with a great despair to see all the life that had been lost.

Just as she was getting used to the feel of flying in the air within the confines of the helicopter, they landed outside of a gated community with a sort of civilization. The houses here looked almost brand new. Grand and plentiful. Fake plastic gardens made it feel like the houses themselves had two faces. Two truths. One on the surface, and a second hidden. They hurried into another black SUV and buckled in.

Seeing the question on her face, he said. "Raven's Glade, where the principal members of our society reside. Engineers, doctors, wastewater plant operators, teachers, and their families. Everyone necessary for this sector to survive."

She nodded, looked ahead, and folded her hands in her lap before he could grab them again. Her skin crawled with so much exposure. She was not used to any of this. Conversation, human touch, the outdoors. Anything that could be considered normal to the average person.

Her head hummed from the tumult of the helicopter. So much to adjust to. Heavy exhaustion weighed on her bones, and it wasn't even noon yet. As the car started to move, she could feel his gaze on her as a deep and uncomfortable sleep overcame her.

Startled awake by Zephyr gently shaking her shoulders, Téa rubbed her eyes.

"We're here." His deep voice eased her from sleep.

She blinked a few times, trying to clear the fog. The trip felt like only moments, but the sun sat low as they pulled onto a paved driveway. The car crawled forward longer than what she felt should be normal. Just when Téa thought they were headed nowhere, a massive rock structure appeared ahead. Growing larger by the second, she thought a giant must live there. When they were mere feet away, Téa finally understood it to be a house. No, a castle. Imposing and sturdy. The elements would have to work overtime to make a dent in the fortress.

"Welcome, Téa, to your new home." Zephyrs' eyes sparkled with excitement as the car came to a stop.

The castle was antiquated yet sophisticated. Gorgeous classical windows covered the resplendent relic. Its spiraling towers and gray stone loomed like a living thing over them all.

Téa accepted Zephyrs hand as he helped her down from the SUV. Gravel crunched underfoot as they made their way through the outdoor walkway. Téa and Zephyr climbed up the bronze brick stairs to a set of iron gates. She marveled at the space they took up. *How could something so grand still exist in a long dead world?*

The great double front entry was at least twice her height. Two armed guards appeared as they pushed the doors open from the inside and remained steadfast until Zephyr and Téa crossed the threshold. The heavy gates groaned as the guards pulled them shut.

They were graced by a sweet fragrance upon entering. It was not the harsh chemical smell she was accustomed to. It was thick and warm, delectable. Inside the grand foyer, light fell in from three stories of arched windows. Dark wooden floors were polished to a high shine. Gorgeous limestone walls, thick and sturdy, surrounded them. It was intimidating yes, but also beautiful and welcoming. For the first time since talking with Hue, her mind and body relaxed. Maybe this change in what she thought her future would be was not all bad. She was in awe trying to take in all the elegance she was so suddenly allowed to be a part of.

Zephyr asked, "Are you hungry?"

She nodded.

He looked at the black strap on his wrist. "I planned an early dinner. It will be ready in about an hour. Eleanor manages Sandstone Estate, she will show you to your room. I assumed you would appreciate your own space until we get to know each other."

Tension eased from her at those words, and she smiled. "That was very kind, thank you Zephyr." She was grateful and relieved they would not be forced into the same room right away, but with a shudder she was acutely aware that it was inevitable.

Eleanor walked towards Téa, she was average height, fair skinned, and refined. A few gray hairs mixed into her tight bun. Small wrinkles scattered the edges of her eyes, and she smiled, exuding a comforting aura around her.

"Hello Miss," she said. "Right this way, please."

Téa followed her. They changed directions so many times, it didn't take long before Téa was turned around and couldn't even tell which way they had come from. The inner maze of Sandstone would take some time to memorize. Trepidation crept within her when she realized that finding her way to the dining hall would consume almost the whole hour.

Eleanor eventually stopped in front of a room and led Téa inside. A panoramic view of the outdoors greeted them. Téa imagined what an incredible sight the outdoor grounds must have been during the bygone era. Thick velvet tapestries framed each window. It was a pleasantly controlled temperature. A plush, sizable bed to her right was piled with blankets and pillows that tempted her to snuggle up in them and take another nap. She could not recall a single moment where she was allowed comfort like this.

Téa fought the urge to find a corner to hide in. The back and forth of excitement and fear was making her nauseous.

Eleanor noticed Téa's hesitation to follow her around the spacious room, and tilted her head expectantly.

Téa swallowed thickly, then asked, "Is this all for me?"

Eleanor smiled, "Of course, now follow me please." She showed her to the walk-in closet. Two of the SUVs could have parked inside with room to spare. It was full of more attire than any one person could ever need.

Eleanor looked to her, "Your measurements were taken from your medical evaluations. Everything will fit."

"I'm not sure where to start with all of this." Téa said with a shudder. "Do you know what I am expected to wear to dinner?"

"There is no dress code when General Strauss is away. I would recommend something comfortable. Your private bathroom is just through here." She gestured to the left of the closet. "Do you need anything else, Miss?"

Téa could have sworn she saw a mist in Eleanors eyes, and the surprising urge to hug the older women threatened to overcome her. But Téa swallowed the lump in her throat and said. "No. Thank you, Eleanor."

Eleanor nodded and left the closet, then Téa heard the bedroom door close from the other room, leaving her alone in the silence.

Téa wandered around the closet, found a pair of blush pink, high-waist, drawstring sweatpants, an impossibly soft cream-beige sweatshirt that would barely cover her stomach, basic underwear, and a silky bra without wires. She had never felt clothes so luxurious. Her clothing back at Steppe Two was stiff and ill-fitting. Téa smiled as she rubbed the fabric between her fingers, but the feeling of eyes on her back never diminished, she kept glancing behind the racks of clothes, and in the corners of the room.

It took some time, but after a few more passes of the room, an unexpected giggle escaped her lips. This was all hers. Téa hugged herself, a smile on her face as she took her finds to the bathroom to prepare for a shower. She stopped short and her mouth dropped. The bathroom was triple the size of her old dorm. All tall ceilings, and shiny faucets. She slowly moved forward, her footsteps echoed as she went to a comfy armchair after walking once around the entire bathroom. She sat down to unlace her military boots and took off her fatigues.

Téa opened the frosted glass door to the shower and walked through. It was the size of another room. She paused taking it all in, there was a clawfoot tub against one side of the spacious shower area. There were two different shower heads and multiple knobs against another wall. She never could have imagined such a thing; a small smile broke through. Téa never had a bath before and was excited at the thought of relaxing in warm water, and decided, why not try it? This might be her only chance, after a day like this who knew what tomorrow would bring?

It took a few minutes to regulate the knobs to the right degree. Once submerged in the hot water, her body relaxed and she sighed deeply. Téa rested her head against the smooth back of the tub, then noticed the different glass bottles lining a shelf next to her. Having only ever owned a bar of soap, she was not sure what each container was for, so she tried a few out in her hair then smothered some on a rag and washed. So many aromas filled the steamed air. It was heavenly.

Téa's eyes weighed heavy as she soaked and nearly fell asleep until she noticed the water had chilled. She reluctantly pulled the plug. With the water draining from the tub, she grabbed a towel and dried off. Never had she felt so soft and clean.

Téa untangled the knots from her hair with a wide tooth comb and let it hang down to dry naturally spiraled, then dressed and found a pair of hard soled slippers. As she contemplated what to do next, she heard a knock at the door. Téa opened it to find Zephyr himself would be escorting her to dinner. When she noticed he was still in his fancy suit, she became suddenly self-conscious, although relaxed a little when she saw that he did take off the tie and left the vest unbuttoned. Téa hugged herself and fiddled with her sleeves.

He didn't say anything when he looked at her.

"Should I go change?" Téa asked and hugged her body tighter. "Eleanor said I should wear whatever makes me comfortable."

"No. Absolutely not." His voice soft, enraptured. "You look perfect. Nothing like a soldier." His smile brightened his eyes, and Téa's cheeks flushed.

He offered her his arm, and she let him guide her.

The dining room was just as cozy and refined as the rest of the palace. A stunning stacked rock fireplace sprawled to the roof at the far end of the room, with an elegant, long, mahogany, table in the center, filled with food.

Her stomach grumbled, and she realized all she had eaten that day were the handful of saltines before their meeting. He pulled a chair out for her, and she sat down. He took the seat next to her at the table.

"I told most of the staff to go home early tonight. I thought it might be nice to have a quiet dinner."

She flashed him a smile. "Thank you." Thinking that she didn't know the proper protocols in a place like this, she was grateful not to have an audience.

"Here, eat up." He started loading her plate.

Téa didn't know real food like this still existed. Beef roast with sauteed onions and au jus, mashed potatoes, caramelized carrots, rolls, and real butter. Farther down the table she even saw a variety of desserts. She tried to refrain from eating too much too fast but did not stop until she was full, so focused on the delectable meal that they did not speak. She could not recall a single time where she felt so satisfied.

When they were both finished, Zephyr took their plates and disappeared for a minute. When he returned, he asked her, "Would you like to sit with me awhile?"

She was exhausted but also did not want to tell him no, not after all he had given her in the space of a day, so she said. "I would like that."

He held his hand out, and she took it. He led her over to the fireplace where there was a couch and two armchairs. She expected him to sit them both on the couch, where she would have to sit close to him again, but graciously he gestured to one of the armchairs and he took the other.

"How are you doing so far, Téa?"

Not entirely sure how to answer that; she hadn't even decided for herself yet how she felt, let alone what to tell him. She settled on being truthful. He had not shown her any malice. The opposite in fact. How he responded would also show her more of his temperament, perhaps prepare her better for how to present herself going forward.

"Honestly, I'm not one hundred percent sure." She shifted in her chair, "I woke up this morning fully prepared for whatever my military assignment would be. I believed I would be a full-fledged soldier. Instead, I was told I would be meeting my assigned husband."

She paused, suddenly her nausea had returned, and with it, an intense need to hide. Her eyes shifted around the room.

Zephyr studied her closely, apparently aware of the sudden change in her body language and pulled his chair closer to hers. Speaking softly, he said, "It's okay, take a breath, only say what you feel like sharing."

She had never been heard before and her words wanted to pour out. She nodded and took a deep breath. "I had heard stories from the men on base, and how they would treat their wives. It was not pleasant. In fact, I don't think I ever heard of any good coming from the arranged marriages. When I was informed that my match was a high-ranking officer, I was scared. There would be no hiding or running from someone so powerful."

She looked away and her next words came out in a rush. "But then I met you. So far you have been kind. I never expected to see a place like this, let alone live in one. I am still anxious of what my...our... life will be, but I also feel a bit hopeful and maybe excited. I am willing to give this a chance."

He was silent for what seemed like an eternity, and she was worried she said too much. She had not spoken more than a handful of words to him the whole day, and suddenly she was spilling her guts to this unfamiliar man. She immediately regretted everything that had just come out of her mouth.

"Are you always so forthcoming?" He smiled at her.

She couldn't look at him. She was terrified of what she might see. She closed her eyes and pulled her legs up to her chest. But then she heard a quiet chuckle and felt his hand on her outer thigh. He had gotten out of his chair, fabric rustled, and was on his knees in front of her. He pulled her calves down slowly and placed her hands into his.

"Téa, thank you. I am so grateful to have been matched with such a beautiful and insightful woman. Please, don't ever stop sharing with me."

She took a full breath and held it before saying, "I will do my best." And she smiled.

"Let me help you back to your room."

He let go of one hand, and they made the long walk around to the sleeping chambers. When they arrived, she hesitated from turning the knob. She was his now, and they were outside her room. Would he try to kiss her? She was not ready for that yet.

Relief poured over her when he let her hand go and said, "That door there at the end of the hall", he pointed, "is my room. If you need anything at all, just come get me."

She nodded. "I will. Thank you, Zephyr."

"Good night, Téa."

She smiled. "Good night."

Téa went inside and shut her door. A million thoughts grappled for attention, but it had been an extraordinarily long day. Full and beyond exhausted, she crawled into bed. Her head sunk into the pillow like a boulder.

# CHAPTER FIVE

# Earth

When Téa woke, it took her a moment to remember where she was. She stretched her neck, arms, back, legs, testing the strength in her muscles. Then went to the restroom, did her morning routine, and decided to leave her hair down again. A simple luxury that was not afforded to her on base. It was long and luscious, and whatever was in those bottles from her bath the night before left her without frizz.

Téa could care less about being attractive. In her life, as the only woman on base, she held a constant state of unease, uncomfortable around every man. Even with giving him clear signals that she was not interested, they would make advances towards her whether she wanted it or not, which she never did. Not *those* depraved men. As a result, her appearance was always a matter of hiding her natural beauty. Hair in a tight bun, fatigues two sizes too big, and a constant frown on her face. It took tremendous effort to not be approachable, and it would have been nice to relax, to be herself and have a friend. But she was betrayed every time she tried. They always, eventually, tried to force themselves on her.

Even though she would no longer have to worry about those unwanted advances, Téa was not free. She belonged to Zephyr now, and even though she still craved freedom, there was a sense of relief in that belonging. The only positive aspect, that no lesser men could touch her now.

There was a heaviness that had started to ebb away from her protective outer shell during the night. Worrying about her appearance had always been a matter of hiding, and self-preservation. Now she could finally do something as simple as smile without giving a man the wrong idea. She could wear cute clothes and feel girly. But not for attractive reasons. Just a freedom to exist. She had never allowed herself to feel pretty or desirable. A defense mechanism against the monsters surrounding her.

She went to the closet and picked out a pair of comfortable jeans that hugged her curves, and a flowery blouse that cinched at the waist. She found a simple pair of white flat slip-on shoes. Ready for the day, she exited her room and headed down the hall to Zephyr. She knocked twice and he answered almost immediately.

"Good morning." He smiled. "Did you sleep well?"

His voice was alluring and confident. She had not spent much time looking at him yesterday, too fearful of the unknown. Now she noticed him. He was perfectly tall enough for her to be able to easily tuck her head underneath his chin. His gray eyes creased at the corner from the kind smile that hugged his lips. His sandy blonde hair was longer up top and faded to a buzz around his ears. He seemed relaxed, not like the Lieutenant General and second in command to General Thomas Strauss.

She felt the smile tug at her lips, "Yes. I feel amazing. I didn't know sleep could be so rejuvenating, I usually wake multiple times throughout the night." She looked off into the distance. "Base isn't exactly *comfortable*." She took a deep breath then shook off the unsettling thoughts, "It must be late though, right?"

His quizzical look lasted only a moment before he grinned. "Not too bad. I would have let you sleep longer. That reminds me, I have a gift for you." He stepped back further into his room, and Téa followed. He headed toward a grand desk, picked something up, and turned to her holding out a black box the size of his palm. He opened it for her, and inside was a black band identical to the one he wore on his wrist.

He helped her put it on. "I know you used an alarm clock back at base, but this is far more efficient." He pushed on the side of the band and a small screen lit up. "Here is how you set your alarm."

After showing her how to use her new smart watch, he said, "Sleeping in today was an exception, but we do have a lot to accomplish in the coming months. It would be best if we decided on a time to start our days together moving forward. I typically wake at 5:00 a.m. Would that be alright with you?"

"Yes. Perfect, actually." The excitement of new things wore off and her words trailed away. "That's what I'm accustomed to." Téa forced a smile. She had forgotten that he would be training her to become the perfect military wife. Slightly less relaxed than a moment ago, she wondered what it was they would be doing every day.

Zephyr clapped his hands once and rubbed them together. "Splendid. Before we get into it, how about some breakfast?"

"That sounds great." She waited for him to leave first so she could follow since she did not know her way around yet.

In the dining room there was a new fresh selection of food. Fruits and pastries, coffee, sugar, cream, and a variety of teas. She made herself a plate as Zephyr watched.

"Are you not hungry?" Téa asked when she sat down.

"Don't you worry about me, I already ate."

She was self-conscious to be the only one eating, but Zephyr was gracious and averted his eyes, entranced in his smartwatch. Only when she was done did he begin to speak. "Shall we?" He held out his arm and they set off down a new corridor.

"As I mentioned briefly yesterday, my work is not all done from the comforts of Sandstone. I must travel often to the different regions of the continent. There are other established communities that need monitoring. I meet with the commanding officers of each sector in person, enforce laws, take inventory of supplies, monitor land growth, and a variety of other tasks as my father sees fit. Often there is unrest in some areas, and we must be prepared for confrontation."

She listened intently as he continued to talk to her. It seemed as though he was doing the work of multiple people, and his tone of voice came across tired and deflated. Téa was surprised at her sympathy for him as she watched his shoulders slump lower the more he spoke.

Finally, when he paused in speaking, she asked. "Your father doesn't delegate more duties to other officials?" She narrowed her eyes. "It seems like so much on your shoulders." She said harshly not intending to insult his dad, but her tone did come across that way.

He took a breath before he spoke again. "There are very few people with my security clearance left in the population. My father trusts me to ensure things are running as they should. It is my duty to serve him." He did not sound angry or offended, more so like a son resigned to the will of his father.

"I see." She took his hand, not fully understanding why she had the urge to comfort him. She was about to say, 'Well now you have me.' But held the words back, and instead said. "You need me to know all the laws and procedures for when we travel together?"

"Yes. But, Téa, it's more than that. There are still combat zones where civilians are fighting Dunamis control. We will have guards, but we'll need to know how to defend ourselves and each other, as one. We need to learn how to anticipate the others' moves. To rely on each other. We are, one day, going to be taking my father's place. We need to be strong together."

The idea of fighting innocent civilians made her stomach churn. The gravity of what he said lodged in her gut like an anchor in mud, heavy and stuck. General Thomas Strauss oversaw what was once the North American continent. They would be in control of a huge part of what was left of the world someday. She was not sure any amount of training could prepare her for a future like that.

Oh God, it came back to her like a freight train. She struggled to keep her feet under her. Commander Hue Hillside basically told her that Dunamis was hiding something from her. A top-secret mission he had said. How could she have forgotten? What was Connex-A? There was so much she didn't know. Hillside had said she was lucky to be matched with Strauss. Did that mean she could trust him? The room spun.

"I know this is a lot to take in Téa. Are you okay?"

She could not acknowledge him.

"Why don't you sit down. You look a little pale."

She sat on the floor, and he slowly lowered himself next to her. He spoke softly, "You know, you are not at all what I had imagined. According to your file, you managed to take down many of the men who tried to violate you. Physical tests were of the highest percentage. Your mental evaluations suggested you were a cold, calculating person. That was part of the reason my father approved our match. That, and of course our DNA compatibility." He reached for one of her hands and squeezed it gently. "I didn't expect to like you so much. You are not cold at all. Forgive me, but you just seem scared, honest, and kind. You don't need to fear me Téa, I would never harm you."

Téa sat quietly for a moment, organizing her thoughts before responding, "My file is not wrong. The truth is, I was forced to defend myself. I wasn't cold and calculating because I wanted to be. It was because I had to be. I am scared, Zephyr, all the time. And being here, assigned to you. I have no idea what to expect. Here, I'm outside of what I'm familiar with."

His voice wavered, "I didn't realize... I didn't know how bad living on base was for you." He squeezed his eyes with his thumb and forefinger, as though her fear was profoundly affecting him. Then raised his head and looked at her eyes. "I want to get to know you Téa, at your own pace."

Those words brought her back down to gravity, *at your own pace.* They calmed her frayed nerves. She took a breath, "Ditto." Gave him a grin and held his other hand.

His megawatt smile caused a warmth in her chest, as he said, "So you like me too, huh?" He nudged her shoulder with his. "My mom used to say that. Ditto. He rubbed the sides of his legs with nervous fingers, saying the next part fast, "She passed away. Car accident." With the words out, he eased, calm with a gleam in his eye as he kept talking, "She said it was how she said, 'I Love You.' Father did not allow the actual words to be spoken. It was how she showed me she cared."

Téa was surprised at his vulnerability. She had forgotten that he was only two years older than her. He had such a commanding presence and was so sure of himself, he had seemed much older. Now with him showing her how open he could be, she could see the possibility of growing close to him.

She felt a small flutter in her stomach as she said, "I'm sure you know already, but I lost both of my parents before I could even remember them."

He looked at her intently now, "You are my family now, Téa. I'll take care of you."

She didn't know what to say to that, so she gave his hands a quick squeeze, and stood, pulling him up with her. "So, where do we start?"

He smiled back and continued to guide them down the hallway while holding her hand, "I was thinking today we would just do some light exercise, test our physical capabilities. Then tomorrow we will put together a workout routine. We will focus on the physical before we get started on intelligence lessons. My father has given us four months to train together, and he has someone taking care of my responsibilities during this time. After that we will begin working as a team for Dunamis. On our one-year anniversary of meeting, we will be married."

The flutters stopped and her stomach clenched. One year. That was what Hillside had said. There was more to what was happening here. Something she was not privy to. She was telling the truth to Zephyr. She really did like him. Téa willed that her feelings would not betray her, and hoped whatever else was going on, that Zephyr did not know about it.

He seemed to sense her distress. He gently grabbed her shoulders and rubbed her arms. "But hey, that is not happening tomorrow, right? Let's just take it one day at a time, okay?"

He was so reassuring and so in tune with what she was feeling without her needing to tell him what she was thinking. Wanting to trust him more than she ever wanted anything in her life. She decided without all the facts, whatever they may be, that she would trust him. She would train with Zephyr and give him everything she had, because even if he betrayed her, at least she would know him as well as he would know her. A fair battle.

"Okay," she said. "Let's do this."

# CHAPTER SIX

# Space Station Luna

Annabelle was in her safe place, the greenhouse, sifting through the batch of dirt that the General had his cronies send up with the last re-supply. It was horrid. The dirt was full of sharp broken glass, nails, and shards of metal. She, Ian, or any one of the apprentices were sure to injure themselves if she did not get it cleaned up. Even using thick rubber gloves and a sifter, it had taken her a majority of the morning just to process the first ten pounds.

Ian stopped by midday to bring her lunch. Something about his light grin and relaxed shoulders always had a way of cheering her up.

"I figured I'd find you in here." He said with an easy smile. "You know I think you'd starve if it weren't for me."

"Haha, Ian." Annabelle laughed and playfully squinted her eyes as she took the offered bowl of soup. "Thanks." She leaned against a counter next to Ian who had his arms and his ankles crossed.

"Yum, broccoli cheddar?" Annabelle asked before gently blowing on a spoonful and taking a sip.

"Yep, Martine really knows their way around the kitchen these days. Eliana says that they are her most promising apprentice."

"Hmm, it shows." Annabelle was quiet in thought and took a few more bites, allowing the comfortable silence to settle around them. Finally, she asked. "Why didn't you ever pick a trade?"

Ian uncrossed his legs and stretched his arms behind him with a groan before he spoke. "I just want to help people. I enjoy knowing a little bit about lots of different things, instead of a lot about one thing." He cracked his neck and kept talking as he walked around the room looking at the various plants. "You know, it's nice to be able to help out in lots of different areas whenever someone needs an extra hand. It makes me feel... useful, fulfilled somehow." Ian stopped moving and looked at Annabelle with mock seriousness. "Not all of us can be child prodigies like Sawyer and know exactly what our calling is as soon as we're born," he said with a wink.

Annabelle playfully gave him a slight shove, "Oh shut it, Ian. She's not a prodigy, Sawyer's just really... gifted." Annabelle paused and tried but failed to hold back a sigh.

"Although it sometimes makes our three-year age gap seem like twenty. She's just so refined, and smart, and cool- it's intimidating sometimes."

Ian kindly rubbed Annabelle's arm before speaking, "Well, I for one, think you two are a perfect match. You even each other out. She needs to lighten up some, and who better than our very own flower child." Ian grinned, and Annabelle mockingly rolled her eyes before laughing. Then Ian declared, "Welp, I'd better get going, Erin has a plumbing issue she needs help with."

"Oh, a *plumbing* issue? Or a plumbing issue." Annabelle asked as she wiggled her eyebrows.

"*Haha*, Annabelle." He took her empty bowl and said, "See you later?"

Annabelle nodded, "See you later, thanks for lunch, Ian." Annabelle smiled after him as he walked away but felt a mild sadness float over her like a thin veil, the room was always colder when she was alone.

Annabelle began crushing up eggshells, mixing them with coffee grounds and banana peels to prepare the mixture for adding into the newly cleansed soil. As she worked her gloved hands, kneading and stirring the compost, her thoughts drifted to the surveillance room. Annabelle never once saw any of the soldiers at Steppe Two eat a banana or drink a cup of coffee. In fact, the more she thought of it, the more guilty she felt. Sure, Luna had its issues, and waiting for supply shipments sometimes stretched the inhabitants thin, but it was nothing as brutal as the lifestyles that were endured by the soldiers, and *her* on Steppe Two.

Annabelle thought back to all the conversations she had secretly overheard from her hiding spot in surveillance. It made sense to her why the resistance on Earth continually brought up the suggestion to evacuate Luna and blow it up. Luna was surviving at the expense of the people living on Earth. If she was honest with herself, she could not disagree with the resistance's desire to end Operation Luna, if Luna was doing more harm than good for humanity. Seeing the way the people of Earth lived broke Annabelle's heart, especially when she was convinced that the inhabitants of Luna could help them. Earth didn't know what Luna knew.

Maybe that's why the surveillance room was off-limits. The older generation did not want the younger generation to know that they were living well at the expense of others. The younger generation might revolt if they knew. Annabelle often thought about turning herself in and blowing the whistle. Spreading the word like wildfire that life on Earth was still declining, not improving due to the research done on Luna like most of them thought.

Hours passed by as Annabelle worked when a knock at the open doorway interrupted her thoughts.

"Hey, gorgeous. Join me for dinner?

Sawyer's sultry voice had a way of making Annabelle blush, *every time.*

*Shake it off woman, you're stronger than that.*

Anabelle cleared her throat, "Um, actually, it's been kind of a long day, I was just going to head home and hit the sack, raincheck?"

She almost changed her mind about saying no when she saw the disappointment on Sawyer's face, but her frown faded so quickly that Annabelle wondered if she had imagined it. "Of course, raincheck," Sawyer said and tapped her knuckles on the wall as she walked away.

Annabelle hated letting people down, and almost shouted to Sawyer that she would be joining her for dinner after all, but she held herself back and let the disappointment congeal uneasily in her belly. If she was truthful with herself, she could feel the tension between them building. She knew that Sawyer was ready to be more physical, but Annabelle wasn't in that place yet and didn't know how to tell her, so instead, she avoided the problem. She didn't want to scare Sawyer into the arms of another just because she needed a bit more time before the next step in their budding romance.

Taking one last look at all she had accomplished for the day, a proud smile on her face, Annabelle shut the overhead lights off, leaving only a green glow from the grow lights, and slid the door shut.

She promised herself that she would go straight to her room and get a good night's rest for once, but like always, the surveillance room called to her. It begged her to come and take a look. To watch. When Annabelle had all the screens up and running, she began her search. Camera by camera she was methodical in locating *her*. But she wasn't in her room. Not in the gym, nor the mess hall. *Where is she?* Panic started to build from somewhere deep within Annabelle, a writhing sickly thing snaking its way through her. Her fear was poison. *I can't lose her.*

She hadn't realized how long she had been sitting until she felt the ache in her back and the stiffness in her legs.

The artificial sun lights were slowly growing bright around her signaling her to the start of a new day. When the shock hit her that she had been up all night, Annabelle finally conceded to give up her search, to accept the fact that *she* was no longer at Steppe Two. Annabelle had to find out what the Luna informants, the people who spoke in whispers while she hid, knew. Had to know what knowledge was being passed to Luna from Earth, to find any clue as to where *she* had gone. But if she asked, then they would know that Annabelle had been sneaking into places she shouldn't, they would know that she had been eavesdropping. Maybe she could do some sleuthing without them knowing. Find out where *she* went on her own.

Annabelle looked at her watch. Only one hour until she had to clock into work. But the idea of working seemed like an impossibility. *Ian.* She hurried to his room and knocked on the door. He slid it open halfway, groggily wiping the sleep from his eyes.

"Belle?" His speech was slurred with drowsiness, hair in a ratty mess, only wearing boxer shorts as he partly hid behind the door. "What are you doing here at this ungodly hour?"

"Can you cover for me today?"

Confusion spread across his face, "Um, yeah, but why? What's up?"

"I'll tell you later. Thanks, Ian!" Annabelle shouted as she hurried down the hall.

Urgency grabbed hold of Annabelle as she fast-walked the brightly lit corridors, gears whirring under the transparent floor, her panic robbing her of breath, choking her, like a villain bringing about her end. She could not explain it but losing *her* would be like losing a piece of herself. Chopping Annabelle off at the knees to fall flat on her face. *I have to find her.*

Annabelle knew from the talk she overheard from her secret air duct, that the first scientist to live on the space station kept detailed records of all of their interactions with the resistance, hidden somewhere so that they would not be found by the General's men during random inspections. She also knew, that same scientist had a lengthy lecture today.

Pushing her urgency down, Annabelle tried to project calm, normal, body language anytime she passed someone in the halls. A smile here, a nod there, 'How are you?' 'Great, and you?' pleasantries as she went along her way. When she arrived at her destination Annabelle waited a few feet from the scientist's door until all was quiet before stealthily sliding into the room.

Once inside the dark space, Annabelle didn't want to risk turning the lights on in case she had to suddenly hide. She used the soft light from her wristwatch to find her way around. Unlike her living quarters, which consisted of a bed, desk, and closet, Professor Trombols' living quarters were that of a fully furnished and functioning apartment. *This is going to take forever.* After at least an hour of opening drawers, peeking behind cabinets, crawling under beds, and rifling through clothes, Annabelle had come up empty-handed.

She was about to give up when she saw it, a loose panel slightly sticking out from the wall in one of the closets.

Annabelle carefully pulled it back and it slipped out easily. Inside the small space was a pocket-sized box filled with about a dozen slim flash drives.

*Shit. This is a lot.*

Just then a bright white light flooded under the closet doors where Annabelle was hiding, and she thought her heart might leap out of her chest. She tried to slow her breathing and remain perfectly still.

Annabelle heard someone shuffling through belongings as they were shouting to another person. "Just one-sec hon, I forgot my notecards." A moment of silence, then "No, that was last week, today I'm going over the effects of microgravity on mouse cells." More rummaging sounds filtered through the closet door where Annabelle was sure Professor Trombol would hear her pounding heart when the old woman shouted again, "Ah here they are!"

The seconds dragged on and sweat beaded on Annabelle's forehead as she held her breath. Then, just as suddenly as they had entered the room, they were gone, and Annabelle greatly welcomed the relief that comforted her nerves. She let out the air she held in her lungs and took another deep breath. *I've got to get out of here.* She decided to risk taking the flash drives with her and hoped that old Professor Trombol wouldn't check on them before Annabelle would be able to return them.

She tucked the box under her arm, wishing she hadn't worn yoga pants today as pockets would have been handy, and quickly and as quietly as she could, she hurried back to her room.

# Chapter Seven

## Earth

The fitness center was a cavernous room with high, domed rafters just as opulent as she had come to expect from all the rooms at Sandstone. Every type of workout equipment imaginable, both high tech and conventional, was inside. Spacious floor mats, and a mile-long indoor track circled above their heads.

"There is a restroom through there", he pointed to the left side of the room. "I had some workout clothes brought down for you. Why don't you go change? I'll wait for you here."

She expected sweatpants. That was not the case. She squeezed her body into purple leggings, a white sports bra, and a pair of tennis shoes. She hugged her abdomen as the air chilled her exposed stomach.

She had never worn anything so revealing. She had always felt strong before. But now she could see how thin her body was, and not in a pleasant way, but a breakable way. She took her necklace off and hid it in the bra.

When Téa walked back out to face Zephyr, she froze, taking in his basketball shorts and bare chest. Smooth clear skin, and ropes of muscle down his arms, and legs. Toned torso forming a V-shape at his waist. Her heart skipped a beat. With nothing covering his muscular form, she saw he was far more solidly built than any of the men back on base.

It dawned on her then, that even though the men there had seemed big and bulky, most were not in fact that large compared to Zephyr. Just bigger than her. It made sense to her now, considering their minimal diets and probable vitamin deficiency. They were probably small compared to what a healthy man could be in size.

He stared at her as obviously as she was staring at him, and he cleared his throat. "Let's start out with a run, shall we?"

"Sounds great." She smiled.

She quickly learned that her daily jog did nothing against the ravages of malnutrition. She had been the quickest person on base, but Zephyr easily outpaced her.

After a few laps, and slowing to a stop he said, "Don't worry, you're naturally quick. A few good meals and you will be hard to keep up with." And winked.

Her chest burned with the effort of pulling air into her lungs. She had to sit down. They took a five-minute break and then turned to the weights. He started her on a simple bench press with one long bar.

"We'll see where your strength is at. Remember, no pressure. We're just getting a foundation to work from."

She laid down on the bench and Zephyr stood at her head. He looked down at her. "Ready?"

"Yep." She put her hands on the cool metal and pushed up. She was able to get the long rod out of its holder, and as it slowly made its way down to her, she realized, alarmingly, that she could not push it back up. She was going to be crushed and die in the most unnecessary way possible. She started wiggling and a strange noise escaped her.

"Hey, hey, hey. Don't panic. I've got you!" He was laughing. Zephyr was actually laughing as he lifted the bar up for her. She could not believe it! Her heart racing, she sat up, turned around, and punched him as hard as she could in the arm.

"Ow! Okay. Okay, I'm sorry. Geez, you do know how to punch. For a minute I thought *all* the reports were going to be wrong about you. Glad to see you have some fight in you."

He was still laughing just a little. But she eased at the compliment, and the mild fury left her system.

"Why don't we call that a day?" he asked.

"Yes, please. I could use a shower." She said and shot him a terse glare.

"Sounds like a plan." He gave her a crooked smile. "We'll get some lunch afterward. Come on."

He held his hand out and she reluctantly took it.

The next day she was awakened by the pleasant chimes of her new accessory, and she was much better mentally sorted. She knew now what to expect from her day, and the knot of anxiety in her belly loosened.

Headed to breakfast, she thought to herself that she could never get past the excitement of whole foods. Real freshly made sustenance that she looked forward to consuming. She did wonder though how they acquired and maintained livestock. She had not seen any on the property. Where did the eggs, beef, milk, and bacon come from? What and how did those cows and pigs eat? She had not seen anything freely growing on the trip here. Birds had gone extinct, or so she had been told, she always assumed that meant chickens as well.

She supposed that was another way high-ranking officers benefited from having dominance. They could acquire things that most people simply could not. She knew Dunamis had taken over food production decades ago, constructing secure facilities where that process took place. She just assumed, given the meals they consumed at Steppe Two, that those facilities were lacking. Téa could see now how wrong she was. The facilities weren't lacking, they were obviously unevenly distributing the food. Bile rose in her throat.

Zephyr was already seated in the dining hall when she arrived. "Good morning." He practically shouted across the great hall, as he stood and waved, excited to see her.

Téa shook off the eerie feeling consuming her, and let his enthusiasm brighten her spirits, "Good morning." She grinned.

It was endearing knowing he seemed to enjoy her company. It made her feel more at peace in Sandstone. She fixed herself a bowl of yogurt, and fresh blueberries, and put a healthy dose of cream cheese on a plain bagel. After she poured herself a glass of orange juice and took a seat.

"So, what's on the agenda today?" she asked him.

"Physical strengthening. We didn't actually accomplish a whole lot yesterday. I want to put you in a swim simulation suit to build your endurance."

Téa had heard about these suits but had never had the opportunity to use one. With clean water depleted, swimming pools were no longer allowed. The leisure activity was only available to those who lived along the coast or near large bodies of water.

She brightened and said, "That sounds amazing! I can't wait."

He grinned at her and motioned for her to finish her meal.

It took an entire thirty minutes to get her laced into the attire standing up. The suit was heavy. *Very heavy.* She was not sure how she was going to be able to move. It was like wearing a giant black balloon filled with gel as dense as lead; cool to the touch and soft on the inside like a silicone that molded to her body.

"Okay," Zephyr said as he secured the last piece. He grabbed long black cords that dangled from the ceiling with metal clips on the ends and held them out to her. "We're going to strap these to the back of the suit. It will hold you a few feet off the ground. Just enough for you to be able to move your arms and legs in a forward motion."

He made it sound so simple. Zephyr hooked the various loops and fasteners to the suit.

When he was finished, he said, "Okay, I'm going to help you lay on the ground. It'll be easier when the cables start lifting you." He chuckled to himself and said to her, "My first time, my assistant lifted my legs too fast, and I was still standing. Face planted so hard I fractured my jaw."

Shock flew through her. "Holy crap, Zephyr. That's not funny!" Her excitement quickly turned to apprehension. "I don't know if I want to do this."

Still softly laughing, he reassured her. "Hey, I'm not going to let you get hurt in a training exercise. I promise."

He placed one hand on each of her shoulders, on the front of the suit and braced himself, "Okay. Lean against me, and I'm going to lower you to the ground."

"Zephyr, are you sure? I feel like this suit will crush you."

"Trust me, I've got you." His tone was solid and sure.

She tried to lean against him slowly and carefully, but the weight of the suit left her with little mobility, and she fell hard against his chest. Terrified of smashing her face, a small yelp escaped her. But true to his word he caught her without a problem. He was a lot stronger than she had given him credit for. Zephyr gently placed her face first on the ground.

"Okay. The wires are going to start lifting you. Don't panic. They are designed to withstand three times the amount of one suit."

A small groan and metallic clanking told her the mechanism pulling her upwards was working. She started rising off the ground, and to her great delight she suddenly felt weightless.

"Once you feel comfortable, start rotating your arms in slow long circles, out in front and behind and alternating each side." He said as he mimicked the motion.

She did as he instructed and was surprised with the immense effort necessary to move her body.

"Good, you're doing great! Now, try adding your legs into the rotation. Slightly bend your right leg and slowly kick it out as you move your left arm. Repeat the motion with your left leg and right arm."

It didn't take long for the strain in her physique to take effect. She struggled to keep up the momentum.

"I know it's hard Téa, but you're doing great! Just a few more minutes. Our goal is twenty minutes for today, ten more tomorrow, and so on until we reach a full hour."

She worked as hard as she could to push herself, until *finally* and gratefully, Zephyr shouted, "Times up!"

Breathing heavy, a joy blossomed in her chest, she was proud of herself. The more they trained and the more she had a balanced diet, she realized she was only experiencing the tip of the iceberg in her abilities. Her former co-inhabitants at Steppe Two provided the basic training she needed in their unwarranted attacks on her person. Now she would have the knowledge and the capability to truly defend herself. She knew as she experienced more of the world, her minor insecurities would be put to rest as well. She was naturally brave; she just needed the knowledge to cement her foundation.

Zephyr looked impressed with her as he said, "You're amazing! I am going to lower you to the ground now." The cables slowly dropped her to the floor, then Zephyr said, "Just lay still and I'll help remove the suit." He straddled her back as he undid the connections, then leaned close to her ear as he spoke, "I am going to unzip the back now, hold still."

The pleasant scents of mint and tangerine from his morning tea wafted towards her.

"I'm going to reach in to lift you out."

Zephyr put one arm next to hers inside the suit, her heart raced. He clenched his hand around her wrist, and she froze. Then he gently pulled back.

"Now, the next arm."

Her whole body tingled, and her arms were limp at her sides, her belly on the ground, she turned her face to the side to hear him better and held herself still. Her heart pumped furiously, and her skin was flushed everywhere he had touched her.

Zephyr wrapped his arms around her chest and whispered, "I'll hold you while you bend your knees and sit up."

Together they eased her out of the thick ensemble. Zephyr lingered a second longer than needed with his arms wrapped around her. Heat spread across her cheeks.

As he stepped away, he asked, "How do you feel about a run? Up for it?"

"Definitely." Her words came out dreamily. She could still feel the pressure where his arms were moments ago and felt a little dizzy. She shook it off and followed him up the steps to the track above them.

Her head spun when they reached the top of the landing. She could hear Zephyr talking to her, but the words were fuzzy. She swayed and collapsed with a thud.

Everything went dark.

# Chapter Eight

## Earth

Téa woke in her room, with a lump on her head. She winced as she gingerly touched the bump at her temple.

"Téa, are you okay? How do you feel?" Zephyr sounded exceedingly worried, his voice caught part way through his questioning, his brow drawn together.

"I think I'm okay. What happened?"

"You fainted."

She was quiet while she processed this information. She put her hand behind her neck, it felt sore, tender, and hot to the touch. Then said, "I don't understand. I would run five miles every day back at base, and most of the time when another soldier would come at me, I took them down. I shouldn't be drained like this all the time."

"Téa, it's different here. Sure, you ran miles, but at your own pace. You overpowered the troops, but in one or two simple moves. You were deprived of basic nutrients for years. The men you were surrounded by, the same." He took a deep breath and continued. "You have only been on a balanced diet for two days. In those two days, I have pushed you physically. Running faster than you are accustomed to. The weights. Now the swim simulation. It is a lot for any person to adjust to. We will keep pushing, but not past your breaking point. Rest for the remainder of the day, and we will start again tomorrow. I will have dinner sent to your room."

She wanted to protest, but his words came out with a sense of finality to them, and he didn't leave her space to retort. He raised her hand to his lips for a kiss, and then departed.

An uncomfortable feeling traveled through her, a stranger in her own skin, unsettled. She was not this weak person. She was the one who safeguarded herself. Who studied and prepared.

Determined to prove him wrong, Téa decided to rest today, but tomorrow, she would get up two hours before him. How did he know what her breaking point was? She would train for one hour every morning, and then rest for one hour before her sessions with Zephyr.

True to herself, Téa rose hours before the sun. She grabbed an apple from the bowl of fresh fruit that always sat in the dining room, chugged some water, and headed to the gym. She would start with the weights. She would not be taken by surprise this time by the unexpected weight of the solitary metal rod; she knew what to expect.

She laid down on the bench and adjusted her grip. Took a few deep breaths and pushed. The bar lifted easily from its place. Slowly, she brought the bar to her ribs and pushed back up. Taking another deep breath, she repeated the motion five more times before her arms felt like jelly.

Next, she did her normal stretches, then headed to the track. She knew she could run for a great distance at her own much slower pace, but she wanted to keep up with Zephyr. So, she settled on two miles, accelerating as swiftly as she could.

Twenty-two minutes later, heart racing, blood pumping through her veins, and sweat pouring down her back, Téa laid down grinning ear to ear, proud of herself. She had just enough time to go back to her room, shower, and rest for a while before Zephyr would be expecting her at breakfast.

When she walked into the dining hall, her nose filled with savory aroma, her stomach audibly growled. She smiled knowing that meant she made progress this morning. Her body needed to refuel.

"You look well." He sounded pleasantly surprised, as though he was expecting to carry a zombie down to their work out today.

"Thank you, I feel great." She gave him her biggest, most exaggerated grin, and sat down at the table. "So, what's on the agenda today?" she asked a bit jokingly, repeating her words from the day before.

He chuckled. "I was thinking we would try out the rock wall. It's great for upper body and core strength. Plus, it's fun."

"Sounds fantastic!" she said enthusiastically.

Zephyr laughed and smiled at her, "Are you sure you didn't hit your head too hard? You seem far too cheery." He winked.

"I'm just ready to conquer this. Conquer all of it. I am not used to being cared for. I prefer to be able to take care of myself."

Zephyr was quiet, and his head drooped. He seemed almost sad or maybe a little mad. "You know Téa, I do not ever want you to feel that I am trying to control you. However, it would be nice to feel more like a team in this."

She had not considered how he may be feeling in this situation. She had never been needed by anyone before, and she supposed it was probably a nice feeling, to be needed.

"Of course, we are a team, Zephyr. I didn't mean it like that. I just want to be able to hold my own. Like you said in the beginning, I want to be your equal, to be able to keep up with you. That's all."

Was that truthful? Was that how she really felt? Or was she still on edge, getting ready for the next attack? She wasn't sure. But she did know she did not want to hurt Zephyr's feelings. So far, this place was the most like a home she had ever experienced. It could not be so bad to let her guard down, if only a little.

He seemed satisfied with her response and said, "Eat up, and we'll get going."

Téa filled her plate with biscuits and gravy and two slices of cantaloupe. The sweet juice from the soft fruit splashed her tongue and tickled her taste buds. It was amazing. She thought to herself that she could live the rest of her life just eating fresh fruit. She cleansed her palate with a refreshing glass of ice water. So complete her toes felt like dancing.

They entered the gym and Zephyr led them to the tallest space in the room. It was covered with different colored fake rocks, bolted into place on the walls. They all had different angles and grooves carved out of them. There seemed to be no rhyme or reason to their disarray. At parts, the wall jutted out sharply, or curved like the underbelly of a great blue whale.

Zephyr led her over to a wall that had a more simple surface from bottom to top, and pulled on long black ropes that hung from the ceiling. "Eventually, you will be able to free climb this. For now, we will take safety precautions and strap you into a harness and helmet. Here, put your legs through here."

He held out what looked like a diaper made of seatbelt straps. She put her legs through the two largest holes as Zephyr held it in place for her. Then he pulled on the strap around her waist, and it tightened. He pulled her close to him, she could feel the heat of his body, and watched the muscles in his forearms flex as he looped a rope through her harness and made a double eight knot with one of the long ropes that hung from the ceiling. Her heart did that pitter patter thing again, that she wasn't sure she'd ever get used to, and she tried to slow her breathing.

There was a stand in the corner that held a white powdery substance. Zephyr said it was chalk that would keep their hands dry. She dipped her hands in and rubbed them together. Little clouds puffed around her.

They approached the wall. "Start by feeling the rocks. Look for the little grooves that you can place your fingers on and test them out, see what feels most comfortable. Grab it and pull yourself up until your foot finds another hold. Go slowly, take your time, and make your way as high as you can. If you are able, climb back down when you are tired. Otherwise, I will be here ready to lower you with this." Zephyr gestured to the rope in his hands that threaded through his own harness and a device he called a grigri, then ran up to the ceiling and wrapped around a cylinder before falling back down to where it was attached to Téa.

Téa's excitement waivered, unsure a singular rope could hold her with just simple pieces of metal connecting her to it, and him. She must not fall.

Zephyr looked at her, "Now, I'm what's called your, 'belayer', when you're ready, say 'on belay', then I'll respond, 'belay on'. Got it?"

Téa swallowed a lump in her throat and nodded.

Zephyr spoke again, "When you're ready, say, 'climbing', and I'll respond, 'climb on'. That's how we keep each other safe, okay?"

She could only nod again. Téa shook her hands in an attempt to shake out her nerves. Preparing to climb, she looked at Zephyr, and said, "On belay."

He nodded, and said, "Belay on."

Then she looked at the wall and said, "Climbing."

Behind her, Zephyr said, "Climb on."

Téa swallowed again and clenched her jaw. She gripped each rock until she found one that conformed to the shape of her hand. The first was a little way above her head. She looked at ground level for a gap in the wall where she could place her foot. She grasped the rock above, pulled herself up a few inches, and steadied her body with her feet, heart racing even though she was only a couple feet off the ground. She could smell the chalk on her hands and feel the cool rocks against her face.

Pulse flying, she reached up, and found her next hold. Time moved slowly. She did not look down, not once. Her forearms burned first. Then her back muscles, under her shoulder blades and her hands started to weaken. She knew then, it was time to make her way back to the ground.

Her fingers were going numb and tingly, her foot slipped, and stomach sank.

She fell.

She thought for sure her head was going to crack open like an egg, yolk breaking and spilling over the floor, the shell unable to be glued back together. But a sharp tug stopped her. She was suspended in the air and breathing fast, then forced herself to look. Zephyr held her steady, barely exerting any effort. A small smile spread on his lips.

His eyes found hers and he laughed. "I've got you. I am going to lower you slowly."

She landed with a soft thunk, then turned to him angrily. "Do you think it's funny I fell? Why are you smiling?" She was hurt and offended that he seemed to be laughing at her expense. That he expected her to fail.

"Woah, calm down killer." He said with a laugh. "I am smiling because you were only two feet from the top. Didn't you notice? You almost completed the entire wall on your first try *and* lowered yourself back down. You are amazing!"

Téa crossed her arms and clutched her sides, a reluctant grin tugged at the corners of her mouth. She was still preparing herself for the worst in everything. It had kept her alive this long. She forced herself not to apologize. She *was* amazing, "Thank you." The words still came out sheepishly.

Zephyr smiled some more, "That's probably enough for today. Unless you are up for a quick run?"

She was not, between her early workout sans Zephyr and now the rock wall, but she did not want to tell him that, so she nodded. "Sure."

At lunch, she could hardly lift her spoon. Grateful it was a soup meal, and easy to eat. Unlike any soup at Steppe Two, this was hearty and filling, full of fresh vegetables, pasta, and warm broth. Her teeth sank into a warm crescent roll the kitchen served with the soup, wonderful flavor caressing her mouth. When she finished eating, Téa was ready for a nap. She willed her eyes to stay open, to focus.

Zephyr was speaking to her. "It has been a few days now, and I was thinking before we get started on intelligence training, we should get a baseline of your geography knowledge. I had some maps brought here from the library. How about a quick study lesson before evening?"

"Of course, good idea." *It was a horrible idea.* She wanted her bed.

He unrolled the long bundles of paper. Everything looked foreign to her. He started with the basics, places she would be familiar with, starting with the seven continents, and then moving to a map of North America. He zeroed in on Steppe Two, then showed her the route they took to get to Sandstone. Pointed out the giant uninhabitable middle section. Apparently, it used to make up multiple states, now it was simply labeled as the Desert Sector. Zephyr showed her the coast lines all along the bottom half of the enormous mass of land, and finally, up North where more than just coastal areas had places for people to live.

They spent a solid three hours going through the colorful charts. By the time they were finished, dinner was set to be served in two more hours. Just enough time for a bath and a short nap.

She knew what Zephyr was trying to impart on her was important, but she was not sure how much of the data stuck. She doubted her decision to add the extra training that morning. Maybe she could ease up and trust the process Zephyr had lined out for her.

Téa decided to take a nap. She slept through her alarm, and Zephyr had dinner brought up to her. She decided to end her secret morning sessions. There was no competition, who was she trying to impress? She had nothing to prove. She only needed progress and growth to be a strong person, not the silent kudos of her ego.

# Chapter Nine

## Earth

It had been a week since Téa had arrived at Sandstone. She had not met Strauss Senior yet, and he was set to make his appearance today. Everyone was on edge. The staff bustled about in a frenzy to get the estate ready. No one laughed, no one smiled, everyone laser focused on their jobs.

Téa had not known what to expect with Zephyr but was pleasantly surprised with his kindness so far.

It was different with General Thomas Strauss; his cruel reputation preceded him. She did find comfort in knowing Zephyr truly seemed to care for her and would hopefully protect her. Their bond had grown every day. General Strauss had also been the one to arrange and approve their match, so if he did not approve of her accomplishments thus far he had to at least accept the choices he had made for them.

"What are you thinking? You haven't said a word all morning, and you've barely touched your breakfast." Zephyr gestured to her full plate; his face twisted in concern.

Téa had been gazing into the distance and shook her head. Shrugging, she said, "I am just apprehensive about meeting your father. I have never been around someone of his status. I'm worried about doing something wrong while he's here."

Zephyr stood up from his side of the table and walked around to her. He held both her hands and looked her directly in the eyes. "This is your home now and I never want you to feel scared here. I promise he won't lay a finger on you or say a single word out of turn."

She looked away, still feeling unsure. He pulled her face back to him gently and kissed her forehead. He had never done that before, and a warmth shot up her sides.

She leaned forward and hugged him. "Thank you, Zephyr. I don't know how, but you always seem to know what to say." She pulled back and smiled at him.

He looked at her earnestly.

"You never have to thank me for being kind to you. And I meant what I said. My father, just as much as us... is bound to the rules of Dunamis he helped to form. I am his only bloodline, and he knows I am aware of this. It's true he is not a nice person, and he rules with an iron fist. But in this home, and when it comes to me and you... he cannot, and I will not let him be in any way unkind." He placed one hand gently on her neck, "You are safe with me Téa, I promise."

The knots in her stomach relaxed, she turned back to her plate and took a bite of her eggs. Still without an appetite, she pushed her serving away.

"How much time do we have?" She asked.

"He is about an hour out. What do you have in mind?"

"I still haven't seen the rest of the Estate. Feel like giving me a tour?"

"Absolutely m'lady!" he stood, dramatically bowing. Laughing, she wrapped herself around his arm and they walked.

He spoke quietly as though they were in a museum winding their way through the corridors. "Before the Decline, the Sandstone grounds were some of the most impressive ever orchestrated in the United States. A great sweeping valley filled with beautiful gardens. Perfectly manicured trees lining the front lawn. Nowhere else could compare. Now, of course, nothing grows."

He stopped in front of two ornately detailed metal doors, intricate flowers wrought into them, with shimmering opal inlays, and gold curling handles designed to look like vines.

"We may not have Genesis here, but we do have our own little slice of paradise." He opened the doors and revealed a room with a small garden.

Téa was speechless. In front of her were flowers of all different shapes and colors. Fruits and vegetables. Raspberries, strawberries, tomatoes, zucchini, various herbs, and so much more. In the very center of the room, a sapling. The room smelled of fresh wet dirt and leafy greens. It was perfection.

"Father was able to source some seeds from Genesis. It took enormous coordination to get the soil that would allow anything to grow. A water filtration system that would keep the plants thriving without using too much. Solar panels to keep the full spectrum lights running."

Téa was curious about the lack of security for the garden and wondered how it could possibly be thriving so well but didn't ask about it.

"This is where most of our meals come from. We are extraordinarily fortunate to have this little oasis. And of course, we feed all Sandstone employees and their families. In exchange, they are happy to help maintain the garden when I am away. Father does not come near the room; he says he kills every plant he touches and worries about harming our food supply. I think he just knows this is the one peaceful place I have in the world and allows it to be mine."

It surprised her that the Strauss family would not be forcing other people to supply their food. It calmed her knowing the whole employ at Sandstone worked together like their own little community, rather than just being servants.

"It's beautiful, Zephyr. I love it."

He stared at her like he was craving to tell her something, his mouth opened then closed, but said nothing and pulled her to his side.

"I am glad you are here with me."

A flurry of joy swept around inside her. She could have sworn she saw something yellow actively bloom in a corner. She gave her head a small shake and smiled at him.

"Are you ready? He will be here shortly; we should be there to greet him." Zephyr said.

She wasn't, but said. "Yes, I'm ready."

Every person under the Sandstone residence was in attendance in the grand foyer when the black SUV arrived. It felt like the oxygen was sucked out of the room with his mere arrival. The front doors were pushed open by the armed guards.

General Thomas Strauss was a big man. Tall, muscular, and intimidating, like he could crush a man with one arm. He obviously did not have a problem with rationed food supply; maintaining this kind of hardened bulk would require an enormous amount of daily calories. Téa had once seen a picture book as a child that had a giant green man, who was rescuing people from a burning building. But The General didn't look like he'd be someone to do the rescuing. He looked like someone who would be irritated by their screams as they burned. His face was covered with benevolence, as if the necessary presence of other people intruded on his private world.

"Eleanor. My messages," he demanded.

Eleanor appeared at his side, took his blazer, and handed him a stack of white note cards.

"Zephyr, I trust your training is going well." It was not a question, but a statement, and the General did not look at him as he spoke.

Zephyr was stiff in his reply, "Yes sir."

"I will see you in my office in thirty minutes." He spared Téa a quick glance, "Miss Garcia, welcome to Sandstone." At that he walked away before Téa had a chance to say a single word, but grateful she wouldn't be forced to exchange pleasantries.

Everyone released a collective sigh. They had all been holding their breath. The staff went about their business and Zephyr looked to Téa.

He laughed. "See, not bad at all."

She smiled at him. "Definitely easier than I had expected."

"Alright," he paused. "I have to brief him on our progress, and I imagine he will give me a report on how my temporary replacement in the field is performing. I'll see you at dinner. Take this time to relax, or explore, whatever you feel like."

"Okay, see you later." She gave him a soft grin, and he winked at her as he walked away, sending the butterflies in her stomach into a frenzy.

She took a deep breath and tried to think of what to do next. Téa was so used to his constant companionship that she wasn't sure what to do with herself. She didn't want to sit idly in her room. The outdoors was not an option unless she wanted to burn or overheat. Téa didn't feel like exploring the closed off portions of Sandstone, not in the mood to get lost. She decided to see if any help was needed in the kitchen.

The kitchen was gorgeous. It had a beautiful stone arch-
way over a large double oven. There was a grand island
that had seating around the edge, with gleaming pots and
pans hanging over the top. The centerpiece was a massive
gleaming copper sink with a pearlescent backsplash.

There were only three people in the large, beautifully
stocked area. A woman and two men. Besides Zephyr, Téa
had only met Eleanor and didn't know their names. She
wasn't sure what to say.

One of the men noticed her and said, "Can I help you find
something, ma'am?"

"Oh no, I was just wondering if you needed any help
here?" Téa asked.

"Much appreciated ma'am, but the food supply is under careful supervision and only distributed at designated
mealtimes. No unauthorized persons are allowed to handle
the fare." He seemed genuinely sorry to tell her no.

"Oh, not a problem at all. I just had some free time, and
I'm honestly not sure what to do with myself." She said with
a shrug.

"Ma'am, have you visited the library? It is quite beautiful
and just on the other side of the living quarters. I could
show you the way if you'd like?"

"Oh no, that's not necessary, I'm sure I can find my way.
Thank you so much, that is a great suggestion, I think I will
do just that." She gave him a kind smile and left the kitchen.

*Finding the library shouldn't be too hard*, she thought to
herself. She had already figured out how to mostly navigate
on her own. The training facility, her room, the dining
room, and grand foyer. If the library was on the other side of

where her room was, it should be fairly simple. She had not even thought about a library being here. She craved books but was not allowed to freely visit Steppe Two's library. She had to sneak in when everyone else was asleep. But she realized now that it was obvious there would be a library in someplace as majestic as Sandstone.

Téa smiled and had a bounce in her step. She was getting excited about the idea of looking into any book she wanted without the fear of being caught or needing to bribe a guard. She had finally passed the thruway that led to her room and was rounding a corner when she stopped in her tracks, overcome with awe.

The pathway leading to the library was wide, and made of marble that sparkled with tiny flakes of gold dust. A tall and vast wall of windows flanked one side with soft cream-colored curtains that drew a line toward a huge door, one that was bigger than the main entrance.

She was scared she would not be strong enough to push the massive thing open. But it surprisingly moved with ease. Rainbow light spilled in from stained glass windows. A large winding staircase curled upward from the center of the room. Books lined every wall four levels high.

She normally went straight to war strategy and fighting manuals. But she didn't need that here; that is what she had Zephyr for. The last time she used her imagination was with picture books when she was in school with the soldier children. She wanted something grown up that she could disappear into.

She perused some shelves next to a large desk near the back of the room and glanced at the titles. Most books were operating procedures for the General, and a few ledger books. She was about to move on when one spine caught her eye.

'*Supernatural Abilities in an Evolving Generation*'

Its title was suggestive of non-fiction, but the word 'Supernatural' definitely belonged in fiction, *right*? It was among what she assumed were the General's books, and she highly doubted he was a leisure reader. She grabbed it and suddenly felt like she was back on base, waiting for someone to walk in on her. She went up the staircase two levels, hurried towards the back, and squeezed herself behind one of the bookcases. She opened the pages at random.

'*It is believed that only select males are equipped with the Connex-B gene. Manifesting through great levels of anger and depression. Abilities can include superhuman strength, accelerated healing, and manipulation of metal.*'

She could not believe what she was reading. This couldn't be real. She flipped a few more pages and kept reading.

'*Connex-A, or more widely known as the Soulmate gene, presents in both male and female humans. Clarity on Connex-A is lacking. What we know so far is subjective. It does not simply require two parties to have the gene, but also compatible DNA, and for lack of better terms, for both parties to be in love, in order to activate their powers. There is debate on the existence of love as it cannot be measured in science. Some claim that the appearance of the Connex-A abilities only become active when met with matching souls. Historically, the existence of souls has also been debated. Supernatural abilities have varied greatly and can be un-*

predictable. We have recorded those individuals who have demonstrated these abilities. They have naturally gravitated towards each other, and as such it is recommended that all persons containing Connex-A be eliminated. It is too difficult to control and monitor an influx of, for want of a better term, soulmate couples; and near impossible to anticipate which abilities will develop.'

Her blood pulsed in her ears, making her body hot and uneasy. She flipped through more pages.

'The suggestion of a weaponized Connex-B carrier has been debated at length. At this time, both genomes only develop naturally. Results have found that a serum to forcibly activate the Connex-B gene is possible but severely unstable. Creating real life scenarios, as opposed to a serum, to rapidly develop the Connex-B gene is preferable. Both genomes are exceedingly rare. Connex-A more so than Connex-B. At the time of this publication there is only one known individual who possesses both genomes. Subject eighty-five. Research is ongoing.'

Téa's vision blurred and spun. She could not read anymore. This was impossible. But then Major Hillsides' voice came back to her, 'Have you ever heard of the Connex-A gene?' It hit her like a sledgehammer. That was real, this was a real thing in the world. How was it not public knowledge? How was this possible?

Her heart sank and her knees went numb.

Does Zephyr know?

Breathing rapidly, she stood up and paced in the secluded space. She could not be found with this book. She rushed and took the stairs two at a time down to the bottom floor.

She carefully found the exact spot she took the book from and put it back.

She decided she couldn't talk to Zephyr about what she had found. Not yet anyway. She needed to know if he was already aware and if she was a pawn on a giant chessboard, just a piece to be used for his every whim.

How could she face Zephyr and the General? They would see the fear written all over her face. She couldn't hide from this, but what could she do? Her heart pounded; her legs shook. Desperation to release some of the tension took hold. She would go for a run.

As she approached the door, the knob turned, her stomach dropped, and she froze. It opened, and General Thomas Strauss walked through.

Fear flashed in her eyes. Grateful for the immense room, he didn't see her yet, at least she hoped he hadn't. She hurried behind a red velvet couch in the far corner and sank down as far as she could, hoping he wouldn't notice her. What if he found her hiding? What would she say? She tried to calm herself. She heard his footsteps rapidly moving toward the desk. He grabbed one of the ledgers and walked back out of the library, he never saw her peeking around the couch.

Overcome with stress, Téa sat in silence, and let the tears stream down her face. She felt small again and at the mercy of those who knew more than her. Those who had more power and freedom than her. Hillside had tried to warn her. He wanted her to know that there were people keeping information from her. The most terrifying part was the fact that these officials had done research on weaponizing humans. Where were these individuals with supernatural abilities? Had they all been eliminated?

She cared for Zephyr and was scared he was not being honest with her, but that book was so blatantly out in the open. It could not be a secret at Sandstone. Who else knew there was a whole generation of people out there evolving? What top secret mission was she being groomed for? Did it have to do with the Connex genes?

She wanted to run away; this was all too much to handle. But where would she go? There was no one and nowhere. She didn't even know how to get transportation and could not cross the desert midland on foot, she'd die.

Téa would not be able to keep this all in and would have to confront Zephyr about it when they were alone. General Strauss was only here for two days. She had to know what they were planning for her. Two days. That was it, she could get through the next forty-eight hours and figure it out from there.

# Chapter Ten

## Space Station Luna

The little box of flash drives tucked under her arm burned with the anticipation of unpacking its secrets. Annabelle knew it was wrong to snoop in someone else's room and belongings, let alone become a thief. A year ago, she never could have imagined crossing that line. But after she caught that first glimpse in surveillance when someone had accidentally left the door open, and then waiting to watch them enter their passcode so she could return later, breaking the rules had become an addiction. She waited for the next opportunity to catch a sliver of something other than the milky bursts of stars outside the windows of Luna, and the porcelain white walls that held her in like a prison. It was a craving so sweet it was impossible to ignore.

To see that life existed someplace other than these plain corridors was a beautiful thing to witness. Sneaking into surveillance made sneaking into Professor Jillian Trombol's apartment surprisingly easy. *This is not good, Annabelle. You should not be enjoying this rush. You did a bad thing.*

"Oh shut up, self." Annabelle said out loud, shaking her head at the same unfortunate timing of passing a tall older man in the halls.

"What was that?" He said with a frown on his face, obviously assuming that Annabelle was speaking to him.

"Oh, nothing! Sorry, just talking to myself- I uh- forgot to turn the grow lights on in the nursery." Annabelle nervously laughed as she hurried faster towards her room. *Keep it together Annabelle.*

Annabelle flew into her room, entered her code on the lock pad, and slid the door shut behind her. Breathing deeply she fell backward onto her bed letting the small box of flash drives fall onto the pillow beside her.

As her adrenaline ebbed away, the sleeplessness began to catch up with her. *I should really take a nap.* Her eyelids fell closed heavily and her heart rate slowed, and just as she was falling into a much-needed sleep, there was a knock at the door.

Annabelle sat straight up, grabbed the box, and hurriedly shoved it into her closet.

"Uh, who is it?" She shouted out.

Sawyer's voice replied, muffled through the door. "It's me, you weren't at work, I thought we could have lunch together. Are you feeling okay?"

*Shit.*

Annabelle dropped her head into her hands and rubbed her eyes. She really didn't want to push Sawyer away, she really did like her and enjoyed the direction their relationship was heading, and after turning her down for dinner last night, Annabelle didn't have the heart to turn her away again. But-sleep, sweet glorious sleep, oh how she craved it.

Annabelle's feet dragged heavy as she took the few steps to her door, she shook her hair back and plastered a smile on her face, then slid the door open.

"Hey, gorgeous." Annabelle said with as much enthusiasm as she could muster.

Sawyer squinted her eyes and crossed her arms. "Are you okay? No offense, but you kind of look like death."

Annabelle laughed incredulously, "Geez, thanks!"

Sawyer put her hands up apologetically as she entered the room, "Sorry, I didn't mean anything by it. It's just not like you to miss work, and you look like you haven't slept in days."

Annabelle grinned and pulled Sawyer into a hug, "It's okay, I was only kidding. But, actually, I am really tired, I didn't sleep well last night,"-or at all-she thought to herself, "and I asked Ian to cover for me to catch up on some sleep."

Sawyer leaned back from their embrace and brushed a lock of Annabelle's dark straight hair out of her face sending tingles down her spine. Then said, "Well, you still have to eat, right? How about I go get us something and bring it back here?"

Annabelle nodded with a half-smile, her bottom lip sucked between her teeth, before saying. "Yes, please."

They slowly parted down to the fingertips while Sawyer said, "Okay, I'll be right back, don't go anywhere."

As soon as Sawyer was gone Annabelle's adrenaline and guilt started to creep back up. She needed to hide the box better. She rushed to her closet and flung the door open. She pulled the box out from a pile of crumpled laundry and looked around her small space for a better spot. There weren't many options. She settled on shoving it underneath her bed into the far corner of the room. Wriggling out from under her bed after it was placed, Annabelle stood up and dusted off her purple leggings.

Annabelle paced her small room as she waited for Sawyer to return with their food. Her mind raced with what she was doing. Stealing. Sneaking around. Lying by omission. This wasn't her. Not the kind of person she was.

*Pull yourself together Annabelle, why does the mystery earth girl mean so much to you? You're being a bit extreme all because your favorite person to watch has disappeared.*

But Annabelle couldn't help it. She had been watching *her* for years. Ever since stumbling into the surveillance room while looking for replacement water tubing for the garden when she was still an apprentice. There was something about this woman from Earth that Annabelle could not shake. Like a long-lost memory, or a forgotten word on the tip of her tongue. She finally understood the old videos she watched of fans screaming and passing out when they would finally meet their favorite celebrity.

*You're obsessed, Annabelle. Don't look at the flash drives. Get some rest. Tomorrow, you'll sneak the drives back where they belong, and you WON'T go back to the surveillance room.*

Annabelle heard light footsteps outside of her bedroom door and stopped pacing.

"I didn't know what you were in the mood for, so I got a little bit of everything." Sawyer said as she balanced a tray of food with one hip while sliding the door open.

Annabelle hurried forward, "Oh, let me help you!" Annabelle carefully took the tray and set it on the bed while Sawyer closed the door.

They sat crossed-legged on the bed across from each other with the tray between them. Annabelle watched a pleased expression flutter across Sawyers' face as she pointed out the items on the tray. "We have our various cheeses, strawberries, grapes, an assortment of crackers, and your favorite-tomato and basil toast."

Annabelle smiled quietly and stared at Sawyer before slowly leaning in and brushing her lips against Sawyers. "You are amazing and beautiful, thank you."

Pink flooded Sawyers' cheeks, "You're very welcome."

Annabelle's exhaustion was stronger than her hunger, but she forced herself to take bites as Sawyer chatted about her morning.

"Remember the patient I told you about that's expecting twins?" Sawyer spoke, "Well, she's only thirty-two weeks and has been in to see me over a dozen times for Braxton hicks. I don't blame her, it's her first pregnancy, but I've tried explaining to her-"

Annabelle's mind wandered back to the flash drives as Sawyer talked. The little black sticks pulled her focus, she wondered what secrets they held, what truths could be discovered within their depths.

"Annabelle? Are you still with me?" Sawyer leaned towards her in concern, her brow knitted together and a hand on Annabelle's thigh.

"Hmm? Oh, yeah, I'm sorry, I'm just so tired." Annabelle said bashfully as she lowered her gaze and was overtaken by a yawn. "I really think I need to get some sleep."

Sawyer patted Annabelle's knee and brushed a lock of her long black hair behind her ear. Annabelle felt a shiver of delight trail under Sawyers' touch.

"Of course, maybe we can catch up over dinner?" Sawyer asked.

"Definitely, that sounds nice." Annabelle answered with a grin.

Annabelle followed Sawyer to the door and softly slid it shut after Sawyer departed. She turned around and stared at her hiding spot while debating on pulling the small box out from the corner of the room, but instead, she crawled into bed, snuggled under her covers, and let her eyelids fall closed.

Ian and Annabelle walked through the garden as he showed her everything he had done in her absence the day before. He spoke animatedly with his hands as they passed each grow box. Then he paused at one in particular and Annabelle came to a stop beside him as she listened.

"So this box here, the troublemakers, I don't think they're going to make it. I added some fish emulsion to the soil, but as you can see, the leaves are still sickly. I just don't think we're going to get any of the Holy Basil to thrive. But the Plantain is thriving, which isn't really surprising, and as you know, they have similar medical uses, so it mostly evens out–but I'll let you be the one to tell Sawyer that her asthma case study will have to be put on hold."

Ian nudged Annabelle and laughed when she didn't reply. He chuckled at her stoic stance before saying, "Yo, Annabelle, ya with me? Where's your mind at?"

Anabelle with her arms crossed turned to face him and said, "I stole flash drives from Professor Trombol the night before last. That's why I needed you to cover for me, I was up all night. I'm a dirty cat burglar, Ian."

Ian was quiet for a second before the laughter started. Annabelle watched in shock as his chuckle built in his chest and boomed out of him until he was gasping for air. Finally, with a hand on her shoulder and leaning over as he wiped a tear from his eye, he caught his breath.

He stood up straight and tried to control his wide smile. "Okay, first of all, 'dirty cat burglar?' who talks like that? And second, you're kidding right?"

Annabelle's mouth dropped open, "Ian, no, I'm not kidding, I'm a thief, and I need you to take this more seriously. The guilt has been eating me up inside."

Ian's face turned serious, and he held her by the shoulders as he said, "Annabelle, you are the best, most kind, and honest person I know. Sure, you did a bad thing, but you are still a good person." He took a deep breath and then said, "I'm sorry I reacted that way. It was just a shock, I never expected those words to come from your mouth. But I'm listening now, and we'll figure it out together, okay?"

Annabelle let him pull her into a tight hug, her head tucked below his chin. "Thanks, Ian."

"Any time, Belle." He gently pulled her away and bent down slightly to meet her eye level. "So, what possessed you to break into Professor Trombol's living quarters? Did you suddenly have a hankering for some old biology lectures?" Ian asked with a playful sparkle in his eye and a laugh caught in his throat.

"Hardy har har, Ian." Annabelle grinned. After a moment of silence, she hugged herself, and her voice dropped close to a whisper. "No, I took them because... I know that she keeps logs of all communication between Luna and the resistance on Earth. I overheard her once when I was hiding in the surveillance room."

Ian slowly blinked his eyes and shook his head. "Hold up." He cleared his throat. "That's a lot to unpack, Belle. Give me a second." He carefully lowered himself to the floor, his arms limply hanging on his pulled-up knees, then patted a spot next to him on the floor. After Annabelle sat next to him, Ian said. "Okay, so you're saying the records room, the only room that is off-limits, where we supposedly store data and send it to the research team on Earth, is not a records room? Also, what do you mean by resistance?"

"Yes, I'm saying it's not a records room, I'm saying the first generation of Luna is spying on a military base on Earth." Annabelle took a deep breath and let it out slowly. "The Earth isn't healing because of our research. It's still dying, and our space station is sucking up its limited resources. It's the General. He's become an evil tyrant and from what I've gathered, there's a group of people resisting his dictatorship."

Ian picked at his cuticles as he sat in silence. Annabelle couldn't take it anymore, "Say something, Ian!"

He dropped his palms to the floor as if looking for mental stability. "Okay, here's what we're going to do." He started tapping his fingers and shoes on the floor, "Right. We have to see what's on those flash drives, Belle. If Earth is still dying after all the research Luna has done, then we need to find out why."

Relief flooded through Annabelle. It was a comfort to not be alone in her secret espionage, even if she did conveniently leave out the fact that her true reason for stealing the flash drives was to locate her missing person. But what she had told Ian was the truth and it wasn't until she had confessed to him that she realized how heavily that knowledge had been hanging on her shoulders. She was no longer alone in her secrets and even had renewed purpose in her life. Her objectives on Luna had become stagnant, knowing that their research was not doing any good, and she wondered if perhaps that was the reason she had become so fixated on the mystery woman. because she had nothing else to hold onto.

With Ian's help, Annabelle would be stagnant no longer. She would find a way to help the people on Earth.

# Chapter Eleven

## Earth

Téa could not deny that she was shaken. The world as she knew it was shifting, and if she did not tread carefully, she was fearful that she would slide right off the edge of the earth. As she fast walked back to her room her breathing came out rapidly. When she arrived, she pulled her door open, hurried inside and slammed it shut, then huddled into a corner with her back against a wall.

As her heart rate slowed, she stretched her legs and arms out, and took a few deep lungs full of air. Her thoughts raced; *how am I going to get through this*? If the General suspected that she was aware of his devious way, would he have her locked up until it was time to produce a grandchild for him? Or worse, what if Zephyr knew how deep the corruption within Dunamis had spread and moved up their one-year timeline. Once there was a baby to consider her chances for escape drastically decreased.

A slow ache blossomed in her chest. She had grown to trust Zephyr, even cared for him deeply. She could not believe that someone as kind and patient as him would be involved in the torture and torment of innocent people. He had not shown even a hint of violent tendencies, and Téa was more attune than most to the warning signs, especially when it came to men.

She shook off any doubts she had about Zephyr and focused on how she was going to get through dinner with the General. Then the thought came to her. Whenever a high-ranking officer back at base wore their dress uniforms, they always stood taller. Something about the nice clothes gave them the appearance of more power than they actually had.

Téa decided it was worth a try, stood up, went into her closet, and found the most sophisticated outfit she could. Her inner strength had faded but perhaps, she could take back some power by projecting confidence. She picked out dark gray slacks, and a silvery blouse that accentuated her figure. She pulled her hair up into an elegant bun with just a few loose spirals to frame her slender face. She was ready, she could do this.

On her way to the dining room, she practiced her most calm, happy expression. She walked tall with her head held high. But when she arrived, Zephyr and his father were already seated. Surprise ran through her like a flood. She thought she was early, and it was a shock to see them already there *and* almost finished eating. General Strauss sat at the head of the table, Zephyr to his left. Téa pulled a chair out next to Zephyr and sat down slowly.

He gave her a curious look as she sat down, "You look nice."

"Thank you." She said and smiled at him as she tried to appear undisturbed. "So, what did I miss?"

Zephyr cleared his throat, obviously taken aback by her premature presence. "You didn't miss anything. Father just wanted an early dinner after his long trip." He said as he tried to avoid eye contact.

Silence.

Téa was losing steam. She suddenly didn't know what to do with her hands. Was she sweating? She definitely felt hot.

"Miss Garcia." General Strauss' voice was deep and intimidating. "My son tells me that your physical aptitude is coming along expectantly."

She was not sure what she was supposed to say to a comment like that. *Thank you?* So she sat up straight and said, "I wish to exceed expectations, sir."

"Nonsense, Miss Garcia, you must only continue to do exactly as you're told. Nothing more, nothing less." His stern voice carried to her as he raised an eyebrow and frowned at her.

"Yes, sir." She looked at her hands in her lap.

Zephyr narrowed his eyes at his father's harsh tone towards her. "Dad..."

"You will address me as General Strauss or Sir." He glared at his son.

Téa was seated close enough that when their arms brushed, she felt Zephyr's muscles tense, and could see the veins in his wrists pulse as he clenched his fists and ground his teeth. She could not let him explode at his father; knowing now what the General was capable of, experimenting on Connex gene carriers and putting children into abusive homes to create *real life scenarios* thus forcing their Connex-B gene to activate. She gently and discreetly put a hand on his leg and gave it a light squeeze. He looked at her, and she locked eyes with him.

He seemed to understand a warning in her glance and held his tongue.

General Strauss spoke to them both, "I will be cutting this weekend short. There is too much to be done at headquarters. I will be leaving first thing in the morning. No need to see me off. Understood." It was not a question.

"Yes, sir." They replied at the same time.

"Miss Garcia. *Son.*" He inclined his head at them and left the room.

When the General was gone, Téa took a deep breath and released it slowly. She rested her head on Zephyrs' shoulder. Zephyr was not bad. She could feel it in her core.

"Are you okay?" he asked softly as he caressed her arm.

"I'm not sure, but I think I will be as long as I am with you." She did not mean for words that intimate to come out, but it was too late to take them back and she did mean them. She raised her head to look at him.

His voice wavered with emotion. "You will never have to worry about that. You will have me, always and forever." He held her face with both of his strong, smooth hands.

"Ditto," she said, her heart racing.

He gazed into her eyes. "Téa-"

One of the kitchen staff appeared and interrupted whatever Zephyr was about to say to her. "Sir. Ma'am. Will there be anything else for you tonight?"

Téa's hammering heart slowed.

Zephyr answered, "No, thank you, Angie. That will be all."

"Téa, I-"

"Please. Let's hold this conversation until tomorrow after your father is gone. There's so much I want to talk about."

He gave a slight frown as though he was a tad let down, but there was still hope and kindness in his eyes as he said. "Okay, tomorrow then. Can I walk you to your room?"

"Actually, I haven't even had dinner yet." She laughed as the nerves left her body.

"Ah, right, well, would you like me to sit with you?" He asked.

"No, I'll be okay. I've gotten rather good at finding my way around."

"Are you sure? I wouldn't mind being next to you for a while longer." He grinned shyly.

"I think I need a minute to myself if that's okay?"

"Of course." His head dropped and his smile faltered.

"But tomorrow, we'll talk?" She said hopefully.

"Yes, tomorrow. Goodnight." He raised her hand to his lips and gave it a kiss.

Alone with her thoughts, she knew they had to leave. They could not keep training for a secret mission where they might be used to try and enslave people with superhuman powers. That must be what all this was about, what else could all the training be for? The *unrest in certain communities* that Zephyr had mentioned. It had to be connected. General Strauss must be preparing them to take control of people with the Connex-A and Connex-B genes.

What were they going to do? Where could they hide? She had to trust Zephyr. She did trust him. She was frustrated that her hands were tied. That she couldn't solve this problem on her own because men in power had kept her trapped since she was child. But Zephyr had been kind and he knew more about the world than she did. He would know what to do. They would get through this together.

After she forced herself to eat, she headed to her room. She changed for sleep, then tossed, and turned as she let sleep take her into the night.

She was awakened by a knock on her door. *What time is it?* She found her watch. 4:30 in the morning.

Too early.

She groaned and shivered as she lifted her warm blankets, the General always had the air conditioning on full blast when he visited. As she opened the door, she could see the shadows under Zephyr's eyes, and took in his disheveled hair. He looked as exhausted as she was.

"Father left thirty minutes ago. I'm sorry to wake you, but I just couldn't wait any longer. I've been restless all night. I could not stop thinking about you. About us."

"Zephyr, please, slow down." She could barely open her eyes. She was cold in her light pink silk tank top and shorts. She crawled back into bed and covered herself in her blankets.

Zephyr stood awkwardly in the doorway.

"Well, don't just stand there, come on in."

He came inside and shut the door.

"Téa. What you said last night. That you would be okay as long as you had me. It... well, it meant a lot to me."

"Zephyr, please wait, there's so much we need to talk about."

"No, let me say this." He paced looking at her pleadingly. He ran his fingers through his light-brown hair. "Téa, I know we have been forced into this situation. This arranged marriage. I wanted to try and make it as comfortable for you as possible. I never wanted you to feel like a prisoner."

He paused and took a deep breath. "After meeting you, this thing between us became so much more for me than just a requirement. I know it has been such a short amount of time, but every day I spend with you, I feel myself craving more time. Every minute you are not next to me, I'm thinking about you. I feel complete and happy when you are near."

His cheeks flushed and he smiled. "You are beautiful. Stunning actually. I know you feel like you don't have a choice, and I have been terrified at the thought of you just accepting this role and not feeling anything for me. Scared of you playing the part without any true emotion. But last night. Last night, I felt it. I felt that you care about me, and I know that's real. Téa, I want to be with you, as more than someone you are forced to be with. I want you to be here because you want to be."

He glanced at her quickly with a desperate, sad gleam in his eye. "So, I haven't figured out exactly how yet. But I want you to know that if what you feel for me, if anything, is not real... then I want to help give you your freedom. I don't think I could handle it if I knew you felt like a prisoner with me."

"Zephyr, please, stop."

He stopped his pacing and looked at her. She lifted the blankets and patted a spot next to her on the bed. He slowly walked over and sat down. She wrapped her arms around his waist and laid her head on his chest. She felt his heart beat a mile a minute, a caged lion trying to claw its way out.

"Zephyr, you're not alone in your feelings. You matter to me; I don't want to go anywhere without you."

He pulled her chin up to look at him. He caressed her face.

A sharp involuntary breath.

Hearts pounding.

He leaned into her, paused, and gently brushed his lips against hers. She parted her mouth and they moved together. Responding to each other's increasing pressure. A quiet moan, and suddenly his hands were under her shirt pulling her closer.

Then, she remembered. She placed a palm on his chest and pushed away gently.

"Sorry," he said. "I was getting carried away." He nuzzled her nose with his.

"No, it's not that." She smiled. "But something happened yesterday. It's important. Can you give me a minute to get dressed?"

"Of course. I'll wait outside." He gave her one last kiss and she shivered again, this time, not because she was cold.

She hurried to the restroom, brushed her teeth, and fixed her hair into a smooth bun. Went to the closet, found a pair of dark jeans, and a maroon sweater, then opened the door to see him casually leaning against the wall with his arms loosely crossed, patiently waiting. "We need to go to the library," she said.

Moments later, they stood in front of the grand doors. "Zephyr, I am not sure I'm ready to go in there."

"What do you mean by that? Téa, what is this about?" He said it gently and ran his hands slowly up and down her arms.

There was so much she wanted to say... *I found something yesterday. Are you going to kill me when I show it to you? Should I show this to you? I've changed my mind, forget I said anything. Everything is going to change. Have you been lying to me this whole time? We barely know each other. The book is out in the open, of course you know. You are just as bad as your father. You were ready to protect me from your father. You are nothing like your father. I feel good when you are around. You make me feel safe. I just want you to hold me.*

No words escaped. Her heart thumped in her ears; her eyes watered as she stared at him with her back against the door.

"Téa, you are starting to worry me. What could be so bad inside a library? Please just talk to me."

She shook her head and opened the door. She walked towards the back where the desk and the shelves with the ledgers were. There it was, at the very bottom end shelf. Exactly where she had left it. She grabbed it and held it tight against her.

"I found this yesterday. I wasn't looking for anything in particular. I was just trying to find a good book to read while I was waiting to meet you and your father for dinner."

Slowly, she held it out for him.

He looked confused as he took the book from her. "What is this?"

"Please, just read it."

He seemed unsure but opened the book. He read the first few pages and then started flipping. He paled. He swayed a little and reached for the chair behind the desk. He sat down and kept reading. Téa paced for what felt like an hour, but was probably only minutes, he closed the book and put his head in his hands.

"I should have known," he said. "It's so obvious now. Téa how much of this did you read? Where did you find this?"

"I didn't read much, just a few passages. Enough to understand what your father is capable of. Weaponizing supernaturals." She pointed. "I found it exactly there. It was just sitting in the open for anyone to find. I thought for sure you must already know. That everyone, but me, must know."

Zephyr shook his head. "No, nobody knows. No one except my father most likely, and probably a handful of his most trusted soldiers. Which, before you ask, no I am not one of those trusted people. I am just a son who does what he is told."

He glanced at her and continued. "I knew of something. High level and top secret. I would see memos to my father coming and going that would mention genes, but I assumed it was related to our standard testing. They never mentioned anything about people with abilities."

He hesitated, then said, "I know there is a place back at Steppe Two. A secret wing with top level security where they perform experimentations. I always assumed it was new weapons, or biochemical warfare of some kind. I know better than to ask my father questions, so I never did." He inhaled deeply, stood, and gently held both her arms while he looked at her. "Téa, he would not just leave something like this lying around. It doesn't make sense for it to be in here."

They were both quiet for a while. She thought in silence before she said, "He almost caught me with it yesterday. I had just put it back when he came in to grab a ledger."

Zephyr's grip on her tightened slightly, a serious look in his eye, asked. "And he didn't notice this, or you?"

Téa shook her head. "I don't think so. He was in a hurry, just grabbed a ledger on the top shelf and walked back out. I was hiding behind that couch over there." She gestured towards the other end of the room.

He glanced quickly then looked back into her eyes. "I'm telling you Téa, he wouldn't leave this here, someone must have planted it. Someone wanted him to know that his secrets aren't safe."

Téa stared into the distance, mind churning, "Or someone wanted me to know," she said. "One of the kitchen staff recommended I check out the library, even offered to show me the way."

He pulled his hands away from her and crossed his arms. "Was it Angie, or William?"

"I don't know any of their names, but there were two men. It was the taller one."

"Two men? Téa, that is not possible. We only have two employees in the kitchen. A man and a woman, husband and wife."

"Zephyr, I'm certain there were two men, and he knew the kitchen protocols. I offered to help, he said the food was on strict lockdown, and that I couldn't help."

He shook his head and began to pace. "That's not true. One of the reasons our garden thrives is that we allow the employees to take what they need. It's how I decided we wouldn't have issues with stealing or hoarding. Otherwise, we would have to install and employ strict security in that section of the estate. Also, how would someone know you would be wandering in the kitchen and direct you to the library? And that you would then even find the book? That doesn't add up." He shook his head.

"Or he was waiting for the right opportunity, and it lined up perfectly? Maybe it was too risky to hand it to me. Why else come up with imaginary kitchen protocols to try and steer me away?"

He stopped, "You need to show me this man, I need to question him. Do you remember what he looked like?"

She nodded, "Yes, definitely."

"Okay, let's go to the kitchen."

When they arrived, a thick succulent aroma sat so heavy in the air Téa could almost taste it. The smell came from something simmering on the stove. Angie kneaded dough in the corner, and William cut a small pile of vegetables. They didn't seem to notice their arrival, so deeply in tune with their art.

Zephyr cleared his throat. "Angie, William? A word, please."

They both startled, paused what they were doing, wiped their hands on their aprons and faced Zephyr.

"Of course, Sir. Ma'am. How may we be of service?" William addressed them.

"Yesterday, there was a gentleman working the kitchen with you. What do you know of him?"

Angie and William shared a glance.

Angie spoke, "Sir, no one was helping us in the kitchen yesterday. A couple of your fathers' guards came and went. But no one assisted us or lingered."

Téa took a step forward, crossed her arms and said, "What about the man who suggested I look at the library? Surely you noticed me speaking to him?"

Angie and William looked at each other, and William spoke, "I'm so sorry ma'am. We don't recall seeing you in here yesterday." Angie nodded, agreeing with her husband.

"Understood. That will be all. Please, if you remember anything else, come and find me," Zephyr said.

"Yes, sir," William nodded.

As soon as they were clear of the kitchen, Téa said. "Do you believe them?"

Zephyr considered the question before replying. "Yes, I do believe them."

"How could they not notice me having an entire conversation with a stranger?"

"Everyone is on edge when father visits. They were probably extremely focused on their work. The General is very specific about his meals."

They were both quiet, walking without direction. Not knowing how to proceed, when one of the guards rushed towards them and stopped just a foot away.

"Sir! Urgent message for you. Password encrypted."

He took the tablet from the guard and dismissed him. Zephyr looked at Téa's questioning gaze and said, "Every high-ranking official has an individual password for top level communication. I have never gotten one before."

He entered his code and read the message, then showed it to Téa, eyes wide with fear.

'He knows. Get out now. You have 45 minutes.'

Téa stiffened with terror, "What does that mean? Who knows? Your father? What will he do if he knows we have information we are not supposed to have?"

"He'll kill us." Zephyr's tone was stone cold.

"But- you're his son." She could not believe the General would kill his own son over leaked information. Information they could not even prove.

"My father does not make mistakes, does not leave loose ends. There is a reason he doesn't want us to know about the Connex genes, and I have no doubt that he would not hesitate to kill me. Last of his bloodline or not, I have always been expendable. I know this because..." he ran nervous fingers through his hair, and gripped both sides of his head, "my mother didn't die in a car accident. He killed her."

She stopped breathing and clutched her chest, "What? Your Mother? Oh, Zephyr." Her tongue was lead, her heart breaking for him. "You said he couldn't hurt us, that he was bound by the laws of Dunamis."

"I was trying to make you feel better. Téa, my father *is* Dunamis."

Téa trembled. "What are we going to do?"

"We run."

# Chapter Twelve

# Earth

T éa was in her room packing as quickly as she could, shoving things into a backpack. Zephyr had given her strict instructions as they raced through the corridors.

'When we leave it will be hot outside. You cannot wear that sweater. Change into something with a lightweight material. Neutral colors. Nothing bright. It also needs to cover all your skin. Pack three changes of clothes. Items you can layer. Wear running shoes. No flats, no boots. You need to be able to run. Pack any other essentials you might need. Pads and other hygiene products. Try to empty your bladder. We cannot stop until we reach the border. Meet me in the garden.'

After she rushed to pack her things, she found him waiting for her just inside the indoor greenhouse with the beautiful flora. Such an odd sight to see something so beautiful during the midst of something so terrifying.

"Did you get everything you need?" He asked her.

She nodded. "I think so, what now?"

"I have packed as much fresh produce as I can. Some for us to eat, some for bartering. We need to get into the pantry for some dry food and water. But we can't risk involving Angie and William. We need to be careful that they don't see us."

They were able to get to the pantry undetected. They packed some bread, granola bars, and dried fruit for themselves. Salt, sugar, and dry beans for trading. As much water as they could carry. One small case for each of them in hand. Backpacks of clothes strapped on. Duffel over their shoulders full of food.

Zephyr whispered, "Okay, we're going out the service entrance in the back. Once we're outside, we still have about a dozen yards to get to the garage. Out there is a truck in the fleet with a camper shell. Are you ready?"

She was absolutely not, in any way, ready. But she had to be. She acknowledged him. "Yes."

Zephyr cracked the pantry door an inch and peeked outside. He gestured for Téa to follow. He ushered her away from the kitchen down a narrow hallway that she had never seen before with smaller high windows letting the sun in to light their way.

He pulled her into a small janitorial closet near the end. He took his watch off, then hers, and shoved them behind a stack of mildewed buckets.

Breathing heavy, he said, "The exit is only a few feet away, but there is nowhere to hide out there. Hopefully, we don't run into anyone. If we do, *don't say a word*, let me do all the talking."

She nodded. "Okay."

He looked hurriedly through the small gap. "Coast is clear." He opened the door, and they darted towards the exit.

Outside, a blast of heat hit her hard. The scorching land was so bland and blinding, she squinted her eyes. Immediately Téa felt the dust in her lungs settle, causing her to cough and making it hard to breathe. Every ounce of moisture was sucked from her skin, leaving her parched. Static from a walkie-talkie came from around the left corner. Zephyr pulled her towards the right.

"Hurry. This way."

They made it around to the other side where there was no cover of shade. The trees, long barren, were mere sticks in the sand.

Zephyr spared a quick breath before he told her, "We have to run, chances are pretty high that someone will spot us."

They moved as fast as Téa could pump her legs. The heavy gear weighed her down as they ran. Zephyr slowed to stay in pace with her. She tensed for a split second but kept going. It looked as though they were running into the desert where they could easily be spotted, but suddenly the land sloped, and ahead there was a huge concrete structure.

When they reached the metal door, Zephyr balanced his case of water on his knee and yanked the gleaming handle.

He grimaced and she knew the door was burning his hand. He held it open for her anyway and she hurriedly slipped inside.

He rushed to two boxes affixed to the wall, one silver and one first aid. He tore the first aid box off and stacked it on his case of water. Next, tugged open the silver box. Inside were dozens of keys. He knew exactly which to grab and led her down a row of vehicles. She saw the truck ahead, it beeped once, and its lights flashed as he unlocked it.

"Throw your supplies inside the cab!" He shouted as he did the same and sprinted away.

He returned in seconds carrying a full gas can in each hand, opened the tailgate, and put them inside.

"See that wall over there?" He pointed and she saw shelves stuffed full of tools, camping gear, and radios. "Go grab two sleeping bags and a tent if you can. I'm going to get a couple more gas cans."

She ran, paused for just a moment, and decided to take a radio as well, clipping it to her pants pocket. She grabbed the items he said, just barely able to get her arms around it all and ran back, shoving her haul in the vehicle as Zephyr closed the lift.

"Get in!"

She hustled to the passenger side, climbed in, and slammed her door shut. He stepped up to the driver's side and shoved the key in the ignition. When the truck rumbled to life, Zephyr jumped down and ran around to the front of the building. He pulled on a long, thick chain. The metal shop door in front of them clanged as it rose with each pull. Bright sunlight stared her down. Zephyr ran back and heaved himself inside. He gunned it and they shot off.

Téa looked behind them but could not see anything with the camper shell. She was going to roll her window down to stick her head out when Zephyr shouted.

"No! Don't! The glass is bulletproof. I can see with the mirrors. I don't think anyone is following us. Not yet anyway."

"What about the front gate?" She asked.

"We aren't leaving out the front. There's a rear entrance to Sandstone. Not many know about it. It hasn't been used in years."

Breathing heavily, she said, "I grabbed one of these." She showed him the radio.

Sweat dripped down his forehead and he smiled. "You are a genius! Switch it to channel four."

She did, and for a full minute it was just static. Then, one of the guards spoke.

'Does anyone have eyes on Mr. Strauss or Miss Garcia? They haven't reported to lunch.'

Zephyr looked at her, surprise across his face. "They don't know we're gone yet."

'Probably in their quarters, getting busy if you know what I mean.' Chuckling, then more static.

Zephyr was quiet before he said, "These only have about a three-mile range. We'll lose signal soon, but at least we will know when they're close."

They approached the rear exit. It was a much smaller, rusted gate that appeared neglected. Zephyr stopped the truck and got out. He struggled with the metal for a few seconds before it finally flung forward. He hopped back in and pulled up a few feet, then got back out and closed the gate. A meek effort at covering their tracks, then they drove on.

When the adrenaline eased from her body, Téa was able to think. "Zephyr, what did we just do? We acted on impulse. Who sent that message? What if it is a trap? What if whoever sent it wanted us to leave Sandstone, to get us out in the open."

He was quiet. "I don't know, we-" He was about to say something else when the radio came to life again.

'General Strauss is approaching the front gate; I repeat General Strauss is back on grounds.'

They looked at each other, like a pair of deer frozen in headlights. The encoded messenger was telling the truth. They made the right call to leave.

They left the radio on as they put distance behind them. As they listened, they were able to gather that his father knew they were missing and had sent a team by boots on the ground to search the castle. No one had reported seeing any vehicles coming or going, so the General must have assumed the two were still inside. When they lost signal, no one at Sandstone had yet noticed that a truck, or any of the other supplies was missing. They knew this would buy them some time.

"We have to keep moving. We need as many miles between us and them as possible."

"Where are we going, Zephyr? Where is there to go? Won't the General be able to find us anywhere?" Her heart thrummed in her ears.

He was silent. When he finally spoke, his voice was gentle again. Calm.

"We can't go to the far south. The big stretch from here to the southern coastline is uninhabitable, we wouldn't make it far before our gas would run out, and we would not survive long under the sun. There are small settlements along the west coast. But crossing the connected space is almost as bad as going south. We cannot go northwest. It's too close to Steppe Two. That leaves Northeast. The north is some of the only land left that resembles anything of what the topography was before the Decline. It is difficult to get access. I'm worried I will have to use my real name to get us in, and that would alert my father. Hopefully it won't come to that."

Téa reached for him and gently rubbed his hand with her thumb, careful to avoid the blisters that formed there from opening the hot metal door. "We'll figure it out, together. It will be okay."

He smiled at her and kissed her hand. "Right now, we just need to get out of Arid Sector. So few people are left, and even fewer have the means to get gas. We stick out like a sore thumb, especially if he gets the helicopter looking for us. If we can drive for at least eight hours without stopping, then we'll have a fighting chance."

She studied him. Chiseled jaw, sturdy hands, and those eyes. She could not recall ever seeing such pure gray. They intoxicated her.

"Zephyr, what you said before, about your mom?" He shifted, a little uncomfortable, but did not drop her hand. So, she continued, "Would you tell me what happened?"

He braced himself before speaking. "I was fifteen. She had started asking father questions. I am not sure about what, but they started to fight almost every day. That's when he began living at base, and only coming home on the weekends." He took a deep breath and let it out slowly. "They never had a loving relationship, but they used to be civil. It had always been a strained home, but the tension seemed to amplify. I actively tried to stay out of his way. Spent almost all my time in the garden or my room.

"One night he came home on a Thursday. Mom and I were reading together in the library. He rushed in. Something had changed, he was exhilarated. He told me to go to my room, but I stayed just outside the door, looking in. He was explaining something I couldn't hear. He was excited, but Mom–she wasn't happy. They started screaming. She slapped him. No one had ever laid a hand on him before, and he lost it. Picked her whole body up and threw her as hard as he could across the room.

Her head hit the stairs.

Blood pooled.

I yelled.

He ran towards me and grabbed me before I could get away. I thought for sure I was done for, his voice was dark, menacing. He said, Mom died in a car accident, that we would never talk about this or I would end up like her." He clenched his teeth and gripped the steering wheel. "Any amount of love I may have held for that man died with my mother that night. I actually hadn't gone back into the library since then, not until today."

She spoke softly, "Zephyr..." She didn't know what to say. So instead, she unbuckled, inched as close to him as she could, rested her head on his shoulder, and listened to his raging heart.

They had been driving for roughly six hours when Téa said, "I don't think I can hold it anymore. We need to pull over."

They drove the empty highways. The people who were still alive rarely abandoned their small towns. With travel too expensive, people had started living where they worked.

"That's fine. I'll fill the truck up while we're stopped."

They had started encountering small amounts of brush along the deserted highways, but nothing for cover. She squatted on one side of the truck while Zephyr filled up on the other. They hurried and only lost four minutes.

Back inside the truck Zephyr opened the glove compartment. Inside were tissues, hand sanitizer and medical grade face masks. "Here you go", he said with a smile. She was grateful for the sanitizer, not willing to waste any of their water.

They had started moving again when Zephyr spoke. "We're only about four hours away from the first North check point. It's just outside of what used to be Chicago." He hesitated. "I am recognizable by name, and no civilians are allowed to cross. That just leaves impersonating a serviceman and his wife. Do you remember the names of any married men from Base?"

She thought for a second, then smiled, "Just one, and I definitely do not care if he gets in trouble because of us. Although hopefully his wife will be spared. Melton Farris. Wife, Stephanie."

He grinned, "Perfect. Of course, we don't have identification. That is where we will have to grease the wheels, so to speak. Most guards are willing to look the other way with a little encouragement."

She laughed, "I'm familiar with that."

He smirked. "You're going to have to elaborate on that."

Téa smiled, "I used to sneak extra provisions all the time when I was younger. I would use the food to give to the guards, so they would let me pass without squeezing my ass, or so they would let me into facilities where I shouldn't be. Pay offs are a practiced skill to me." She winked.

He kissed her head. "So full of surprises."

Night had fallen by the time they reached the checkpoint. Streetlights illuminated inky hard tar and a single guard was stationed at the simplistic kiosk. The gate was one thin bar that lifted like a crooked grin. Téa thought they could drive through it easily if they had to, but Zephyr had told her about the small bits of metal that stuck out of the ground ready to puncture their tires. They needed the guard to lower them. If he did not let them pass, she worried about what she and Zephyr would have to do to the unsuspecting person.

Their lone vehicle pulled up.

Zephyr looked straight ahead as he spoke. "Good evening, Melton Farris and wife Stephanie, new transfers from Arid Sector."

"Welcome to Timber Sector, I'll just need your ah, identification." He was thin and young, his uniform hung off his frame, pimples dotted his chin.

"I accidently packed it in the back. You'll understand that I don't want to wade through my belongings to find it." Zephyr handed him a bundle of raspberries and a small watermelon. "For my apologies."

Téa remembered the food on base. He had probably never had fresh fruit before.

The young man's eyes were big as saucers as he took the offerings, "Right. It's so late, I ain't wanting to rummage in the dark neither. Lemme just run your names in the system, no ID necessary." He grinned.

Téa froze, she whispered to Zephyr when the guard walked away. "What will happen when he finds out Farris is not a transfer?"

"Don't worry. The computers are outdated. Most of the time, documents and pictures won't download so most don't even try. He'll see that Farris, and his wife are indeed assigned to the Arid Sector and let us go."

Zephyr did not seem confident as he shifted in his seat, eyes flashing from side to side, Téa ground her teeth.

Seconds ticked into minutes. Zephyr gripped the steering wheel so tightly Téa was sure he was kneading finger indentations.

The guard came back. "All set. Have a good night y'all." He raised his arm and popped a raspberry in his mouth, smiling as pink saliva dribbled down his chin.

They had gone about a mile when Zephyr stopped and yelled with enthusiasm. "We made it!" He pulled her to him and hugged her tightly.

Téa laughed. "I told you it would work out!"

He released her, beamed his gorgeous smile, and continued driving.

"Where to now?"

"There is a community about five hours further north. It's of minimal importance. The General doesn't pay it much attention. We should be able to rest there for a short while. Then we'll make our way east to shipping ports. Try to get to another continent."

Téa's heart was heavy despite having so many miles between them and the General. "It feels impossible that we made it this far." Her brow creased with worry.

He grabbed her hand and gave it a gentle squeeze before releasing it. "Hey, it's okay. We'll camp just outside the town to be safe. Just for a good night's sleep. We'll wake up early and we'll keep moving, stay ahead of them until we're out of my fathers' reach. As long as we're together, I know we can do this."

Zephyr's optimism was enough to slow her breathing and calm her mind. She grabbed them each a handful of granola and a bottle of water and opened Zephyr's for him, put their waters in the cup holders and passed his food to him.

# Chapter Thirteen

# Earth

They pushed through until they were finally outside of what used to be Wawa, Ontario, and set up camp in a field outside of town. They made sure they were far enough away to be unseen by the locals, but close enough to be alerted to any trouble. The township was small before the Decline. Now it housed just a couple dozen families.

Téa was grateful for the tent and sleeping bags, she was so worn out her bones hurt. She rolled up some extra clothes to make a pillow, and Zephyr followed suit.

They laid down inside the tent on their sides facing each other. Zephyr looked at her while he spoke. "You know, this whole area used to be surrounded by rivers. It bordered a great lake, teeming with fish. Clear and sparkling like a diamond. Trees so thick it was hard to walk through."

Téa tried to picture it and longed to live in such a world. "How do you know so much about before?"

"My mom. She was convinced the world could be as it was some day, lush and full of lives with freedom, better than what it is now. She used to travel with her family when she was a girl to so many places. She was passionate about describing the lands and when she talked about them, they would be vivid in my mind."

Zephyr tucked a strand of hair behind Téa's ear. She tingled at his touch, and she whispered, "Would you tell me more, maybe where your moms' favorite place was?"

Zephyr smiled ear to ear. "That's easy. Cape Perpetua in Oregon. She said she and her family hiked along the beach there, listening to the waves crash against the cliffs, watching the seagulls fly, and then she had found a tide pool."

Téa scooted closer. "A tide pool?"

"Yeah, it's this shallow little pool of saltwater, usually along rocky shores. It's full of small aquatic life. She said it was brimming with living things, snails, crabs, and anemones... seagrass that was soft and silky. Her favorite find was a bright orange starfish." Zephyr paused and looked at Téa with mock seriousness. "Which she was sure to warn me, never take it from its home out of the water. Doing that will kill it."

Then he smiled as he combed his fingers through her hair, igniting a fire deep within her, and he spoke. "It's a sea animal shaped like a star, rough to the touch, with these little round suction cups underneath that'll grab hold, and attach themselves to you, but they're so beautiful you won't ever want them to let go." Zephyr stroked her cheek. "Kind of like you. You've grabbed hold of me, Téa, and I don't ever want you to let go." He kissed her fingertips. "My sea star."

Téa had a lumberjack in her chest trying to break free, heart racing, warmth spread up her sides.

He took a breath and let it out slowly. "My mom said the ocean was like her own secret world that she could disappear into. She'd spend the whole day by those tide pools until the sun set and her breath chilled."

He turned to lay on his back, keeping hold of Téa's hand, and placed it on his heart. "Now there's nothing left where we are but large ponds. Elsewhere, rivers are dried up, oceans devoid of life, forests sparse instead of dense." A single tear rolled down his cheek. "All because of some poison in our atmosphere that no one has ever been able to explain."

Téa reached out and wiped his tears away, replacing them with soft kisses, and lay her head on his chest, listening to his breathing. Laying next to him made her feel anchored and safe. She was sure he must be able to hear her heart beating. "The world is still beautiful to me," Téa said. "Genesis was the first time I saw grass. Maybe your mom's wish will come true? Maybe Operation Luna could fix things?"

The muscles in his jaw twitched before he replied, "I wish it could. Operation Luna is nothing more than a lifeboat for humankind. A backup generator. There is no easy fix for Earth. The damage is too extensive." He looked down at her, caressing her face.

The thumping in her chest increased in pace. "Zephyr, how long can we run? Eventually, your father will find us."

Overcome with emotion, desire, fear, her tears fell. He gently wiped them away and pulled her closer, placing a warm gentle kiss on her lips. He then unzipped both their sleeping bags, and rezipped them together. He held her tight and breathed her in. His strong arms wrapped around her, and she thought she could live in the heat of this moment forever. They comforted each other until the rhythm of their beating hearts synced as one.

"Téa, I can't promise he won't find us. I can promise that I will do everything I can to keep you safe..."

She could feel his pulse quicken under her hand and he said, "Téa. I am in love with you."

She saw the tenderness in his eyes, felt the truth of his words in the center of her being. Téa knew, as sure as the sun was hot, that he was genuine. She cared for him but didn't know what love was. Could this be it? He protected her and was kind. She knew she was attracted to him. She had a longing in her heart for companionship and when he touched her, however, innocently, her whole body vibrated.

He pressed his lips to hers as though she could disappear at any moment. "I want you Téa... Do you want me?"

*Want?*

She did want to be near him, to know him. She felt good when he was close, but she knew that's not what he meant. Then he brushed his hand down her arm and left pleasant shivers in his wake.

She never wanted his caresses to end. "Yes, I want you, Zephyr."

His lips were on hers again, gentle, and sweet. Then their kisses intensified. She didn't want him to stop, she did not want him to ever stop touching her.

He grabbed behind her thigh and lifted her leg over his, and she thought for sure her heart would leap out of her. He combed his fingers into her hair, gently massaging her scalp. A pleasant sensation crept through her. His weight against her was firm and sure as they continued to kiss. He breathed heavily as he lifted his shirt over his head. She ran her soft fingers over his tight chest.

He started to raise the hem of her shirt when she was suddenly alert. She was not ready for him to see the silver chain around her neck, so she held his hand, and he stopped without hesitation.

"Do you want to stop?" he asked.

She shook her head and all she said was, "leave the shirt," then pulled him back to her.

Zephyr rolled her from her side to her back and put his arms around her. Their kisses deepened as they explored each other's bodies. Zephyr was gentle and took his time. He moved in response to her every motion. They were passionate with one another, and at last, they fit together perfectly, they rose and fell together.

They breathed each other in and held each other close. Téa never wanted to let go, she never wanted to leave this moment. When her breathing slowed, happy and content, she pulled her clothes back on, then Zephyr did the same. Zephyr wound his fingers through her toussels of curls, and lightly brushed his hand across her arms.

"Zephyr?"

"Hmm?" He smiled and nuzzled her nose.

"Don't ever let me go," she said. This man had tenderly grabbed at her heart and intertwined it with his own.

"Never, my Love. Get some sleep." He pulled her close, sharing one last soft kiss, and they fell asleep in each other's arms.

Dawn broke. They could not have gotten more than a few hours of sleep. Téa sat up, still groggy, when a cry sounded in the distance. The noise was so faint she wondered if it was just the wind, but Zephyr shot up straight from a deep sleep awake and alert.

"Téa, they're here! We have to go now!"

He grabbed the sleeping bags from under her, and shook her shoes out, "Leave the tent. We have to move!"

Téa silently cursed herself for not putting her shoes back on last night, precious seconds lost.

She ran towards the passenger door when Téa saw them in the distance and stopped short. Across the field, far enough for a sprint, but close enough to see clearly, a soldier had come out of a small log home. He dragged a woman by her long blonde hair through the mud. She kicked and screamed. The soldier raised his weapon. Téa heard the sharp crack reverberate around them. A perfect red hole sat between the woman's eyes.

Silenced.

The woman dropped like hot rubber.

Téa blanched, limbs frozen stiff. Zephyr shook her, screamed something at her, someone, more soldiers, behind them. The world spun.

Someone yanked Zephyr down by his neck from behind. General Thomas Strauss stood over Zephyr where he lay on the ground coughing. Heat radiated off the General's massive body, spittle flying from his beard. Eyes wild.

The world sped up, sounds became sharp again, bringing Téa back into the moment.

"Did you think I wouldn't find you?!" Strauss blared. "And taking HER with you!" He bent down and dragged Zephyr by the collar then kicked him hard in the ribs. "You should know better than to cross me, boy!"

The sight of Zephyr holding his body in pain broke Téa free of her shock. She threw herself at the General. He released Zephyr and yanked Téa off, violently putting her to the ground. "Don't even think about it, *little bitch.*"

Téa felt a desperate desire to keep Zephyr safe, she screamed at him. "Kill me! Leave him alone and kill me. He's your son!"

This got Zephyr's attention and he stood up, "NO! Do not touch her!"

Strauss laughed, so hard it brought tears to his eyes. He doubled over and howled so loud Téa's ears split. "Ah, so the little love birds have spirit! Don't worry, I won't be killing my greatest *assets.* Not today at least."

Téa and Zephyr looked at each other with confusion as two guards grabbed their wrists, pulled their arms behind their backs, and handcuffed them. The cold hard metal was too tight and bit into her skin.

The General barked orders. "Take them to town. Get them loaded on the copter."

Hearing that, Zephyr ducked down and quick as a whip swung a leg out and around, bringing his guard to the dirt. He ran headfirst at the second guard holding Téa so hard that the man's body left a dent in the truck behind him, and the guard collapsed unconscious.

Zephyr's father bellowed. "ENOUGH!" He snatched a handful of Téa's hair, pulling roughly against her scalp, she grimaced.

Zephyr reached down the back of his legs, pulled his cuffed hands under and in front of him. Then he grabbed a handgun from the limp guard and aimed it at his father.

"Let. Her. Go."

His fathers' face flushed with hate, eyes slits. "You do not want to do this, *Son*."

The first guard rose, and Zephyr shot him in the leg. He wailed like a dying cat and hit the ground.

Zephyr pointed the gun again at his father. "I said, *let her go*. Now."

The General shoved Téa towards Zephyr and raised his hands "You have the keys boy." He growled.

Zephyr crouched, kept aim on Strauss, and took the keys for the handcuffs from the pocket of the still unconscious guard, while the injured guard continued to scream in the background. Zephyr released his hands from their confinement, and then Téa's.

"You will not follow us or call for help. I will shoot you."

"Well, you better do it now Son," the General declared, ice in his voice. "You will never have another chance, I can assure you of that." The General spat.

Zephyr held his hand out. "Téa let's go."

Heart racing and palms sweaty, she grabbed him and they backed away. As soon as they were a safe distance, they ran toward town.

"Zephyr what are we going to do!?" She screamed as terror tore through her.

"We're going to steal their helicopter." He shouted.

Pure hot adrenaline coursed through her veins. As she ran beside Zephyr, she could see the fear and focus in his eyes. They approached the first house on the edge of town, where the spent female body lay, that golden hair and scarlet-covered face would forever be etched on her mind.

"This way!" Zephyr pulled her along as they sprinted.

They rounded a corner and were about to run directly into the back of a soldier. The same one who shot the woman. The soldier turned as he heard their feet pounding the ground. Zephyr shot him before he had a chance to raise his weapon. Téa's ears rang from the blast. Her teeth started to chatter.

Zephyr slowed and held a finger to his lips. They were close to the settlement center where the metal bird waited.

He whispered. "I know my father's pilot. He will not give up the controls, but I don't want to kill him, he's a good man. Since I know how to fly, I am going to try and take him by surprise. Wait here and stay quiet."

Zephyr darted on light feet to the open doors of the copter. He tucked the gun into the waist of his pants, then climbed up without a sound. In a flash, one forearm wrapped around the pilot's neck. With his other hand, Zephyr pushed the pilot's head forward. The pilot swung wildly, trying to make contact, but it was futile. Within minutes, he was put to sleep. Zephyr pulled his limp body from the helicopter and drug him a few feet away.

Zephyr motioned for Téa to come forward. She jumped up from her hiding spot and sprinted towards him. Shouts rose up in the distance, and gunfire erupted hitting the ground next to her, spraying dirt into her eyes.

"NO!" A familiar voice cried out. "Hold your fire! I repeat, hold fire! Do not kill the girl! The General needs her alive!"

She paused for a split second, sparing a glance behind her, and saw Commander Hue Hillside.

They caught each other's eyes for only a moment, he nodded his head at her as if sending her some sort of acknowledgment that he was on her side. Téa pushed away her hesitation and leapt into the helicopter.

"Strap yourself in!" Zephyr yelled from the front seat, set to take off.

Téa looked back at Hue as they lifted. He was talking to his wrist. General Strauss approached from behind and whacked Hues' head with the butt end of his gun. Hue fell.

Téa trembled. The General stared at her, his gaze unwavering, as they rose to the sky. The *chuff chuff chuff* and whirring of the copter drowned out all other sound. She stared back until General Thomas Strauss was nothing but a pinprick.

Zephyr shouted but flying at full power she could not hear what he said. She remembered the headphones. She looked around and found a pair just behind her seat and put them on.

She could hear him now. "Téa," he said. "Are you okay? Are you hurt?"

"No, I'm not hurt, I'm okay."

He was quiet for a minute, then said. "We won't have enough fuel to make it to the coast, so we need to travel as far Northeast as possible. I've heard rumors of people living off the grid there. Maybe, if the rumors are true, and we find them, they can help us."

Téa's eyes burned with fatigue. It felt as though she had just fought her way through a storm. The breaking water, ever constant and deep. The adrenaline and tension slowly eased away, but fear lingered. It was too much to process. What would they do now? They had no supplies, no plan, and nowhere to go, what if the rumors of these people were just that?

She distracted herself by taking in the landscape. They flew over mostly deserted territories. The trees thickened. She had always been told there was nothing left. But here, in the far North, there remained life. Perhaps not as pronounced as the previous generation would recall, but maybe all hope was not lost to this Planet.

After an hour, a short, single high-pitched and repeating tone warned her of a problem.

The blades stuttered, and the cabin shifted. They were tilted almost sideways.

Fear flooded through her as Zephyr screamed. "This is going to get rough! Hold on!"

Images rushed past too fast to decipher. A blur of green, blue, white, and brown flashed past the windows. The air assaulted her like a hurricane. They crashed into the forest, the metal crumbled and glass shattered.

The world darkened.

# Chapter Fourteen

## Space Station Luna

Their steps tapped along the floor like morse code as Annabelle and Ian scurried along the corridors to her room, bumping into multiple people along the way. Once there, they threw themselves inside and shut the door.

"Well, it's decided, we are not built for stealth." Breathing heavily Ian flung himself back on Annabelle's bed with his arms splayed out above him.

Annabelle laughed as she leaned against her closet door trying to catch her breath. "You can say that again. I blame you! I've managed stealth just fine on my own, but you come along and suddenly my nerves are on fire and we're walking like a pair of puppies who haven't found their feet." She bent over leaning on her knees as she tried to contain her nervous laughs.

Ian sat up, his breathing slowed, "So we're definitely not going to use the recreation room to look at the flash drives. Where did all those people come from? Don't they have jobs to do?"

Annabelle and Ian had retrieved the flash drives after their talk in the greenhouse and had decided to go through them in the recreation room, which was one of the only places that didn't have cameras in every corner and was typically empty this time of day. But their plan quickly unraveled when one of the guys Ian had recently gone on a date with showed up with a handful of his buddies.

She crinkled her nose and frowned. "What did you even see in that guy?" Annabelle asked, "He was so nosy-and sweaty."

"Did you not see those muscles though? I mean what human could turn *that* down." Ian said with a tone of voice that clearly stated what an obvious choice it was to date, *John from human resources.*

"Ugh, that's a *no* from me, I can't deal with all that body hair. One of the many bonuses of only being attracted to women, much less hair." She winked. "Which reminds me, whatever happened to Stephanie? I had high hopes for her, she was really sweet."

Annabelle moved to sit next to Ian on the bed as he answered, "Yeah, she was nice, and I mean that body-" He grinned as he wiggled his eyebrows, "but we just didn't connect up here." He tapped his forehead knowingly. "There was no spark-ya know what I mean?"

"Yeah, I do." Annabelle thought back to a time not so long ago when she had yet to accept herself for who she was. The men she dated never produced a spark, but with Sawyer, it was instantaneous.

Silence sat between them before Annabelle asked, "So what now? We can't look through the drives in here, Sawyer could show up at any minute."

Ian raised his eyebrows, "Really?"

Annabelle gave Ian a small shove, "What? We've been spending more time together lately." She shrugged then took a deep breath and continued, "So, our bedrooms and restrooms are the only other places without cameras. I am not going to stand in a toilet stall for hours on end, and you have a roommate."

Ian was quiet for a moment, "True. However, Jeff has been spending most nights with Daphne, and we do have the ol' *sock on the door* understanding, so we could probably use my room." He said with a shrug.

Annabelle chucked a pillow at his face, "Why didn't you say that sooner? We could have avoided all this nonsense, Ian!"

"Really? Nonsense? Annabelle, you really are starting to sound like a *posh lady*." He grinned and stood with his hands on his hips as he swayed side to side like a proud peacock.

Annabelle threw a second pillow at him, and he caught it easily as he laughed and said. "Alright, so my room it is. Are you ready for this?"

Annabelle thought of all the things she had already seen the General do and the things she had already overheard.

None of it was good, and whatever was on the flash drives was probably worse–otherwise, why keep it a secret?

"No, not really." She said, having no idea what she would do after discovering what was on the drives, and wondering if she really wanted to know. But there were too many critical pieces in motion that she could no longer ignore. Determined, she stood and faced the door, "But let's get to it anyway."

Annabelle and Ian were huddled together on the floor of his room with his laptop propped in her lap, The bright lights that simulated daytime had already faded, and the glow from the screen created a white halo around the pair in Ian's darkened room. Her heart raced, pulsating in her ears turning them flush as she scrolled through the text of data before her.

"The General has a son? How is that possible? How could that be kept a secret so well?" Ian whispered next to her.

Annabelle's words came out in a rush. "I don't know. I've never seen anyone in surveillance that he has ever treated like a son. I've been able to figure out that there are some wings at Steppe Two where we don't have a video feed. Maybe he's been there before, but I don't think I've ever seen him." She looked at Ian's confused face, then said. "I mean, obviously I wouldn't know what he looks like, I'm just saying no one of 'son' age has ever hung around the General when he's on base, and all the upper military are older." Annabelle shrugged her shoulders.

Ian pointed to a spot on the screen. "Well according to these reports from whoever informant X is, the son may actually be a decent human being. He seems to be an unwilling participant."

"Yeah, but still a participant." Annabelle scoffed with a hint of sadness.

"Take it easy, Belle. Look at all this shit the General has done. We have no way of knowing what kind of person his son is, if he's been free to make his own choices or not." Ian was quiet while he sat back and stared at Annabelle. He sighed deeply before asking, "Hey, Belle, how long has this been going on? The sneaking around?"

She didn't look at him, unease wormed its ugly way up through Annabelle's stomach. "Why does it matter?"

Ian rubbed his scalp and said hesitantly, "It's just that, all the plants that have been failing lately, the Holy Basil, the ginger, tomatoes... you know as much as I do that our mood has a real effect on things."

Annabelle's guilt wiggled around inside, and her cheeks flushed with shame. "Let's just keep looking, Ian. Professor Trombol has another lecture tomorrow. I'll be able to put these back, so we only have tonight."

Ian leaned back in to stare at the screen while Annabelle scrolled. She heard the sound of his slow breathing and felt the weight of him on the bed next to her; she took comfort in his unwavering friendship, even if she knew he was worried about her. She also knew that he would always have her back.

She pointed again at the screen. "Nearly ten years ago, it looks like Operation Luna sent its findings to the General." Annabelle crinkled her brow in confusion, "But why then has nothing improved on Earth?"

Ian tapped a different part of the screen, "Look here, there are notes dated a couple of years later."

Annabelle read it out loud in a hushed voice.

*"The lack of action taken by the General has confirmed our worst fears. He has no desire to heal the planet. In order to stop the poison from spreading, he would have to give freedom back to the people. He claims doing so would cause more harm than good. He still believes the people need to be controlled for their own survival and safety.*

*We have requested help from the resistance to spread the truth. They are too fearful that it would take too long to see results and they insist their own survival and safety can only be guaranteed if the General is no longer in power. They will continue to grow their communities as best they can in secret, but we fear this is a short-term solution. Worldwide healing can only happen if the entire planet knows the truth.*

*While we have been able to hack into the video feed from Steppe Two. We have been unable to find a way into the universal broadcasting system. As such we are unable to spread the truth ourselves. The General is still paranoid and sends his guards to inspect the space station periodically, and he has forbidden any Luna personnel to return to Earth. Luna cannot survive independently without regular ship-ments of supplies from Earth. Our only option is to follow the General's orders. Our only hope is to keep Luna operational long enough for the resistance to fight back."*

Annabelle took a deep breath and looked at Ian with wide eyes, "So that's why the Earth is still dying."

Ian responded with disbelief in his voice, "What about the part where it says we can't return to Earth. We're stuck here, Belle, and at his mercy."

Annabelle looked at him silently. She thought back to when she proposed ending operation Luna, that's why no one agreed with her. The first generation knew that it wasn't up to the space civilians to decide. The General would not have allowed it even if they did agree. And the rest of the community believed their research was making a difference.

Ian narrowed his eyes at Annabelle when she didn't say anything and asked with a questioning voice, "Wait a minute. Belle? You knew the Earth wasn't healing? Why didn't you tell me?"

Annabelle shrugged, wrapped her arms around her legs, and nervously tapped her toes. "I don't know, Ian. It's been a lot just finding out that the first generation of Luna has been keeping so many secrets from us. I don't think I knew how to react." While that was true, she also hated admitting to herself that she didn't want to share *her* with anyone else. She couldn't explain it, but there was something about this woman that made Annabelle protective.

"Do you ever wonder who your birth parents were?" Annabelle asked as she continued to tap her toes.

"No, not really. I mean there were so many of us, yourself included, that were given up for adoption when the Earth started dying. I like being raised by the community. There's a sense of comfort in having so many people to turn to, but also a sense of freedom." Ian dropped his chin to his chest, staring down, and sighed. "Nice change of subject though, Belle. I get it. You could have come to me, but you didn't, for who knows how long." He raised his head with his eyes closed and rubbed his temples. "For the record, you *are* my family, Belle, and it just hurts that you'd keep something so massively huge from me."

His words pierced her like a needle to the chest. She hadn't even thought about how Ian might feel once he found out she was keeping so many secrets. She hated seeing him look so betrayed. She was floundering looking for the right words to say, to comfort him. He was her family too.

She started scrolling the files again, and just when the emotional choke was loosening,

and she was finding air in her lungs to say the right words to make things better between them, Ian cleared his throat.

"I don't think I can look at any more of these files, it's too much." He said as he gave his

head a shake.

"Ian, I'm so sorry-" Annabelle searched for the right words, but they wouldn't come. So she scrolled again and gasped in shock, "Oh my God, Ian, look at this."

The tension between them instantly fled as they both leaned in to stare at the screen. Annabelle read in a rush.

"*Informant Alpha has informed us of an impending 'planet killer' meteor on a direct collision course with Earth. How-ever, informant Alpha cannot confirm how they obtained such information, and our advance warning systems have not picked up any threats."*

"When was this dated?" Ian asked with fear in his voice.

"It doesn't say. But it's with all these older files, it can't be new information." Annabelle said, with uncertainty in her eyes as she continued to scan through the file. "There's no other mention of any meteor or asteroid of any kind, it must not have been credible information."

Ian stood up fast and began pacing the room. "What if it *is* credible, Belle? Could you imagine? We're *years* away from making Luna self-sufficient, without the Earth..."

He trailed off, but he didn't need to say it, she knew what he meant, they would all die. Operation Luna was ill-equipped to be the last hope for mankind.

Annabelle stood and went to Ian, grasping his arms to stop his pacing. "I'm sure it ended up not being a credible threat. And Ian, we don't need Luna, we just need to get back to Earth. I know the soil there can still hold life."

She took a breath and looked at him, but he seemed unconvinced, so Annabelle said, "Also, the General may be cruel, but there's no way he'd let the entire planet die. Those wings at Steppe Two where we can't see what's going on, I bet you anything he's working on a cure."

"Belle, we have the best scientists in the world right here on this ship and they haven't found a cure. If they haven't figured out how emotions could suddenly seep out of human pores and turn to poison that only affects plants, then there is no hope. And if a meteor is heading our way, maybe it's nature's way of telling mankind that our time is up."

He shrugged her off and walked past her, "I love you, Belle. But I need a break. I can't look at these files anymore." He left the room, leaving silence in his wake.

Annabelle tried to push away the despair that was trying to eat her up. Everything felt off kilter. Her feet unsteady, she sat on Ian's bed and looked around the room. His side of the small space was just as unkempt as her own bedroom. Old movie posters hung haphazardly around the walls, shoes and clothes strewn about, and a plate of old food sitting on his desk. His roommate's side was perfectly tidy, not a speck out of place.

Ian was just like her. Messy and a little wild on the outside but wholly intact and content to help and love others on the inside. She knew him as well as herself. And she knew now how much he must be spiraling because she too was having a hard time hanging onto anything that even resembled normalcy.

# CHAPTER FIFTEEN

# Earth

Téa woke first. She could smell the sweet benzene and the danger they were in. Heat pressed against her as the fire burned greenery nearby. Mangled, warped metal was strewn into an art form around her. Oil and gasoline leaked from the defeated mechanism, primed to explode.

She had to move, but when she tried, Téa realized she was upside down and still buckled in her seat. She released the harness and braced for the impact. She smacked into turf; the roof of the helicopter was gone. Téa gasped and coughed. Her rib cage burned with every breath, and she could feel a flickering just below her heart and to the side, a muscle spasming for purchase.

She held her torso and struggled to stand. Desperate to find Zephyr, Téa combed the area, lifting what pieces of metal and debris she could. The heat from the fire increased. It didn't take long until she saw him at the edge of the debris, still upright in his seat, eyes closed.

She stumbled forward and tried to release him from the chair, quickly realizing that his fastening was jammed. She started to panic. The fire crackled and snapped as it ate away at the twigs and branches.

"ZEPHYR! WAKE UP!"

She tugged on the tough webbing, but it refused to release him. She slapped him as hard as she could, the movement in her ribs caused her intense pain and she yelped. His eyes fluttered open. Téa sobbed through the snot, soot, and blood.

"Knife." His voice came out in barely a whisper.

"What?" She shrieked.

"Knife. There's a knife inside my boot."

The snip-snap and woosh of the roaring inferno overwhelmed her ears. She pried the knife free and sliced the polyester that trapped Zephyr. It was sharp and he was released immediately. He tried to stand but made a noise of painful realization and howled.

"My leg is broken." He looked at her with defeat in his eyes. "You need to leave me."

Panic flashed through her; she couldn't leave him behind to be burned alive. "No. We can do this, let's go! Now!" She heaved and clamped her teeth together, straining the already torn muscles in her ribcage.

He mustered the will to help her move his body away from the growing blaze. They limped and hobbled together until they collapsed a momentarily safe distance away. They lay on their backs and gasped for air.

Zephyr struggled to talk. "We have to keep moving. The fire, it'll spread faster than we can run. I saw some water before we lost power. It's about a mile further north. It's the best chance we have."

Red liquid poured out of his leg from a thick gash in his calf. "You won't make it if we don't stop that bleeding." Téa said.

She took her shirt off, wearing just a bra, and ripped the bottom half of the lightweight material twice. She held two long strands of fabric and tied one above Zephyr's knee, hoping it would stop the blood flow in his lower leg, then tied the second around the gash. She put what was left of her clothing back on, wrapped his arm around her shoulders, and trudged on.

They stood at the base of a great mountain; the sun blocked by incoming clouds. A chill crept around her from suddenly being away from the fire and sun, but when her teeth started to chatter, she realized the chills were more than cold-related. They had survived the crash and stared death in the face. They made terribly slow progress as they stumbled through the trees and brush. The weight of Zephyr's body felt heavier and heavier, slowing them down.

Finally, she saw the glittering, muted rainbows dancing on top of the lake. They made it. Téa eased Zephyr to the ground, his back against a tree, and took stock of their surroundings. Just a few yards away she saw an abandoned cabin. Shelter.

"Zephyr, there is a house a few feet away. See?" she pointed.

He didn't respond.

Téa's already pounding heart started to slam against her chest, her breathing came out rapidly as she looked at his closed eyes.

"Zephyr?" His quiet tore at her. "Zephyr! Please, no. Not now. We are so close!"

His silence brought her to her knees. A soundless scream of pain escaped Téa floating away into the empty wind, and she collapsed on his chest. She cried out what was left of her will, her hope.

"There, there. Shhh. It's okay," said a voice beside her.

Téa's head snapped up, and mere inches away was a gentle, soft face of wrinkles. She hadn't heard them approach. Téa took a breath and let it out slowly, she placed two fingers against Zephyr's neck and when she felt a pulse she could not hold back her smile and tears of relief.

"He's lost a lot of blood. Please help me," Téa whimpered.

"Ted. Over here. Help me get this boy into the house." The old woman called over her shoulder, and then looked back to Téa. "You are in luck, darling. My son is a nurse."

Ted lifted Zephyr with ease and walked towards the house.

Téa suddenly remembered. "The fire. There's a fire about a mile back where we crashed."

"Oh, don't you worry yourself about that. The Vida Brigade already smothered it out." The old woman smiled reassuringly.

"The what?"

"Vida Brigade, dear. That is what this sector calls the resistance."

"Resistance?" She asked, confusion creasing her brow.

"Oh my. We do have a lot to talk about, don't we? Come on then. Let us get you inside."

Téa struggled to her feet, holding her chest. She would love to dive into the cold-water mere inches away and wash the ash from her lungs. Maybe later she would get a chance. She followed the old woman, who was surprisingly fit for her apparent age.

Téa stood in front of the porch of the brittle, rotten structure. It appeared as if not a single soul had passed the threshold in years. Small and almost empty inside, the front window was cracked, and leaf carcasses littered the floor. Téa stepped into the home, taking care to follow the old woman's steps exactly to avoid falling through the rotten areas, and peered into the house. The only furniture was a broken lamp in one corner, and a solitary, mildewed chair in another. After taking in the house, Téa realized that she did not see Zephyr or Ted. Her pulse quickened.

"Where are they!?" She turned to face the old woman, but she didn't see her.

"Over here, dear."

Téa hurried around the corner to the next room. The old woman held up a slab of the flooring on hidden hinges. Téa started down a set of rickety stairs. The old woman followed and closed the hidden passageway, tiny streams of light filled with dust slipped through the minor cracks in the wood above.

"Watch your step, dear. We can't risk light during this stretch of tunnel. There should be a string to your left. We have not used this outpost for quite some time. Feel for it."

Téa could smell the cold dirt as she touched the damp wall. "Yes, it's here."

"Good, good. Hold tight and it'll guide the way."

"Where's Zephyr? I'm not going anywhere without him."

"Oy. You are stubborn, aren't you? Ted will be running with him just a little way ahead. You are going to have to trust me," she said in a placating voice. "Now we must move. Your friends won't be far behind."

"What friends? The General's men?" Téa tensed, "They are not our friends." She said defensively.

The old woman chuckled. "Has sarcasm gone extinct as well? What a sad day indeed."

Téa clenched her teeth and started to move. She had no other choice. She didn't know where she was, she had no resources to help Zephyr, and watching him slowly die from his injuries was not something she was prepared to do. The fact that they even found other people out here in the middle of nowhere was miracle enough.

Resigned to accept the help, she asked. "Where are we?"

"We are in an abandoned mining tunnel. It trails under the forest. Dunamis does not have it on any of their maps. The Claybelt mine was an illegal operation before the Decline. Now it is completely deserted. It serves us well to come and go when we are forced to leave the Sanctuary."

"What is the resistance, and what is the Sanctuary?"

"The word 'resistance' is self-explanatory, is it not?"

When Téa did not say anything, the old woman continued. "When the Earth had begun to die, and Dunamis started taking more and more control years ago, pockets of civilians resisted their takeover. But, as the population depleted, so did our resources. We merely survived as best we could, in secret.

"Eventually, we discovered that Dunamis had greatly exaggerated the expiration of our planet. While it is true that the center areas of this continent are no longer viable, in less densely populated sections of the planet, nature was still thriving. I have even heard that in tiny parts of Guatemala there are birds, and bees in Africa."

Téa stopped short in surprise and gasped. "That's not possible."

"And why is that dear? Because it is what you have been told? Or have you seen it with your own eyes?"

Téa was quiet. There was nothing she could say to that.

The woman continued. "You must believe in good. Only then can you see the beauty the world still has to offer."

The old woman's voice came out a little raspy, but patient, as she shuffled forward. "You know... when the air stilled, back when mass amounts of birds fell from the sky, everyone had to come to terms with the fact that Earth was dying, because that was something that was impossible for even Dunamis to control.

"People panicked. That's when Dunamis was able to take complete control. The people divided were weak. Further division spread like wildfire. Arguing over what went wrong rather than working together to fix the problem.

"Dunamis, not understanding how to heal the dying planet, only how to maintain their supremacy, needed a backup plan. They looked to the stars. That is when Operation Luna started."

Téa stopped again and faced the old woman, even though she could not see her. "How do you know about Operation Luna?" She asked. "That's classified."

Téa could hear the old woman's deep sigh, "Dear, Dunamis is not as secretive as they would like to believe. Most soldiers are children who enlist as soon as they are of age, just to have a bed and a meal. They are surviving just as the rest of us are. Most are not loyal to Dunamis."

The old woman gave Téa gentle pats in the darkness, motioning for her to keep moving. "You know, I miss birdsong the most. With the loss of the Aves, came silence. The pleasant chirps and sing songs were something that I had taken for granted, something I did not notice until it was gone. Suddenly, silence instilled fear. Instead of coming together in a time of crisis, disillusionment and seclusion settled in like rot.

"Without their natural predators, aphids, worms, and spiders, multiplied beyond capabilities of being contained. They thrived. The crops of the world fell below sustainable levels. That first year, the world population dropped by forty percent.

"Not long after the quiet began, it was replaced by noise. Not the beautiful melodies of my so missed vertebrates, but a constant buzz, growing to levels so loud, no one wanted to leave the indoors, the safety of their cars, and brick boxes. Moving from one place to the next without pausing to appreciate what nature remained. Eventually, most of the bugs died out as well, but not all."

Téa tried to imagine such a world, so filled with beautiful life that was taken away so rapidly. She had read about everything she could whenever she had a chance, and it was almost as though she had lived it herself, but hearing it from someone who had actually seen the Decline as it happened, broke her heart.

The old woman quieted again, Téa asked, "And what is the Sanctuary?"

"It is our home. There are other sectors that have resistance communities as well, but the Sanctuary is ours. It's protected by the immense forest. Dunamis does not travel this far by foot, there are no roads, on any maps anyway. Even if they did decide to follow you this far, partway to our destination, the tunnel goes under a giant rock mountain. They would need an experienced mountain climber to reach us, or they would have to go around, which would lead them entirely past the Sanctuary."

She sounded as though she were talking about an adored child. The old woman continued. "You and your friend, I am guessing, ran out of fuel in your helicopter?" The old woman did not wait for an answer before continuing, "There are no fueling stations anywhere near here. The mechanical wings do not reach this far before splatting like a fly."

"What about jet planes, or drones?"

Téa heard the old woman stop moving. "How do you know about such things?"

She shrugged even though she knew the woman could not see her. "I like to read."

The old woman let out a small laugh. "Well, before Dunamis took complete control of food production, there was a small window of time, months really, where the people had to spend entire paychecks on food. Sustenance was so hard to come by. Businesses like airports went out of business. Jet fuel production became limited and manufacturing the parts to maintain the jets became impossible. The drones of course are completely controlled by Dunamis, and they do use them to spy on the people. But our canopy protects us. Helicopters use much less fuel and are easier to maintain, which is why the General is such a fan."

The sarcasm was thick in the old woman's voice at that part, "Plus, the General funnels massive amounts of materials to his launchpad, so he has to conserve elsewhere. Crossing continents of course is only done by water. But enough about all that dear."

The pair were silent for a while after that, and Téa stumbled along in the dark. Finally, she asked. "Will you be able to help Zephyr?"

"If Ted gets him there in time, yes. We have a fully functioning hospital." Téa imagined the old woman beaming with pride and joy. "It won't be much longer now."

"What's your name?" Téa asked.

"Florence Young." The old woman laughed again, "The irony is not lost on me, but we are as young as we feel are we not?"

Téa missed light. It was disconcerting walking for so long in the dark. She wanted to see her feet again.

"Why haven't you asked my name?" Téa asked. "Or any questions at all about me? What if I am a Dunamis spy?"

Florence guffawed. "You are a hoot, my dear. I will enjoy our conversations."

Téa was deeply confused but didn't know what to say after that. Her feet ached as though hours had gone by when Téa finally was blessed with some luminescence in the distance. She picked up her pace, nearly running when she could see the path in front of her and knew she would not trip.

She burst through the opening into fresh air and daylight, then collapsed to her knees and stretched her arms to the sky, taking a deep breath and staring at everything before her. It astonished her.

# Chapter Sixteen

## Earth

The Sanctuary was built into the forest to protect the canopy above. Bridges and platforms overhead connected tree to tree. Rounded huts big enough to house three to five people each, dotted the open spaces, and it looked as though they were halfway buried into the ground with curved wooden roofs and sides. Téa marveled at the unique structures and itched to peek inside. She peered further ahead and realized The Sanctuary must have stretched on and on for miles, further than she could catch sight of.

"How many people live here?" She asked Florence

"Five hundred and forty-three souls live within our boundaries." The old woman had a shimmer in her eye like a doting matriarch. "That includes the unborn growing in bellies, currently twenty-eight kicking and thriving in their wombs."

Téa's eyes widened in surprise. "That's bigger than some of our sector capitals. How do you have so many DNA matches? Do many pregnancies fail? How do you all survive?"

"The only DNA matches here are of the heart, and no, very few of the pregnancies fail." Florence paused and turned to look at Téa with intent, "Dunamis has been pulling the wool over the people's eyes for decades. We survive by working together, by accepting one another, by supporting each other with love and understanding. It takes every one of us to contribute." Florence pointed towards the sky, "See those platforms above? Some are used for community meetings. Some are for entertainment; we do like to shake our groove thang every now and again."

She laughed and swayed her ancient hips as though she were a schoolgirl. "Other platforms are for storage. Most creepy crawlies eventually died out after the start of the Decline, but for the ones still rooting around, keeping our stores up high keeps most away. Down here, for every one of these dwellings you see, there is one used for gardening. See how some have holes in the top where others do not? Bedrooms do not have the holes, for privacy's sake, if you catch my drift." The mature lass waggled her thick gray eyebrows.

"Zephyr." Téa's heart raced again. With her fatigue and amazement, she momentarily forgot how he must be fighting for his life. "Where is he? I need to see him now."

"Of course, dear, please calm down. Follow me."

People stared at Téa as Florence led the way through the labyrinth of The Sanctuary. Some ushered their children away in a hurry to be clear of her, and others stared in wonderment like she was someone of importance. She hugged herself, uncomfortable in her own skin. They had been walking for at least ten minutes when they came upon the largest semi-sphere Téa had seen yet. Florence opened the door, and they walked down a short set of wide stairs. Téa's jaw dropped.

Inside was a fully functioning hospital. She glanced up and saw small holes in the much bigger dome sealed with glass. Natural sunlight streamed in. The walls and the floor were all polished wood. This hospital felt much more comfortable than anything she was familiar with, nothing like the tiled and sterile medical wing-back at Steppe Two. Nonetheless, it housed all the same equipment, medical beds, and stretchers. Defibrillators, crash carts, patient monitors, and various other supplies.

Unlike a traditional hospital, however, there were no metal detectors or security guards. They did have a sort of check-in desk, large and hand-carved with a solitary filing cabinet. A middle-aged man with brown skin, his hair graying and close-cropped, sat behind the desk filling out a form and muttering to himself.

"Ahh. Here's Jessop. He is our primary care doctor, and we are lucky to have him." Florence told her cheerfully.

Jessop did not look up as he spoke to the old woman. "Now Florence, don't go flattering me. You know I don't do well under pressure." He chuckled softly then stood up. Looking Téa in the eyes he reached out his hand to introduce himself.

Téa shook his hand. "Hello, I'm Téa. Can you please tell me how my friend is doing?"

"It's a pleasure to meet you Téa." He took a deep breath. "It's hard to say right now. He is in surgery with Doctor Anderson. He had a badly broken leg, but that was not our main concern. He also had internal bleeding and a severe concussion. It will be a few hours until we know more. With your permission, we would also like to have you checked out for any injuries."

Téa wasn't sure what to say at first and was quiet for a moment as her pulse thrummed in her ears. Then she said, "Will he live?" her voice came out anguished and scared.

"We are optimistic. I will make sure you are the first to know his prognosis as we receive information."

Téa nodded, "Thank you." She considered his request for an exam for a moment. "I suppose an exam would pass some time. But I really think I'm okay."

"I'll take it!" Jessop chuckled again and said, "Right this way."

*Why was everyone so happy here?* The idea crossed her mind that it might be a trick, a show for her benefit. But the people she saw looked vibrant. No sunken cheeks or downcast faces. Everyone had color in their spirit, no one had a sickly pallor. They passed a handful of male and female nurses, only noting three patients in the mostly empty spaces.

Following Jessop, Téa appreciated the stretched gleaming timber around her. They moved by several rooms, little alcoves all made to accommodate at least a few people each, snug yet homey.

Jessop stopped and gestured for Téa to enter the exam room. He asked her to sit on the medical table. He was gentle but thorough. Taking her temperature, tapping her knees to test her reflexes, and listening to her lungs and heart through her chest and back. He nodded, pleased with hearing clear airways and normal rhythm. Lastly, he peered into her deep brown eyes through an ophthalmoscope, then checked her blood pressure.

He asked permission before doing each task. Something the doctors at base had never done while they invaded her body.

Seemingly satisfied with everything he found; Jessop assisted her down. "You were right, almost nothing to report. Looks as though you are extremely lucky. Just a few mild cuts and scratches, bumps, and bruises; and some torn muscles around your ribcage. You will need to take it easy for a while. Florence has graciously offered to host you during your stay here. I'll send you with a couple of painkillers, and an ice pack, but then you are good to go."

The thought of leaving Zephyr alone in this place terrified her. "Thank you, I appreciate that, but I would much rather stay here until I know more about his condition."

Jessop averted his eyes and nodded with a slight smile. "I can respect that. You are more than welcome to keep me company in the front while you wait. Can I get you anything? Are you hungry?"

She didn't think she could eat even if she tried. "No, thank you."

"Well, at least some water. I'm certain you are dehydrated after your journey here."

After he attended to her injuries, they made their way back to the front of the hospital. A few nurses whispered as she passed. Téa took a seat in one of the dozen hand-carved wooden chairs that were surprisingly comfortable even without cushions. Jessop brought her a large wooden cup of water. She took a sip. It was refreshing, not as cold without the ice she had grown accustomed to at Sandstone, but there was no chemical afterbite. It was the best thing she had ever consumed.

"Thank you, Jessop."

"You are very welcome. Now if you will excuse me, I have some patients to check on. I'll be back as soon as there are any updates with Zephyr."

Téa silently acknowledged him as he walked away. How did he know Zephyr's name? Was Zephyr conscious when he arrived? She had mentioned Zephyr's name in front of Florence but not Jessop or Ted. These people seemed to have a lot of knowledge about them, more than they were letting on. It felt as though this community was expecting them. As Téa glanced around the hospital, she realized that Florence had not followed her and Jessop to the examination room. and she had assumed the old woman would be waiting for her but she was nowhere to be found.

Téa busied her mind by cataloging everything she saw. There were flowers and plants everywhere. Wooden vases full of them, as though they were not a precious commodity but easily cut and placed for enjoyment. Something about the feel of the place put her at ease. She should be a tight ball of fear, but she wasn't. Perhaps it was the lack of guns; not a single person held a weapon. Or perhaps the ease of nerves came from the lack of demands of her. Whatever the reason, she was too tired to think about it much. Slowly relaxing into the earthen seat, she let her eyes fall closed.

*She was back at base, knocking on her bedroom door, gloating, drunken voices cutting through with rude laughter devoid of glee. Shadowed footsteps reaching her. Arms, so many arms, tangling their slimy growths around her, pinning her to the cot. Shrieking curses to any God who would hear her. Red eyes and grotesque bodies fighting for pieces of her skin, tearing and biting and breaking. Cold metal slab. Paper sheet providing no protection. 'Hold still this is going to hurt.' Drilling into her skull, so loud as the metal ground against bone, alone, picking at the exposed pulsing pink of her brain pulling away like foam.*

Screaming.

Panic.

"Shush, shh, shh, shh. It's okay, dear. You're okay. It is only me. Take a breath. There you go. See, only us."

Florence gently rubbed Téa's arms, smoothing her curly frizzed out hair, her tranquil voice drawing Téa out of the nightmare, pacifying the demons in her view. Finally clear of the dream, Téa looked around. It was dark; the sun from the skylights no longer bathed them in warmth. Small orbs of kind light radiated from the corners. Téa was stiff. She must have been out and unmoving for hours.

Florence spoke again when Téa stilled. "Zephyr is out of surgery. He will survive. However, he will need to remain in a coma to allow his body to heal."

"A coma? For how long?"

"Dr. Anderson is not certain. He is hopeful for just a few days, but it could be weeks."

"Weeks?" Téa's stomach dropped.

Florence nodded. "You will be staying with me until we can build a home for you. Would you like to see Zephyr before we go?"

"Build a home?" Téa asked, incredulous. "We live here now? Just like that?"

"Yes, dear. You are not a prisoner. You are free to leave at any time, but where would you go? You are safe here, darling, and there is much you have yet to learn."

Florence was so nonchalant about it all. As if Téa's world was not spinning on a top. Orphan, soldier, fiancé, enemy of the state, and now apparently civilian of The Sanctuary. Who was she meant to be? Existing. Floating along, doing as she was told. What other choice was there?

She didn't know these people. But they had helped, opened their doors with no strings attached as far as she could tell. She did not feel threatened here and decided to force her anxiety down in order to take it one minute, one hour, and one day at a time. *Accept, watch, and observe, it's how you'll stay alive.*

"Yes, I would like to see Zephyr before we go. Thank you, Florence.

A chill crept around her skin as they walked to his room. She froze at the sight of him. Zephyr was pale and mottled with bruises, but clean. Someone had cleansed all his wounds and the open gash in his forehead had been stitched together. Leg set in a cast. Ventilator pumping him full of oxygen, tubes and needles falling from his arms and torso. The only sign of life was his chest slowly floating up and then down, a barely discernible flutter under his white hospital gown.

Téa gently dragged a finger down the length of his chin. She couldn't stay here. Seeing him like this was cracking her heart from the inside. She leaned forward and placed a soft kiss on his temple, squeezed his hand, and whispered, "See you soon." in his ear.

She turned back to Florence, "I'm ready."

# CHAPTER SEVENTEEN

## Earth

Téa followed Florence outside to the fresh night air. A slight breeze chilled her bones and a shiver crawled down her spine.

Florence looped her arm through Téa's. She winked. "Help keep an old gal steady, would you?"

Téa doubted the woman needed her assistance, but her warmth was comforting.

Téa looked around curiously, the various paths of The Sanctuary were all lit with the same gentle orbs as the hospital. "What are all these little glowing balls?"

"Solar lights," Florence whispered. The entirety of The Sanctuary runs on solar energy. While we could have livestock, it is safer to not keep animals here. We consume only the fruit, vegetables, and grains that we grow."

"How... how is all of this possible?"

"I assume you are not asking how to garden." Florence stopped in front of a gorgeous oval door that no doubt led into her home. It was carved with swirls and geometric patterns that intertwined as would the melody of classical composition, elegant and beautiful. "There is much to discuss, first we rest." She opened the door and gestured to Téa. "After you."

Her living space greeted them. Florence's refuge was like the hospital, in that very surface was highly polished wood. A small couch was pushed against a wall next to the front door. The living room had an open space with a small table and two chairs near the back, which led into a kitchenette with a single cupboard, sink, stove, fridge, and short wooden countertop. A single hallway continued past the kitchen with two doorways on either side. It was warm and cozy.

"Down there is the bathroom and my bedroom." Florence pointed at the doors in the hallway. "You will be sleeping in the living room here."

Florence reached for a solitary rope hanging on the wall and pulled on it, revealing a hideaway bed complete with a mattress.

"I will grab you some bedding."

She wandered off down the hall and returned a few minutes later with a wide bundle. She handed Téa a sheet, a fluffy bright yellow blanket, and a pillow.

Téa smiled gratefully. "Thank you."

"You're welcome, dear. Let me help you." Florence bent down and helped Téa make up her bed. It was simple, soft, and inviting.

Florence looked at Téa with a grin. "Now that's settled, follow me. I gathered some things for you. Right in here." Florence gestured to a small bathroom. "There are some pajamas there for you, a towel, and some clothes for tomorrow. I am done wore out for the day and I am hitting the sack. If you wake in the morning, and I'm not here, help yourself to whatever you would like in the kitchen, and feel free to explore The Sanctuary." Florence grinned. "Goodnight, dear, I'll leave you to it."

"Thank you, Florence. Goodnight."

Téa was alone with the quiet. She shut the bathroom door and looked in the tub shower combo. There was a single small shelf that held a bar of soap and two glass jars. Not as elaborate as Sandstone, but far better than Steppe Two. Téa decided a quick rinse would probably do her some good as she tried to remember her last shower. Was it yesterday morning that she and Zephyr had gone on the run? She remembered drawing a bath the night before that, after a strenuous workout, but that seemed a lifetime ago, not mere days.

She was thorough in ridding herself of the dirt and grime as the water rained down on her. Téa watched as the mix of mud and Zephyr's blood swirled down the drain. She smelled the smoke from the plane crash leave her as she lathered her hair and rinsed her body, scraping under the tips of her fingers to discover that most nails were broken, and one pinky pooled with purple underneath the nail. Multiple bruises revealed themselves as she scrubbed away the soot.

Her mind wandered. Never in her life had she seen the light shot out from between a living thing's eyes like the blonde woman. Téa had her womanhood and freedom threatened every minute of every day, yet she had never lived through the very real possibility of simply ceasing to be because a man deemed it so. Had not experienced the pain of every rib, every muscle, every fiber of her being aching in torment. Her suffering was deeper than the holes no doubt littering her sinewy body. The one thing that made it all help just enough was the knowledge that she now had someone who cared whether she lived or died, and that was Zephyr. She had to keep going for him.

Tingling numbness spread through her shoulders, her arms shook, legs with no strength left, stomach empty. Despair and loneliness took hold and weighed on her. She sat into the curve of the porcelain tub, wrapped her arms around her legs, squeezing her chest, and rested her head on her knees. As the water pounded her back from above, she cried.

After some time, her tears slowed, and quietly mingled with the water until there was no heated water left. Finally, she turned the shower off, climbed out, and toweled off. Téa dressed, crawled into the graciously given place to slumber, wrapped up in the fluffy yellow blanket, and let the moon lull her into a deep sleep.

The sun did not know that Téa wanted to rest until her bones crumbled and the world stopped spinning. It did not know that she was folding in on herself. Nevertheless, the sun shone. It rose high in the sky, smiling at its friends scurrying along the surface of the wondrous blue and green ball called Earth.

The fogginess in her mind began to clear. Was this sense of safety that the community stirred within her another elaborate façade? Were the timber walls solid and strong, or merely kindling for the fire to come?

Her belly grumbled and cramped with hunger. The bit of motivation she needed to get out of bed. She wandered into the tiny kitchen. The cupboard held plates, bowls, a single pan, and a cutting board. On the counter sat two bread boxes. In the first, a homemade bread loaf. The second held various fruits and vegetables and dried herbs. A solitary drawer held silverware, a butcher knife, and a spatula.

She grabbed the loaf of bread and sliced off a thick piece. Cut a tomato and heated the pan with some oil from a glass mason jar labeled 'Sunflower', on the counter next to the boxes. After a few moments, the oil spit and popped. She placed the bread in the pan and counted to thirty while it sizzled, flipped it, and topped it with tomato seasoned with some fresh basil, and counted to another thirty seconds. The aroma was enticing the joy buried within her to make an appearance. She slid the tomato toast off the pan and onto a plate and walked back to her bed, savoring the fresh ingredients as they filled her core.

She ate every crumb, washed her plate, and made her way to the bathroom. The clothes Florence left for her were simple and functional: a pair of loose-fitting blue jeans, and long sleeve basic shirt. She folded up her bedding and lifted the hideaway back into the wall, tied the laces on her shoes, and left the hut.

The sun blinded her. *It must be close to noon.* Florence had said to explore, so she started walking, thinking that maybe she could figure out how the people living in The Sanctuary knew so much about her, perhaps find out what they were hiding, and how they thrived. She wanted nothing more than to accept the help and the kindness without question, but her years of self-preservation had taught her to doubt everything.

The light spaced out every few feet breaking through the treetops. Everywhere she looked, there were cheery people. Waving to each other, talking, working. A man carried buckets of water, a woman peeked out of a gardening dome where she was filling a basket with its splendors, children built daisy chains and laughed with one another. These were not the hollowed citizens of Steppe Two, not the downcast people of any town she had ever seen. Granted, she had not seen much. What she had experienced was lethargy and sadness, people conceded to a life of routine, misery, and hunger created by Dunamis.

She would never go back.

Standing in the forest, surrounded by peace after being denied it for her entire life, Téa decided to try to give life in this community a chance.

She noticed Florence from a distance striding in her direction. The old woman smiled and waved. Téa returned the gesture. When they were a foot away, Téa could see that Florence seemed practically giddy, a woman in her twenties rather than the abuela she was. Her long silver hair swished around her waist. Eyes crinkled at the corners from years of glee. Beauteous face that was no doubt alluring in her heyday.

"Good morning, deary! Splendid day isn't it? How long have you been out and about?"

The old woman brightened Téa's spirits, "Good morning. Not long. Just got up."

"Wonderful, just peachy keen! You can come help me then. I have a new batch of fish roe I am dying to show you."

Téa smiled. "I'd love to see it. I thought you mentioned the community didn't harvest meat?"

"You are right dear, however, on occasion we do keep a fishpond. It is a commodity, a special treat if you will. Easy to maintain, minimal resources required, with no fear of escapees. This season is going to be plentiful! We'll be having fish for summer solstice."

They arrived at the fish hatchery. The same semi-sphere type dwelling as the rest within the community, but smaller. Inside this one was a ring of compressed dirt encircling a rock pond. Téa could smell the crisp scent of moss mixed with stagnant, fishy water. The surface was dark with a faint, green glow caused by a dozen of solar orbs around the edge. Occasional splashes rippled across the top of the pond.

"It's so peaceful in here." Téa smiled.

"It's one of my favorite places." Florence's soft voice echoed through the darkened sphere, "This way." She said as she pulled on Téa's elbow, leading her to a spot a few feet away. "Here they are. Look right there."

Florence pointed to a clutch of fish eggs, perfectly round, translucent orange, and small. Too many to count, clinging to the edge of the pond just below the surface.

"It's amazing, Florence."

Florence patted Téa's back and smiled at her. "How would you like to visit Zephyr?"

Téa stilled. "I'm not sure." Her mind flashed to the image of his broken body. "It was difficult for me to see him that way. Close to death, I mean. I know he is going to be okay, that the coma is good for him, but it's still hard to watch. I think I would rather explore a bit more. Care to give me a tour?"

Florence grinned and placed her hand on her heart. "Of course, dear. It would be my honor."

Téa enjoyed Florences' company, not needing to worry about what came next, and instead living in the moment. Florence knew everyone in the community. She waved as they passed, greeted them by name, introduced Téa, and asked about the intimacies of their lives as only a grand-mother could.

The head gardener, Phillip, and his wife Mia made the preserved products, like jams, jellies, even wine and brandy. Torrence and Seth, husband blacksmiths, managed the forge. Tess and Louis oversaw the grade school. There were so many others each playing a part in keeping the community thriving.

All of it enlivened Téa, reminiscent of a time forgotten that she had only ever read and dreamed about.

"Florence?" she asked when they walked along a path alone. "Torrence and Seth... the community does not ban same-sex coupling?"

"Of course not, dear! That is all the doing of Dunamis, another way for them to control the people. As I mentioned, there is no need for DNA coupling. The human race continues on as it always has inside this community. By love. Everyone is free to love whomever they wish as long as they are consenting adults."

Love. Was that the cause of the happiness seeping through the colony? No one forced into an unwanted marriage. No one forced to have a child they couldn't care for. Real solid food grown with their own hands. Houses built piece by piece. Everyone moving at their own speed, all contributing to the success of life. It was all there, right in front of her, and still she struggled to see it.

"It all seems so perfect. So harmonious."

Florence dropped an octave of spark as she said, "Nothing is perfect dear. We are, after all, still in hiding. Still scavenging for medical supplies. Fighting a battle we did not ask for. We manage well enough outside Dunamis control, but some things we cannot manufacture. We grow herbs that do wonders for healing, but for major trauma, like what Zephyr has endured, we must sneak into Dunamis facilities. When the solar panels and energy storage need to be repaired or replaced, we must also steal those. Every time we leave the safety of our boundaries our livelihood is at risk. No one should have to live in fear. We should all be free to live our lives however we see fit."

After a few moments of silence, Florence continued. "The Decline was real. However, the cause behind it has been a subject of intense debate, as has the extent of the damage to our Earth, or lack thereof. There is a lot we need to share with you, but there is time for that later. Enjoy these quiet days, soak in the peace surrounding you, for it will not last. What is coming for us all, is already in motion. It cannot, and will not, be stopped."

Téa shivered in fear, "Florence, what do you mean? Are we in immediate danger?" her voice came out quiet yet shrill.

"Hush, child. You are safe, for now. We all are. Rest, learn, enjoy. I must get back to my chores." Florence winked and nudged her shoulder. "I'm important here, you know. Do you know your way back to the house?"

Mind racing and thoughts fumbling, Téa nodded and Florence left her. How was she supposed to 'rest and enjoy' when the old woman was saying things like that?

# Chapter Eighteen

## Space Station Luna

She could hear her pulse thumping in her ears as she waited for Ian to open his door. They had parted on unstable grounds last night, and Ian had always been her one reliable constant. Without his reassuring presence, Annabelle's whole world felt as though it were flat and tipping sideways, with her moments away from slipping into a dark and unknown void.

When he didn't answer she knocked again. Relief flooded her body down to her toes when he slowly slid his door open and peeked out, but that reprieve was short-lived with only one glance at his bloodshot eyes and hunched shoulders.

"Hey." he said without eye contact and his voice scratchy.

"Hey." Annabelle replied as she lightly tapped the door-frame with her toe, her hands behind her back.

She was about to speak and cleared her throat to do so, when Ian opened the door all the way and leaned against the wall with his arms crossed and interrupted her, "Look, Belle, you know that old saying? Ignorance is bliss. Well, I get that one now."

"Ian, I'm sorry–"

"No. I mean... look, I'm not mad at you for telling me, and I'm glad I was the one with you when you went through those flash drives." He took a deep breath and blew it out slowly. "It's just... I don't know. What are we supposed to do with all this?"

Annabelle still felt bad about busting Ian's life open wide like a sledgehammer through watermelon, but she could not fight the happiness that warmed and emboldened her. He wasn't mad at her, and right now, that was the only thing she cared about.

She smiled wide, flung her arms around his neck, and laughed in relief.

He stood stone still with his arms still crossed and confusion creased his brow. "Um, Belle? Did you crack?"

She laughed again and took a step back, "No. I'm just so relieved you're not mad at me."

He relaxed his arms and the confusion on his face deepened. "Mad? On what planet would I be mad at you? None of this is your fault."

Annabelle hugged herself and said, "I know the things that are happening aren't my fault, but you knowing about them all, is most definitely my fault. And you were so upset last night-"

"Belle, stop." He smiled. "Of course I'm not mad at you, yeah, I was upset, but not at you, and I mean who wouldn't be after learning that humanity is doomed essentially all because of one evil tyrant and a possible looming asteroid? I mean what do we even do with all this information?"

Reality sunk back in, and Annabelle felt a little queasy thinking about the severity of their situation, but with Ian by her side, she mustered the courage to say, "We blow the whistle. Tell the whole Luna Station everything that we know."

Ian gaped at her and she could almost see the wheels turning in his mind before he said, "That's why you proposed shutting down operation Luna all those months ago!" He said quickly as his voice steadily increased. "I just thought at the time that you were being typical impulsive Annabelle, that you wanted a change of scenery or something."

Annabelle gave his shoulder a shove and laughed as she said, "What do you mean *typical impulsive Annabelle*?"

He raised his hands in surrender, "Oh nothing, nothing at all." He said with a sly grin.

Annabelle narrowed her eyes at him with her head tilted, then asked with a more serious tone of voice. "So, we tell everyone, and together we come up with a solution?"

Ian was quiet in thought until he finally spoke with hesitation. "There's obviously a reason the first generation didn't want us to know all of this. I think given how big the situation is, we should talk to one of them first. Maybe Professor Trombol. Confess to taking the drives and confront her."

Annabelle nodded her head in agreement then smiled, "My my my, Ian. How wise you have become."

"I do have my moments," he said with a wink.

Annabelle and Ian nervously crisscrossed each other as they paced out front of Professor Trombol's door.

"Are you sure her lecture was over at 17:30?" Ian asked for the tenth time.

"Yes, Ian, I'm sure. She must have gone somewhere afterward. We'll just have to wait." Annabelle said with a note of irritation in her reply.

"Alright, alright, got it, Belle. You don't have to roll your eyes at me." Ian said as he over-dramatically rolled his eyes in return, eliciting laughter from Annabelle.

"You're such a dork." She said with a chuckle.

The sound of approaching footsteps silenced them both as they practically held their breath.

Professor Trombol was a stout woman with fashionably short white hair, appearing to be in her late fifties. "Can I help you?" she asked.

Annabelle gulped and wrung her hands, "Um... y-yes... uh..."

Professor Trombol walked past them, her eyes heavy, and tapped her entry code on the touchpad. Then turned to face them as she stood in the open doorway. "Well, spit it out child, I've had quite the long day." She said with a tired voice.

Annabelle floundered; the right words absent from her head. Ian looked at her as though to say, 'this is your show'. She suddenly blurted out, "I stole from you!"

Professor Trombol straightened as though she were given an electric shock. Ian audibly cleared his throat and then said. "What she means to say, Professor, is that we'd like to speak with you. May we come in?"

Annabelle could see suspicion build within Professor Trombol, but there had never been any crime or violence on Luna, understandably so, with so few occupants and everyone knowing everyone else. Plus, it was common knowledge on the space station that their survival rested in maintaining a peaceful order. As a result, Space Station Luna was like its own little bubble of controlled happiness, with the exception of the occasional visit from the General's men sent to 'scare' them. But even that never amounted to much, seemingly because the General prized Operation Luna.

After a few moments of silence, Professor Trombol said, "I suppose so, but let's make it quick, shall we?"

Professor Trombol stepped aside to allow them to pass and turned the lights on as she set down a stack of folders stuffed full of yellowed paper with curled edges. Seeing Annabelle notice them Professor Trombol spoke, "Gilly hates the sound of me rustling my papers and she tells me nearly every night that I should go digital. You know. Scan all these into a smart device? but I just can't seem to let them go. Something about the feel and smell of real paper brings me back to what normalcy was once upon a time."

Annabelle and Ian stood awkwardly near the door until Professor Trombol said, "Well, don't just stand there." She gestured to the couch in the middle of the room. "I'll put the kettle on."

They took a seat next to each other on the cream-colored leather sofa and waited patiently while the Professor busied herself in the kitchen. Annabelle nervously bounced a leg up and down and wiped her sweaty palms on her jeans. Ian gently cupped his hand around hers to still her twitching. She forced herself to stop fidgeting and took a deep breath. She couldn't stop the repeating reel of thoughts running through her mind.

*I'm going to be the first prisoner on Luna. They're going to lock me up and throw away the key, or worse, they'll send me to Earth to face the General.*

That thought sent chills down her spine and brought the queasiness back. Annabelle was grateful when the Professor finally emerged and set down a tray full of biscotti, a piping hot tea kettle, sugar cubes, a small tin of cream, and cups.

Professor Trombol did not help herself but placed her hands in her lap and looked at them expectantly, "Now. What do you mean, 'you stole from me'? What exactly did you steal? Test scores for active students? Trying to trade for extra provisions?"

*Oh this is so bad, so bad. She has no idea the depths I've fallen to.*

Annabelle could see the irritation on the Professor's face when she said, "Well, speak up girl. Come out with it."

Annabelle tried to talk, but her voice came out as some kind of garbled squeak. She cleared her throat and tried again. "Um, no. Nothing like that. I, um. Well, I broke into your apartment and stole the flash drives you had hidden." Her last words came out in a jumbled rush and heat flooded her cheeks.

Professor Trombol's eyes widened. "You what now?" She seemed to be searching for the right words. "How did you get past the keypad? How did you even know those flash drives existed?"

Annabelle gulped. "Well, I got in your apartment the same way I got into the surveillance room, I waited around the corner and watched until you entered your code." Shame flooded Annabelle's core as she dropped her head to her chin avoiding eye contact.

The Professor seemed to be lost for words. So, Annabelle unraveled her whole clandestine story, barely stopping for air, while Ian looked on in surprise at her boldness.

As she came to the end of her tale, she slowed down her pace of words and said with more confidence, "So we understand that everyone on Luna is at the mercy of the General, because we need regular supply shipments, and because we don't have our own means to return to Earth. We also know how lucky Luna was that the first resistance informant was the one who noticed that Luna hacked into the surveillance feed and started funneling information between us and the resistance. We know we are basically powerless until the resistance decides to fight back and overthrow the General." Annabelle took a deep breath and at last said, "But what we don't understand is, why keep all of this secret? Why not trust the Luna community to help find a solution?"

Professor Trombol nodded as Annabelle finished talking and said, "I see."

Annabelle stared in disbelief, "Is that it? Don't you have anything else to say?"

"Well, miss Annabelle, if you give me a moment to gather my thoughts, that was quite a lot to take in." Professor Trombol sat up straighter, head held high. "What do you suppose would happen if we told everyone on Luna? Told them all that Earth is doomed and our research has been for nothing? What do you suppose that would accomplish?"

Annabelle felt a flush of anger, "People deserve to know the truth, no matter how terrible it is."

The terse stare the professor tossed her way was enough to make Annabelles' toes curl. The professors voice came out sturdy when she replied. "That may be true. But people are real, with very real emotions. They do not react and behave how you would want them to. Not all would be empowered to do something productive. Some would fall into a depression; some would become angry. Productivity would surely drop drastically. Our survival depends on Luna remaining a well-oiled machine with *everyone* doing their part."

Annabelle scoffed, she couldn't believe this person that she had looked up to, this person who had been one of the adults who cared for her would be so dismissive. "You sound just as bad as the General, thinking you know best!

Thinking it's up to you to decide what is best for people, to control them!"

The Professor stood swiftly, her fists clenched, "You know nothing, *child*."

Annabelle stood up too, her bravery growing with every second, as if challenging Professor Trombol. She turned to look at Ian, "Come on, *Ian*. Back me up here! You haven't said a single word."

He stayed seated with his eyes wide, adams apple bobbing in his throat. "Professor Trombol, she's right. You can't control people forever, eventually, someone else will realize their research isn't working. People already wonder why we don't receive images from Earth. Annabelle isn't the only one who wants off the space station. There are others."

Ian averted his eyes as Annabelle stared in surprise. *Why didn't he tell me there were others?*

Professor Trombol unclenched her fists and shook her head, "You don't understand. It's not that simple."

Annabelle's head snapped back to the Professor. "Why, Professor? Explain it us."

"I'm not at liberty to say."

Annabelle huffed, "Oh come on, Professor." She shook her head, "Don't you think we're past *liberty*?"

Professor Trombol sighed deeply then plopped back down into her recliner. "Why don't you sit back down for this, Annabelle?"

Annabelle hesitated, but her curiosity piqued, she sat, ready to listen.

Professor Trombol looked them both in the eyes as if measuring them both up and deciding if she should say whatever it was that would come next. Finally, she spoke. "You apparently didn't go through all the files on those drives." It wasn't a question, and she didn't wait for them to answer. "Have you ever heard of the Connex genes?"

Annabelle and Ian looked at her blankly, and when they both shook their heads, she continued. "Some time ago, back on Earth, our scientists discovered a new gene in some humans, mostly appearing in persons who were born with a Y chromosome. Over time it became increasingly apparent to some, mainly the General, that these people were powerful, and possibly dangerous."

Confusion flooded Annabelle's mind. "Why? What do you mean? Why would someone who has this gene be dangerous, is it related to why human emotions turned poisonous?"

Professor Trombol leaned forward in her chair and spoke. "We don't know if it's related, but we do know that the people who present a Connex gene have supernatural abilities, powerful and sometimes dangerous, uncontrollable abilities."

The Professor's words opened up a brand new flood gate of questions within Annabelle. Her mind raced looking for the first question that she wanted to ask, but Ian spoke first.

"Who else knows about this?"

Professor Trombol looked at him intently, as though deciding if she should answer him or not. But considering how far they had already come, she answered. "On Earth, only the General, his team of scientists, and a select group of individuals." She ground her teeth as if holding back more she wanted to say about the matter, but seemed to decide against it and kept talking, "And on Luna, only the first-generation research team, and of course the medical personnel."

Shock coursed through every nerve of Annabelle's body. *Sawyer.* "What do you mean medical personnel? All of them?"

"Well, there's not that many of them to begin with, but no, not all of them, only the doctors. Their aides and nurses are unaware. But you see, the Connex gene activation seems to be emotionally triggered, mostly due to severe trauma or anger. Even though the Connex gene is rare, there are a handful of individuals on board that have the gene. If there were ever to be an outbreak of those genes being activated up here, the entire Space Station could crumble in moments. That is how powerful some of these abilities are. The medical team would need to be aware of what's happening and act quickly by tranquilizing and restraining them. It would be our only chance."

The Professor kept talking, something about two different types of genes and a bunch of scientific terminology that Annabelle wouldn't understand anyway. But Annabelle couldn't hear her. Everything was muffled. She only had one thought in her mind on repeat.

*Sawyer's a doctor, Sawyer knows.*

Annabelle had a fleeting thought that maybe she should be having a bigger reaction to learning there was a whole new species of human, but she couldn't concern herself with what they might be thinking of her lack of response to this bombshell of information. All she could focus on was that Sawyer knew. She lasered in on that knowledge as though it were the only thing that mattered.

The Professor was still talking when Annabelle quickly stood up, "Thank you, Professor. We'll be leaving now." Annabelle pulled out the small box of flash drives she had hidden in her pocket and thrust them at the Professor.

Professor Trombol nearly dropped the cup of tea she had fixed herself while she had been speaking when she took the box and then set it and her cup down, a small bit of liquid spilled over the top as she hurriedly blocked Annabelle's path.

"Now hold on–*Annabelle*. Do you understand the delicate nature of this situation? Really, truly, do you understand?" Her voice had the ferocity of a thousand angry abuelas. "You cannot under any circumstances tell anyone this information. Do I make myself clear?"

Annabelle clenched her jaw, nearly spitting her next words out. "Yes, Professor, I understand. I will not tell anyone *who does not already know*." She cut around Professor Trombol and nearly ran out of the apartment with Ian quick on her heels and mumbling some sort of acknowledgement and apology to the Professor as they left.

They hurried away down the hall outside of the apartment. Ian shouted after her, "Annabelle, hold up! What's the hurry?"

Annabelle did not stop. Speaking over her shoulder when Ian caught up she said, "Sawyer knows, Ian. This whole time she's been lying to me."

Understanding settled on Ian's features. "Annabelle." When she didn't slow down, Ian gently grabbed hold of her elbow to stop her. She spun around holding back the tears of frustration and betrayal that wanted to fall.

"She knew, Ian. This whole time she's been helping *them*, the first generation, keep all of their secrets. All their betrayals against the rest of us."

Ian grabbed hold of Annabelle's arms and looked her square in the eyes. "Belle, I get it. I do. But just think about it from her perspective for a second. What reason would she have to tell you? I'm sure you haven't been telling her about all *your* extracurricular activities. And besides that, I'm sure keeping the Connex genes a secret was an explicit part of her training."

Annabelle angrily wiped a tear away that had stubbornly made its way out of her held back well of emotion. She knew Ian was right. But it didn't matter. The woman she might have been falling in love with was keeping Annabelle at arm's length. It didn't matter how hypocritical her feelings were, because after all, Ian had a point, Annabelle was holding back too. But Annabelle's secrets were ones that she had stumbled upon, ones that she didn't know what to do with. Secrets that were incomplete. Sawyer's secrets were told to her from the beginning, ones that Sawyer chose to keep. Annabelle didn't know if that made much of a difference if one was more wrong than the other. All she knew was that she had to see Sawyer.

She had to confront her.

# CHAPTER NINETEEN

# Earth

Téa was not ready to sit alone at Florence's house. Despite how the sight of Zephyr made her feel completely heartbroken and useless, she decided to make her way to the hospital.

No one was there to greet her this time, so her footsteps echoed, a quiet thud with each step. She passed two nurses and they smiled as she went by. She recognized one as Ted, Florence's son.

Téa was a short distance from Zephyr's room when she heard a young woman's frustrated yell. She looked to her left, around the corner of the single small nurses' station, and saw a streak of yellow hair.

The woman seemed about the same age as Téa. She wore cut-off shorts and her slender form was unhealthy looking.

Her knobby knees clacked together as she bent down to grab a pink baby blanket that had fallen. A small child sat on her hip. The woman's bright blue eyes screamed defeat as she rushed past Téa down the hall and towards the exit.

Téa could hear the nurses whispering behind her as she entered Zephyr's room. She shut the door behind her, closing out the noise, taking a breath as she leaned against it.

He was so fragile looking, so broken, so pale. It was hard to believe that he was going to be okay. Fear of his death squeezed her like a vise. It seemed like everything bad in the world was targeted at her, barreling in her direction until it wiped her out. The hushed room was swallowing her whole. She could not look at Zephyr. She could not stay in this solitude. The sadness held her heart tight. She felt for the handle behind her, and pushed her way out, trying not to stumble. Once outside, Téa pulled her shoulders back, brushed the curls out of her face, and paced back to Florence's house on shaking legs.

Téa's heart calmed to a steady pulse as she walked back. When she arrived, she heard voices, one of them unfamiliar, murmuring behind the door. Téa hesitated with her hand halfway to the doorknob and then knocked. Footsteps grew louder then Florence opened the door, greeted her warmly with an embrace, and stepped aside.

The young blonde from the hospital sat at the table holding a cup of warm tea and pumped one skinny leg up and down. The toddler sat on the floor, clutching her pink blanket with one hand while trying to fit pieces of a simple wooden puzzle together with the other.

Florence introduced them. "Téa, this is Emma and her daughter Nora."

"Hello, it's nice to meet you." Téa smiled at Emma and held her hand out but got nothing in return.

Nora mumbled to herself in her own little language, apparently pleased with something she said, then giggled as a tiny bubble formed from her mouth.

Florence cleared her throat. "Emma and Nora stay here from time to time. I was just explaining to her that I would find another bed for them—"

"Let's go, Nora. We're not wanted here."

"Now, that's not true Emma. Just hold on—"

Emma set her cup down loudly on the table clearly not listening to anything Florence had to say. She hurriedly scooped Nora up and turned towards the door. Nora startled, started to whimper and held her arms out towards Florence as the pair ran away, slamming the door behind them.

Téa felt uncomfortable, an intruder. "Florence, I don't mind staying at the hospital until Zephyr wakes up. The chairs are really not that bad."

"Hush now. You don't worry about that. I will sort it out. Are you hungry? I was just starting some lunch." Florence didn't wait for an answer as she made her way to the kitchen, clearly unmoored.

Téa knew she was a stranger here, and it was none of her business, but she couldn't help herself. "Florence, why don't Emma and Nora have their own home? Where's the father?"

Florence's body tensed. "Emma has never said whom the father is. She and Nora live with Emma's father, Dr. Anderson. He is the Sanctuary's only surgeon, the one who worked on Zephyr."

Téa sensed there was more to say, but perhaps it was not Florence's to share, as she did not offer any more on the matter, and Téa knew when to stop asking questions.

Silence fell as Téa and Florence ate their lunch of fresh blueberries mixed into homemade peanut butter with a side of sliced portabella mushrooms baked in sunflower oil. Partway through, the gentle sound of water tapping on wood grew to thick, thud thud thuds, splashing outside, bringing the fresh scent of forest rain, come to wash their sins clean and start the next day anew.

The morning arrived and Téa decided she could no longer avoid the hospital out of fear. She would be brave, shove anxiety aside, and find her inner seven-year-old, the fearless one who conquered a military base, scavenging its secrets, and navigated it to her advantage. That part of her that never allowed the system to crush her.

She would visit Zephyr and she would not allow his broken condition to scare her. Just because he was the only person in the entire world with whom she had any sort of connection, did not mean she couldn't survive without him. She would thrive with or without him. His condition meant nothing. She could forge a new path in The Sanctuary on her own if it came to that.

Reality of her overwhelming emotion for him crashed down on her, she didn't believe a word of what she was trying to tell herself. The truth was, she would feel lost without him.

She sat on a bench outside the hospital tapping her fingers and grinding her teeth. She could not lose him. This one and only human who cared whether she lived or died. They needed each other.

The wind whooshed through her hair as if trying to pull her to her feet. A patch of daisies swirled, waving at her to go inside. She stood and walked to the front door, her reflection in the window, seven-year-old Téa giving her an encouraging smile. *You got this.*

Dr. Anderson was in Zephyr's room when she walked in. He introduced himself. He seemed overly proper, like the political candidates who visited the base in an attempt to gain military support. Those candidates failed every time. Not one of them could bring democracy back. The military was solidly in charge.

He flashed rows of white teeth, with that fake feeling lingering behind the mask, an invisible shield hiding his true nature. "How are you feeling during all of this?" Anderson asked and grinned again through that veil masking wolf teeth. "I hear it was quite a lot to go through in a short period of time. How are you adjusting?"

An involuntary shudder coursed through Téa, and she forced a grin, "I'm doing fine. It's wonderful here. Everyone has been very welcoming and extremely helpful. Dr. Anderson, please, just tell me, when will Zephyr wake up. *Will* he wake up?"

Realization flashed in his eyes. "Oh, of course! I am deeply sorry. I should have led with that." He smiled. "He will be good as new. The surgeries were a success, the coma was medically induced, just a precaution to allow his injuries to heal. As a matter of fact, we will be waking him today. We were just waiting for your arrival. We assumed you would want to be here. He will, however, have to remain in the hospital for a while longer. His internal damage was extensive."

Téa sighed, with all the relief of a person given a second chance at life, "Thank you, thank you so much." She held back tears of gratitude.

The anesthesiologist, a kind woman who introduced herself as she explained in a joking manner that she also served as an obstetrician, and pediatrician, arrived moments later. She messed with a contraption with tubes coming out of multiple ends, like a wiggling octopus on wheels for a few seconds, then wheeled it out of the way.

The procedure was done in moments. She informed Téa that it would take a better part of the day for him to show any activity and that Téa should go home and rest for a while. But Téa knew she could not bear to leave him today.

She was alone with Zephyr again. She tentatively walked over to Zephyr's sleeping form, touched his arm, and whispered, "I'm sorry I wasn't here for you yesterday, but I'm not going anywhere now. We'll get through this together." He remained unresponsive as Téa continued to talk. "It's wild here, Zephyr. I wonder if you've ever seen anything like it? The people are thriving without Dunamis control. They grow their own food, love who they want to love. It's like a dream. The little houses are so cool, they're halfway underground, like little spheres half below and half above. Supposedly it helps maintain climate inside the homes, never too hot or too cold. And it's a huge community, Zephyr. Over five hundred people! Can you believe it? I think most cities these days average around two hundred, right? Even Steppe Two only had just over three hundred. I cannot wait for you to see it all. They say they are building us our own home, that we could live here. It seems too good to be true. I don't know, maybe, with you, together we could find our place here."

Téa wondered if Zephyr could hear her. She sat quietly after that, rubbing his arm and holding his hand, mulling over her thoughts.

"Téa."

Zephyr's voice sounded far away, and her head was foggy. She must have dozed off for a while. She heard Zephyr say her name again. Groggy, she opened her eyes and looked over at him.

*He's awake!*

"Oh my God! You're awake!" Téa launched herself at him and hugged him tightly. He hissed and winced. She pulled back but held onto his forearms, rubbing gently. "Oh, I'm sorry. I wasn't thinking about your injuries."

Relief flooded every pore of her tense body.

His raspy laugh came out softly and he tried to sit up but was not able to. He tried to talk, nothing but coarse breath came out. He cleared his throat and tried again. "Could you get me some water?"

Excitement coursed through her. "Definitely. I'll be right back. Don't go anywhere!" She pointed at him, narrowed her eyes mockingly, with a smile on her lips.

Téa spent all afternoon with him. He had not heard her when he was sleeping, so she told him everything again about the Sanctuary and how amazing it was that it even existed. She gushed about the beauty of seeing happy people everywhere, the flowers, gardens, and mole-like homes. He was still weak, and didn't say much, but smiled as he listened to her enthusiasm about it all.

"I think we could build a home here together Zephyr, you and me." She held his hand, and there was a desperation in her grip, as though frightened he would float away, never to be seen again if she let him go.

"Anything for you, Love." His eyes drooped, and his words quieted. "I'm sorry...but I'm so...tired." His words trailed away and she quieted as he drifted into sleep.

The day turned to evening, and they napped together, Téa laying on the far edge of the bed, scared to hurt him. They woke sometime in the middle of the night and Téa found a nurse who brought Zephyr vegetable broth and Téa a bowl of hearty vegetable soup. Afterward, Zephyr encouraged Téa to go and get some real rest, reassuring her that he wasn't going anywhere, and he would see her in the morning.

She caressed the side of his face, ran her fingers through his hair, and gave him a gentle, soft kiss. He was smiling as she pulled away. "I'll be back first thing tomorrow. Promise." She nuzzled him. "Goodnight, Zephyr."

"Goodnight, my Love."

The next day, after she showered and had eaten a grape-fruit and oatmeal breakfast, she was ready to head out the door when Florence grabbed her attention.

"Wait, dear. I was wondering if you would like to have dinner with me tonight at Ted's place, with him and his family? Do you remember, Ted? My son, the nurse?"

"Of course, I remember." Téa smiled. "I am so grateful to him. He's the main reason Zephyr is still alive, getting him help so quickly. I would be honored to have dinner with you all."

Téa gave Florence a quick hug and ran out the door, eager to get to Zephyr's side.

# Chapter Twenty

## Earth

Zephyr looked like a new man. Within only a day, color returned to his cheeks, his words were coming more smoothly, and he could stomach real food.

"Good morning, Sunshine." He flashed her one of his gorgeous smiles and patted the bed next to him.

She sat and he placed gentle hands on either side of her face. Zephyr looked right into her the way only he knew how, as though he saw her entire mind, body, and soul, and kissed her. A real full-on kiss. Not one of desperation, not a gentle quick one, not on the forehead. But a real honest kiss, as though nothing could be wrong in the world as long as they had each other. It stole Téa's breath away and the flutters in her chest awakened.

"I want to wake up kissing you every day for the rest of my life, Téa."

She leaned into him and breathed deep, content, and secure in his arms.

"Love, I wanted to ask you," Zephyr said "Do you remember right after the helicopter crash, when you needed to stop the bleeding in my leg?"

Téa tensed and pulled away. *Why was he bringing this up?*

Zephyr continued. "You were wearing a silver chain with a ring on it. Where did it come from?"

Téa was quiet. She looked away for a while, debating. On what, she wasn't sure. The necklace was the only thing that was ever truly hers.

She took a deep breath and let it out slowly, then looked at him. "I've had it for as long as I can remember. I don't know where it came from. But I have always felt the need to protect it. Like someone was waiting to snatch it away. So, I kept it hidden all these years. My own little secret."

She gave him a small grin, and he pulled her back to him. "It's beautiful, Téa."

Needing a change of topic, she said, "Florence has invited me to dinner with her family tonight."

"Is that so? Making friends already?" He smiled and rubbed her arm. "I wish I could go and get to know everyone with you."

She lifted her head to look at him. "Me too, but you will soon. Just focus on getting better, okay?" Téa kissed his cheek and snuggled in tighter.

They passed the time daydreaming together, building an imaginary world that felt suddenly possible. Talking about the possibilities of what a future together could be at The Sanctuary, maybe even start a family of their own, and what skills they could contribute to the community. Zephyr spoke of working the gardens as he did back at Sandstone. He knew his way around the dirt. Téa liked the idea of maintaining the fishpond.

Each time Téa had to leave Zephyr, it became harder. She hated to be away from him. She had never had a person to cling to, who wanted her in return.

The night was cool as Téa and Florence strolled together toward Ted's house. Florence's arm draped around Téa's waist. The breeze pushed pine needles side to side, blowing the sharp scent from the surrounding hills. It was tranquil here. The stars lit their way from above through the gaps in the trees, and small orbs glowed at their feet along the path lined with smooth round rocks that snaked through the Sanctuary.

"Everyone is so excited to meet you. Thank you for joining me tonight, dear." Florence smiled.

"Of course. Thank you for inviting me. I'm excited to start making connections here."

Téa thought back to her school days, how she was never allowed to play with the other children. She was hopeful about the possibility of making a real connection with someone, outside of her relationship with Zephyr.

Ted's home was a larger sphere than Florence's. Téa heard children screaming and giggling behind the door. Florence didn't bother knocking, she opened it and stepped inside.

"We're here!" She shouted. Florence held the door open for Téa to pass through then closed it behind them.

"Grandma!" Two adorable little girls with curly, dark red hair flew at Florence. They toppled her to the ground in a great ball of laughter and hugs.

"Careful now, girls," said a woman who appeared a few years older than Téa, as she walked down the hall to greet them. "Grandma is a little more breakable these days."

The woman was gorgeous, shorter and fuller than Téa, more of a heart-shaped face as opposed to Téa's oval-shaped face. But she had the same long curly hair, dark brown eyes, and golden skin tone as Téa, perhaps a little darker from days working outside. Téa tried not to stare. She had never seen anyone else who looked like herself.

White males dominated at Steppe Two. Téa knew of the different races when she learned about them at school and had always guessed her heritage was Hispanic. While learning about the history of the southern part of North America, the school taught her that she was lucky to be alive. That her race was weaker, and that most people like her did not survive the Decline. The teachers called her 'unclean' and told her she was unfit to mix with the other children.

Everything made a lot more sense to her after that revelation. Why some of the men harassed her so much. Why she didn't look like the other people around her. Always an outsider. Unworthy.

"Hello. I'm Gabriela. You must be Téa. Welcome." Gabriela's voice overflowed with warmth.

"Thank you so much for inviting me into your home." Téa said, following Gabriela down the hallway to the kitchen.

Ted was cooking something that smelled absolutely divine. Steam rose from a pot on the stove. When a timer on the oven rang out, Ted opened it while leaning back a bit to avoid the escaping heat.

"Téa. Nice to see you again. I hope you like squash!" He smiled as he used his mittened hands to place the hot pan on the counter.

"Smells delicious, Ted." Florence had escaped the clutches of her granddaughters and entered the kitchen to help her son.

"Hey, Ma. Can you spread some of that herbed oil on the bread over there? We're having spaghetti squash, with tomato sauce, and garlic herb bread, courtesy of yours truly." Ted waved a hand towel through the air like he was a grand matador ushering his bulls through the arena.

A sharp cry rang out from deeper within the home, Gabriela said. "Oh. Sounds like Miles is awake. I'll be right back."

Miles was too precious for words. Dark-haired like his mother, but also straight textured hair and blue eyes like his father. Drool ran down his chubby baby rolls, and he wore only a cloth diaper. Gabriela sang to him in another language that Florence whispered to Téa was Spanish. Gabriela danced around the room to shake off the sleep. Miles shrieked in delight, slapping, and pulling at his mothers face. Drooling more on his hands and kicking his feet against his mother's side, happy in his mamas' arms.

Dinner was a joyous affair. The family loudly talked all at the same time, laughing and smiling together. The granddaughters reached into the breadbasket when they thought no one was looking after Gabriela had told them no more. They giggled and ran off together after successfully ferreting away their spoils. Ted fed Gabriela forkfuls of spaghetti squash as she nursed the baby at the table.

Téa felt like she finally understood what a home was meant to be. This was it. Love, comfort, happiness, family. Téa wanted a family. For the first time in her life, she wasn't terrified of the idea of bringing a child into the broken world. Motivation to live, more than ever before, swelled within her. Not just to live, but to help heal the planet. For them. For the children who deserved to keep their home.

After dinner, Miles fell asleep again. Gabriela disappeared to lay him down and check on the girls who were playing quietly in their room. When she returned to the table, Ted handed her a glass of wine. She thanked him, then looked at Téa.

"So, Téa. Florence tells me you and Zephyr are former military. Is that correct?"

The question took Téa off guard, her heart began to race, and she clenched her fists underneath the table. She cleared her throat and said, "I actually was never military. I was an anomaly, really. An orphan who lived on base. Zephyr defied his father when we escaped together. He saved my life, so I wouldn't consider him part of Dunamis anymore." Téa said the last part perhaps too defensively.

Gabriela held a hand up and swallowed a mouthful of wine. "Oh honey, I didn't mean anything by that. I'm just trying to get to know you is all. We're all happy you're here." She smiled and patted Téa's knee.

Téa relaxed. "Sorry. It's been a rough couple of weeks," Téa said sheepishly. She didn't want to come across ungrateful to these people who had been kind enough to take her in.

Gabriela looked at Téa sternly. "Don't you ever apologize for sticking up for yourself or the ones you love. Not to me. Not to anyone. Do you understand?"

Téa nodded earnestly. Gabriela was the kind of mother needed in the new world, one who would raise powerful women and protect her family at all costs. Téa was in awe; Gabriela's presence gave her goosebumps.

A short while later, Téa and Florence thanked Ted and Gabriela for the delectable dinner and said their goodbyes.

Téa smiled the whole way home.

# CHAPTER TWENTY-ONE

## Earth

Two more days went by, and Zephyr continued to heal in the hospital. Téa visited him every morning and every night, telling him about her day, and how she could not wait until he was out there with her.

The morning of the next day came as it always did, piercing her eyes with its golden rays seeping through the skylight.

Téa understood The Sanctuary a touch better now. The community shared everything and supported one another. They all contributed to the community gardens and daily chores. As Téa traveled below, she looked above at the walkways that interconnected the forest, marveling at the craftsmanship. She passed ladders that were attached to the trees every few feet serving as a quick and efficient way to navigate.

However, there was one door that Téa had not been allowed to enter yet. The plain and simple door with a tiny earthen hump behind it sat closed, as always, as though wherever it led was completely underground. This feature was in stark contrast to the rest of the dwellings, which were only partially beneath the surface.

Almost all the solar panels were between the hospital and this seemingly going nowhere gateway. Téa asked Florence about it while they ate a breakfast of fresh sliced watermelon.

Florence gulped, "Well, I'm glad you brought that up, dear. I think it's finally time that I filled you in on some things. There is much to be discussed." Florence stood and grabbed their plates, then said. "Why don't you go get dressed?"

Téa's heart raced. The unknown had always been a dangerous variable in her life. She did not like surprises. She got herself ready, met Florence by the front door, then they were headed to the mystery entrance.

Téa's stomach twisted into knots. She hadn't forgotten about Florence's multiple warnings of danger headed their way, or the reminder that there were things still that Téa didn't know.

When they arrived at the mysterious door, a booming voice shouted at them from above. "Stop right there!"

Florence looked up and waved her hand. "Oh, calm down, Stuart. The girl is with me."

Stuart dropped from a short tree and landed gracefully like a panther, shaking his shaggy hair from his dark eyes. "Florence, you know you need council approval to bring her in there."

Florence shot him a warning glance and crossed her arms. "And what exactly do you think our impromptu meeting was about the other night, Stuart? She has approval. Now step aside."

He glared at the two women but did as he was told and moved out of their way.

Florence opened the door, and before them was a polished wooden staircase that declined steeply downward into darkness. Glowing orbs illuminated the steps. The earthen scent of dirt filled the air, and it took a couple of minutes to reach the bottom. They entered a long, tube-shaped room, well-lit, but without the nicely polished wood floors and roof like the huts, just packed soil and stone walls. Three other people occupied the space with Téa and Florence, computer monitors and desks lined the walls.

Three men at the end of the room spoke together in hushed tones.

"—I don't think we should trust her."

"—What other choice do we have?"

"—We can handle this on our own. We've been doing just fine."

"Ahem." Florence cleared her throat so loud, it echoed throughout the room.

The three men jerked around to face Florence, two with wide eyes and the third with his eyes downcast. They'd been caught clucking like a flock of hens, and they knew it.

Florence gestured towards the men, "Téa this is Howard, Frank, and Jung Hee."

"Florence! So nice to see you." Howard, a short, balding man with glasses, recovered faster than the others. When he approached, Téa saw the profuse sweat on his brow. "And this must be Téa."

"Hello, *Howard*." Florence looked at him like he was carrying a virus she did not want to catch but was forced to interact with.

Frank, the youngest of the group, stood at average height with a slender build. He glared at Téa, refusing to speak.

The third man was the only one who held his hand out to Téa to introduce himself. Jung Hee smiled kindly. "Welcome Téa," he said. "We are so grateful to have you here."

Téa was still on edge, eyeing Frank uneasily and leaning away from Howard. But she returned Jung Hee's smile and said, "Thank you. Although...I'm not sure what 'here' is."

Jung Hee gave Florence a sideway glance and furrowed his brow, as though he were under the impression Téa knew what was happening. "This is operation central for The Sanctuary. It is mostly counterintelligence. Surveillance of Dunamis and," he puffed out his chest, "Communication hub for the Vida Brigade."

Frank snickered. "And now apparently the new hottest tourist spot for un—"

"Ahem!" Florence shot him a look of warning.

"Right. Why don't we all take a seat?" Jung Hee gestured to the many open chairs around the perimeter of the room, and everyone sat down, swiveling their chairs so that they were all facing each other.

Florence took control of the room addressing everyone. "Let's start, shall we? Téa, I have brought you here today because you've been in the dark for far too long. We'll start with the basics. Hue Hillside."

Téa's eyes widened. She wasn't expecting his name to be spoken in an underground room, hundreds of miles away from Steppe Two.

Florence continued. "Hue was one of us, along with a handful of men he personally recruited. The book, 'Supernatural Abilities in an Evolving Generation' was planted on his order. He knew you were a learner, a literary, and he figured it was only a matter of time until you found it. He reported back to us when you located the book, but we are not sure how much of it you had a chance to read. He infiltrated Dunamis to keep an eye on you specifically. You are more important to this world than you know."

Téa's thoughts were spiraling, she found that awfully hard to believe, "Me? Why me, what's so special about one orphan girl?"

"Everything, dear. You are, as Dunamis calls you, Subject Eighty-Five."

Téa's stomach dropped to her knees, the room spun. She stopped breathing and turned her focus to taking in relaxing, deep breaths. In, then out.

Florence saw the change in Téa's body language. "This means something to you? How much did you read, dear? What do you know?"

Téa took a couple more breaths before talking, rubbed her legs in an attempt to bring feeling back into them, then looked at Florence. "I didn't read the whole thing, but enough. It talked about some people having Connex-A and Connex-B genes. How when those genetic markers were activated, it gave individuals superhuman powers. Subject Eighty-Five was the only known subject to have both Connex-A and Connex-B, but I never thought...it said only males could have the Connex-B gene. This can't be true; it can't be me."

Téa shook her head and looked at her feet. Florence rose from her chair and moved to Téa's side, rubbing her back in a motherly gesture, bringing calm to Téa. "It is you dear, and we believe you have the power to save us all."

Téa's eyes went wide and she froze in disbelief and fear as she listened to the old woman explain.

Florence went on to tell Téa about Dunamis using the Arranged Marriage Act as a cover to eliminate people with the Connex genes. How they purposely attempted to let the population who carried the genes die out, arranging only those people who were not a threat into marriages. How Dunamis kept selecting individuals with Connex-B for study. Purposefully putting the boys who carried the gene into abusive homes, believing it to be the only way to activate their powers. Dunamis never had an outreach program or intentions of helping orphans when they took her from Jefferson Home for Girls and Boys. They only wanted her.

"Téa," Florence continued. "Dunamis is corrupt. They always have been, all the way back to the beginning of the

Decline. When Dunamis took control of all food production and distributed it *equally.*" Florence used air quotes when she said the word, 'equally.' "They withheld resources from minority populations. They claimed that it was not true, but the truth was in the graves."

Téa's vision blurred. Her head pounded. "Can we take a break, please? I need a minute."

"Of course, dear. How about we go get some lunch?" She smiled and helped Téa to her feet.

Outside in the cool air, Téa watched the civilians of the Sanctuary continue on with their day as if Téa's brain wasn't exploding with revelations.

"I know this is a lot to take in," Florence said by her side, "but Téa, dear, it is important for you to know. We'll take a break, but then we do need to go back."

Téa nodded in understanding.

Back at Florence's they sat in silence, eating some left-over sweet potato hash, so flavorful last night but now lacked all taste. She chugged some water, used the restroom, and then had no more excuses to stay away from the hole in the ground.

"Okay, I'm ready," she said to Florence.

They returned to 'Operation Central' as The Sanctuary called it.

Frank looked at Florence when he said, "Is the princess ready now? Can we get this over with?"

"Oh, shut it, Frank." Florence sighed in exasperation. "Téa, Hue told you about a secret mission. One you would be training for without your knowledge, correct?"

"Yes." She nodded.

"That mission was to take place aboard space station Luna. General Strauss only recently became aware of some mutiny on the space station. He thought it would be an ideal opportunity to test your Connex abilities. He thought that he would be able to turn you into his own personal weapon. Send you to the stars and force you to eliminate all traitors in your midst."

Florence took a moment, as though what she had to say next was critical. "Hue believed Zephyr to be good, but Zephyr knew of his father's plans, Téa. Zephyr has the soulmate gene as well."

Waves of shock hit Téa like a punch to the gut. She forced herself to hold still and listen to the rest of what Florence had to say. "His father hoped the two of you would make a connection, that you would be soulmates, and that through your training, both genes would be activated. He also hoped your love for Zephyr would grow and activate your Connex-A gene.

"Then he was going to send you two to the worst parts of Dunamis. Make you witness atrocities so severe that your Connex-B gene would awaken as well. He wanted both parts of you alive when he sent you to space, and he wanted you on his side. He thought Zephyr was the key to control you."

Téa's mouth ran dry, and she struggled to swallow. Tears of anger and betrayal sprang to her eyes. "He knew? This whole time?"

"Yes dear."

# Chapter Twenty-Two

## Space Station Luna

Annabelle's heart rammed against her ribs, begging for freedom to unleash its chained adrenaline. When Sawyer didn't answer the door immediately, Annabelle knocked hard three more times and shouted, "Sawyer!"

Sawyer opened the door with panic in her eyes. "Annabelle, what's wrong?" She said with urgency in her voice.

"You knew about the Connex genes this whole time and you didn't tell me!" The fight left Annabelle's body and tears took the place of anger. "You lied to me."

Sawyer's eyes widened as she looked both ways down the hall. After seeing no one else around she took a step toward Annabelle and wrapped her arms around her then said, "Shh, shh, shh, now. Come on inside, we'll talk about this."

Annabelle stiffened in her embrace. She was mad at her own body for betraying her, for craving the comfort that she knew Sawyer could provide. She reluctantly allowed Sawyer to gently pull Annabelle inside and shut her door.

Sawyer's room was not a full apartment like Professor Trombol's, but it was bigger and better equipped than Annabelle's. Sawyer guided Annabelle to a small living area with a two-person couch and sat them both down.

Sawyer rubbed Annabelle's back in slow circles and said in a kind and calm voice. "Annabelle, I'm not even going to ask how you know about that. But I will say, it is imperative that you keep that knowledge between you and me. You can't even tell Ian."

Annabelle looked at Sawyer like a mouse caught in a trap.

Sawyer sighed and said, "He knows already, doesn't he?"

Annabelle could only nod as a tear dropped from the tip of her nose.

Sawyer took a deep breath and pressed down on the couch at both of her sides. "Okay, how did you find out? Who else have you told?"

Annabelle fiddled with the sleeves of her floral blouse and felt the edges of her skinny jeans dig into her sides uncomfortably. She laughed on the inside at her attempt to 'look presentable' for Professor Trombol, and wished she was comfy in her yoga clothes. She sniffled and wiped her eyes on her sleeves. "No one else knows. Just me and Ian." Annabelle pulled her legs up to her chest and leaned back against the yellow corduroy couch. "I was walking past the surveillance room one day. Someone had accidentally left the door open. I snuck inside and caught a peek at what they were watching. Once I realized it was Earth, I wanted to see more. So I waited until I saw someone enter their passcode, and I started going back to watch."

Annabelle hesitated, but Sawyer didn't say anything, so she continued. "I was hiding in the vents one day when Professor Trombol was downloading files onto flash drives, that's how I knew about them. The other day I broke into her apartment and took them."

Annabelle heard Sawyer's sharp intake of breath, but Annabelle kept talking without acknowledging her reaction. "Ian and I confronted her and she told us all of it. Everything. That's when I realized you knew. You know about it all and decided to keep this huge thing all to yourself."

Annabelle was surprised when she saw what looked like remorse spread across Sawyer's face. Sawyer tilted her head and looked up at the polycarb ceiling before saying, "I've debated for so long. Wondered if it was the right thing to do, keeping these secrets."

She turned to face Annabelle and pulled their hands together. "But it came down to survival. If I had told everyone, you, what I knew, then there was no telling how people would react. Their emotions, their shock or anger could have activated their Connex gene. Then that person or persons, might not have known how to control their new powers. They could destroy Luna in an instant without even meaning to. And without a way to escape back to

Earth, we have no choice but to keep up the charade. We can only hope that we can convince the resistance on Earth to start fighting back someday. Until then, we have to keep working. We have to keep Luna operational."

Annabelle leaned into Sawyers' shoulder and sniffled again. "How... how do we keep going on as though nothing has changed?"

Sawyer wrapped her arms around Annabelle and whispered, "Well, I think we find strength in each other. I'm here for you now, and you'll be there for me."

"We're living on a ticking time bomb, Sawyer," Annabelle said quietly.

"I know, babe, I know."

Sawyer kissed the top of Annabelle's head and pulled her closer. They held each other until their hearts slowed to a normal rhythm and Annabelle's tears stopped. The mystery woman on Earth no longer plagued Annabelle's thoughts. Annabelle was now wrapped in the world of belonging with Sawyer. Her only thoughts were of how to survive in this impossible situation, and how to do it together. For now, she would do what Sawyer said, bide her time and find comfort with this person that Annabelle was most definitely in love with.

# Chapter Twenty-Three

## Earth

Téa seethed and red blurred the edges of her vision. Her fists balled, ready to go through steel. It all made sense now. How could she be so blind? The dots were all there, so easy to connect. She gave him everything she had. Her love, hope, and trust.

She bolted to Zephyr's hospital room, trying to restrain herself into a semblance of control. She failed. No longer containing her anger when she reached his door, she flung it open and pointed a finger at him, shrieking. "YOU!"

Zephyr curled away from the rage directed at him as Téa continued shouting.

"You KNEW! This whole time, you were in on your father's plans. You knew what he had planned for every person with the Connex genes. Turning men into monsters! Seducing me. You and I were simply an elaborate scheme to bring out our Connex powers. You never cared." She paused, took a breath, and roared. "YOU WERE JUST USING ME!"

"Téa please. Let me explain—"

She couldn't stop screaming. "No. Explain what exactly Zephyr? Explain that you're innocent? Deny that you knew all along, that this was just a game that you would cheat your way through until you won?"

Zephyr's voice cracked and eyes glistened, "No! Téa please. Please don't do this. Give me a chance. Please."

Téa pulled herself together by reeling in her anger and straightening her shirt. Despite her vexation, she wanted to know why, so with arms crossed, she let him speak.

Zephyr gulped and sat up straighter. "First of all, and this is important, I did not seduce you, Téa. I fell in love with you. That night meant everything to me.

"Second, I knew you weren't my soulmate, but I fell in love with you anyway. Father is desperate for power and that makes him more susceptible to suggestion. I suggested to him that the soulmate connection can take time to mature.

"To buy *us* some time. Though soulmate connections are rare, we have studied enough to know that the connection is instantaneous. Something fundamental is felt by both parties the moment they touch. A simple brush of the cheek, a handshake.

"I knew from the beginning that you were not meant for me. But for a reason I cannot explain, I could not tell father the truth. I couldn't allow him to eliminate you. I meant what I said when I told you I would find a way out for you if that's what you wanted."

Téa shook her head in frustration and disbelief, "Liar! You just wanted to use me for yourself and take control from your father!" She felt that was not true, could see how genuine Zephyr's words were, hear how much sense his words made, but she was irrational and hurt. If they weren't soulmates, there was no reason to use her. Plus, he ran from his father, too, and his reaction to the book had been real. He could not have possibly known the extent of his father's experiments with the Connex genes.

"No, Téa, that's not true. I do love you. I am in love with you. Soulmates are not the only kind of love that exists."

Téa fumbled over her words in her mind. *Love.* The butterflies in her stomach betrayed her, but how could she trust him, or anyone, ever again? "Zephyr, I need a minute. I can't even look at you right now." Zephyr tried to say something else, but she turned away from him and walked out the door.

Emotionally wounded, and confused, Téa's internal branches, her lungs, seized from lack of oxygen. She needed fresh air. She hurried back through the hospital and out the front door. Walking to the bench near the entrance, she let the warm rays soak her skin. Focused on pushing air in and out of her body.

Florence meandered her way over and sat next to her on the bench. "How are you holding up, dear?"

Téa remained quiet. Florence nodded in understanding. "You know, not everything is always black and white. If you think Zephyr is telling the truth, but you are not sure, you do not have to trust your brain, you only need to trust your instincts."

Téa stared at the old woman, "You heard all that, huh?"

Florence laughed. "Dear, the whole community heard all that."

Florence chuckled some more, then looked her in the eyes, body language serious. "Téa, a person can make a wonderful first impression or a horrible first impression, but rarely does it accurately speak to the whole verity of that individual."

She took a breath and continued to speak to Téa. "Humans are complex machines. They have hopes, dreams, and regrets all the same. No one person is exempt from the multitude of experiences life has to offer. At some point in their journey, tides will shift, circumstances will alter.

"Good and evil, that is a constant my dear. Who has hold of that good or evil, that changes as well. A person's soul can be corrupted, can be healed, power can switch from one person to the next.

"In war, you must migrate as the salmon do... upriver, through the rushing water. You must battle the rocks and waterfalls in your path and keep your eyes new to the modifications that conflict brings. We are at war, dear. Eons old, going back to when stardust fought to create life. We do not yield, we do not surrender, we must continue. Existence itself depends on it."

Téa was still as stone. The magnitude of what she faced hit her like a shotgun to the chest. What she did next would no doubt set the course of the tides of humanity for decades to come. Zephyr was essentially second in command of the entire world.

If indeed the North American continent held the majority of the world's power, and General Thomas Strauss contained that power, then his son was surely equally as important. No matter if Zephyr said his father was willing to kill him, Strauss himself said Zephyr and Téa were his greatest assets. How much of her and Zephyr's relationship was an act? How much of a fool was he making her out to be? Could she afford to make an enemy of him?

Such a simple task held a mountain of repercussions. If she chose to hold on tight to her anger and betrayal, would Zephyr turn vengeful and bitter, or would he see the error of his ways?

If she went down the path of love and forgiveness, would he take advantage, or embrace his virtue within? Téa was terrified of making the wrong choice. There was no sure-fire way to predict the outcome of her next move.

She knew one thing for certain, she was no liar. He would see straight through her if she tried to manipulate him. Only one option remained. Honesty. She would be honest with him and hope for the best.

Dragging her feet, she made the walk back to Zephyr's room long. Téas' stomach was in knots. Her fingers fluttering with her sleeve ends, stretching, and pulling. Cracking her knuckles one at a time with her thumbs. She stopped just outside his door and tried to settle her nerves. She pushed it open slowly. Seeing the pure panic and regret cobwebbing his face melted her heart to a puddle.

"Téa, I'm so sorry, I am so deeply sorry. Please, you have no idea how many times I wanted to come clean. Immediately after meeting you. That first night with your hair in wet spirals. When we..."

Téa did not listen, she simply let her body guide her. Her feet moved slowly to the bed, she lifted the light blanket and crawled in next to him. She wrapped the cover around them both. Hearts facing each other, she snuggled in close, patiently waiting for her nerves to calm. He held her tight, and their breathing slowed. He brushed the top of her head with his lips and rubbed her back. A single tear landed on her nose, but her eyes were dry.

Zephyr was crying.

Finally, when she mounted the strength she needed, she looked at him and said, "I don't know if I love you the way you love me. But I do love you, Zephyr. I love your kindness and your strength, your heart. You were the first person to ever show me what grace could be. You are my home. It only took days, and you became my safe place. You saved my life. I don't want to do this without you. I forgive you. Not because I have to, but because I believe you. I believe *in* you."

He held still, listening to her words as she continued, "Do you think that we could be more than friends without being lovers, at least for now? A type of family, maybe? Can you be happy for me if I do find my soulmate someday? Will you fight beside me? For me? Because I know I could do that for you. I know I would die for you. I can move forward in this life with you. I just need to know... can you stay with me in this way?"

Zephyr squeezed her to him and his silent sobs shook their bodies. They stayed connected until his tears ran dry.

When he finally calmed, he smoothed her hair and kissed her forehead.

In a quiet and heavy whisper, Zephyr spoke. "I will always want you, in whatever way you will have me. No one has ever accepted me completely the way you have. No one has been more truthful with me than you. I want from my life only to be useful, meaningful, to make a difference. I will fight *with* you, and *for* you. I'm not going anywhere, my love."

He chuckled slightly as he continued. "Although, I don't know how I will feel if you were to find your soulmate, but I'll do my best not to burn the world down." He let out a small laugh, but then said seriously, "I only wish for your happiness."

Now Téa was the one laughing and crying. Knowing in her heart that she made the right choice. She could not be Zephyr's enemy. They stayed in each other's arms, whispering together until the sun went down. Then they fell asleep, content.

Téa woke sometime in the middle of the night. She eased out of the hospital bed, careful not to wake Zephyr. Tiptoeing to the door, slowly turning the handle and slipping out into the hall. She did not want to breathe life into the emotion Zephyr held for her and thought it best not to greet the morning together. Even though her heart ached as she walked away, her head told her to put some space between them, at least for now. She was determined to make their new relationship work, and that included not leading him on, until she knew for sure that she could give herself completely to him again.

Now that the can of worms had been opened, she needed to get back to the Sanctuary mainframe, operation central. She needed to sort through all the new information. A battle was coming, and she needed to be ready.

# Chapter Twenty-Four

## Earth

Florence was waiting for Téa at her house. The two women ate their breakfast together in the quiet. Téa freshened up and put new clothes on. When they left, Téa's feet fought her the whole way back to the secret's imperium, the tube-like room that knew everything about everyone, computers whispering their knowledge, preparing them for their fight against Dunamis.

"Welcome back, ladies!" Howard seemed jovial, more accepting of them today.

Jung Hee smiled and waved. Frank said nothing, still glaring from his corner of the room.

"Nice to see you too, *Frank*." Florence said, sarcasm thick in her voice.

"Are we done with the history lesson yet? Can we get to the point now?" Frank growled in return.

Florence angrily shushed him, then looked to Téa. "We are not Dunamis. We aren't going to manipulate you into activating your genes, but we would be appreciative of your help".

Téa was unsure if this was the path she wanted to go down, but she thought back to dinner at Ted's house, his family, his home. The Sanctuary needed to win. They were the only chance at a real future, the only hope for change. "What do you need me to do?" she asked resolutely.

Florence looked her dead in the eyes, body tense. "We want to destroy space station Luna. We want to take away the Dunamis lifeboat and force them to focus on healing this planet, our home, for all of mankind."

Téa lost feeling in her toes as Florence stared at her waiting for a response. She rocked slightly in her seat. "How?"

Florence took a deep sigh of relief. "There is a supply crew leaving in two weeks headed to the space station. Their shuttle will depart from a launch pad not far from the General's residence. We hope to sneak you and a small team onto that space shuttle. Upon arrival, you and your team will sabotage Space Station Luna."

Téa's eyes widened in surprise. "Me and my team? You expect me to lead this? I don't have any real combat experience. My training has mostly been from books. I only trained for a few days with Zephyr. You can't really believe I could handle this?"

Florence reached out and patted Téa's knee with a placating smile. "Téa, I misspoke. Of course, I don't expect you to lead the team. Most everything has already been planned anyway. But, I do expect the others to respect you, and I need you on this mission." Florence pulled her chair closer and held Téa's hand.

"But, why, Florence? Why do you even need me?"

Florence took a deep breath and focused on Téa's eyes. "The reason General Thomas Strauss believed you and Zephyr were soulmates was not only because you both possess the Connex-A gene, but also because you have compatible DNA. We know now that you and Zephyr are not soulmates. But you did have a connection. You do have feelings for him do you not?"

"Yes, I do care for him." Téa hesitated, "I think I even love him. Just maybe not in the way he loves me right now."

"Right, dear. So, a close match. Zephyr is not the General's only son."

Téa's body went numb. *No, not again. Not more secrets.*

Florence seemed to sense Téa's fear and said, "Don't worry, Zephyr is not lying to you still. He does not know that he has a twin. The General kept Zephyr in the dark as much as he could, and essentially forced him to do his bidding by threatening his life. Zephyr only knew what the General wanted him to know."

Shock froze Téa momentarily before she dropped her head between her legs and focused on her breathing. Her heart hurt for Zephyr. She knew all too well what it felt like to live a life that was not your own. Then, the rest of Florences' words sunk in. Téa spoke quietly without sitting back up. "A twin? Zephyr has a twin?"

"Yes dear, and we think *he* may be your soulmate. We wish for you to retrieve his brother from space station Luna before your team destroys it. Then back here on Earth, we will at long last have the upper hand in this war."

Finally, when Téa raised her head, the room blurred. All she could see clearly were her own hands. A pawn. She was only a pawn in the battle for Earth. She would never be free. Living a family life inside the Sanctuary walls would remain a dream. She would never have her own purpose. Never have control of her own life.

Florence kneaded Téa's back in slow circles and waited for her to reply. Téa wondered what would happen if she were to say no. Would the Sanctuary kick her and Zephyr out? Or something worse? Did she really have a choice? It didn't feel like she had an option.

With more strength than she felt, Téa sat up straight, jaw set, and looked at Florence. "Okay. What's next?"

Florence exhaled as if she had sensed Téas' hesitation and sighed with relief. Téa briefly wondered what Florence was prepared to do depending on how Téa had responded. She shook the thought from her head as Florence said. "We introduce you to the Vida Brigade."

Téa had never seen any military presence around the Sanctuary. Florence explained that they were stationed five miles away. A precaution in case Dunamis ever located the

Sanctuary. It would give the Sanctuary time to prepare for an attack while the Vida Brigade defended the border.

Florence spoke as they walked toward the outpost. "The Vida Brigade has done wonders with what they have. Most of their equipment is twenty years old, from before Dunamis had complete and total control. Military supplies have the most Dunamis security, and therefore are the most difficult to steal, so we only attempt a heist if we are desperate. Several years ago, we ran out of bullets and lost two civilians during that supply run." Florence's eyes glossed over, she stared into the distance before she continued. "But they have kept us safe all these years."

At least they didn't need to use the old miner's tunnel. Téa's skin crawled at the memory of walking underground with her senses muffled by the darkness. The Vida Brigade was on the opposite end of the Sanctuary, and she was grateful for the fresh open air of the thick forest. They were quiet the rest of their walk to the site and Téa took in these final moments of solitude, etching them into her memory before the chaos that was sure to come.

They finally arrived at a line of trees that were painted with red stripes marking the Vida Brigade territory. Where the forest thinned out, a rag tag group of soldiers stood at attention with their weapons. There were a dozen or so troops, more intimidating than Téa could have imagined, and they formed a semi-circle at the border. It reminded Téa of the militarized Steppe Two and a chill ran down her spine.

A tall dark-haired man with a full beard and thick shoulders dismissed the other men and rushed to greet them with his arms outstretched and a smile plastered across his face. Drawing out the old woman's name his voice boomed playfully. "Florence, you old geezer! When are you going to retire?"

Florence squinted her eyes, "Javier, I swear to God, if you call me an 'old geezer' one more time, I'll shoot you myself."

Javier howled his laughter to the sky and said, "Okay, okay, don't shoot." Still laughing, he looked at Téa. "And you must be our new queen, come to save the day." He winked at her as if he were the cleverest man on Earth.

Florence shook her head and rolled her eyes as she walked forward. "Where's the rest of the crew headed?"

"Chow time, mamacita! Care to join us?"

"Yes." Florence stated. "We'll be bunking here too. It's too late now to make the trek back."

Téa stopped, stuck in place with surprise. "Wait. We aren't going back to the Sanctuary tonight? What about Zephyr?"

Florence huffed and waved her hand as though she were flicking a bug away, and for the first time her tone of voice seemed annoyed with Téa. "Zephyr will be fine, dear."

Téa's eyes began to water for reasons she couldn't understand. Perhaps it was Florences sudden shift from caring grandmother figure to harsh militant. It triggered Téa in a way she wasn't ready for, and forcing her away from Zephyr, her safe place, was too much. Florence stared at her and sighed before saying, "We have walkie talkies for emergency use. I'll have Ted check in on him and inform him that you won't be able to visit tonight."

Téa dried her eyes, heat warming her cheeks. "Thank you, Florence. I appreciate it."

Florence didn't say anything in response, and still seemed irritated as they kept walking. Téa felt chided, like when she got in trouble for peeing the bed at the orphanage. The nun had slapped her face and made her sleep in her urine for two nights before they finally replaced her bedding. Téa dared not ask Florence anymore questions and followed along silently, her nose to the ground.

They came upon the largest tree in the area and climbed the ladder attached to it. Above, there was a log house structure built across multiple trees, big enough to fit six large grizzly bears. They walked in. Inside they did not have the glowing orbs for light, instead gas lanterns lit up the space. Two long rectangular tables were set up near the front of the entrance with seating. A makeshift kitchen waited near the back.

'Chow' consisted of some kind of meat on a stick, charred greens, and boiled potatoes.

They gathered their plates of food and took spots at an empty table. Javier sat across from Téa and waved his meat in Téa's face. "Hunted these little rodents myself. Nasty little pendejos sneak into our gardens."

Téa squinted in disgust and stiffly eased back from his beacon of splendor.

Javier laughed. "Rapido, chica. Eat before it's all gone."

Javier huffed, shook his head, and left her when she was no longer entertaining enough for him. Florence took his spot and smiled. "It's wonderful out here, isn't it? Being above the ground. It feels like flying, I get so tired of sleeping in the dirt."

Téa nodded but didn't know what to say. She did not feel like she was flying. She felt like she was falling.

Florence grunted, perhaps a little disappointed in Téa's lack of enthusiasm. "After dinner we'll give you the grand tour, then tomorrow I'll introduce you to the team. You'll be spending most of your time here from now on, so that you can prepare."

Téa could sense Florence's frustration with her, so she tried to perk up, "Sounds great! I'm excited to help the Sanctuary."

The women smiled at each other. Florence seemingly pleased with having won Téa's devotion. "We'll accomplish great things together, dear."

Téa smiled and nodded even as her stomach rolled. They finished their dinner in silence while Téa did the best she could to put on a brave face.

After dinner Javier gave her a tour as Florence followed along. The Vida Brigade's homes were not the semi-spheres of the Sanctuary but little cabins up in the trees. Téa counted about a dozen, possibly more.

After the tour, Téas' relief spread through her limbs when Javier and Florence showed her to where she would be sleeping, gratefully, *alone*, and took their departure. Téa was worried she would have to bunk with Florence. She didn't know how much longer she could keep up the charade of being the dutiful savior, so being alone with her thoughts was a gift.

Téa tossed and turned, miles away from a restful sleep. The treehouse they assigned to her for the night was empty except for the bed, which consisted of square piles of hay that stabbed her through a single sheet. The lumpy pillow smelled of body odor. She flung off a thin blanket that wasn't doing anything for warmth, and decided to go for a walk to warm herself up. She climbed down the ladder nailed to the tree.

Almost everyone was asleep above her, some of the treehouses still had lights on, but they were quiet. She passed a fleet of vehicles parked on the top of a big hill with an open field below. It was an impressive collection of various trucks, a van, a firetruck, and two tanks. As she neared the end of the Vida Brigade area, she saw that only one cabin sat on the ground, brightly illuminated. As she got closer Téa heard gruff, masculine voices laughing within.

Téa slowed then tiptoed up to the small simple log hut, trying to make herself unseen. She leaned against a corner of the cabin to listen to the men inside but couldn't hear much. Then she saw an open window near the back, she quietly crouched towards it and peeked in. She saw multiple television screens against one wall, and two men facing away from her, seated in chairs watching the displays.

Blueprints of Dunamis holding facilities that looked like food storage, laid on a table between her and the chairs the men were sitting in while they stared at the TV's. Below the blueprints were lists of supplies, amounts of explosives, and times. She continued to scan and saw another paper with a layout of what had to be space station Luna. It also had a supply list below it, including a quantity of explosives.

Téa froze, her heart raced as she realized what this meant. The Sanctuary did not just want to destroy Operation Luna. They wanted to destroy Dunamis food supplies as well. Bringing Dunamis to its knees, and in the process starving the hundreds of thousands of citizens who relied on Dunamis for food. So many innocent people would die of starvation. Defenseless men, women, and children.

Téa ducked down out of sight and her heart raced when one man's chair groaned as he swiveled around. She listened to the two men talk to each other from where she hid below the window, their voices rough and loud.

"Did you hear? Dr. Anderson is requesting more Rohypnol during our next supply run."

"Damn," the second man said as drew out the word. "That man goes through more roofies than a pimp."

The first man laughed. "You're not lying. If I had a sweet little thang like Emma in my home, I'd be riding her all night long, too."

At those shocking words Téa risked a peek through the window again. The man inside held his hands out between his legs as if gripping an imaginary girl and thrusted his hips.

Their disgusting laughter receded as Téa stumbled away terrified. Her stomach rolled. She made it a few more feet then vomited behind a tree. Dizzy and panicked she stood but was only able to walk a few more feet before the urge to empty her stomach again overtook her.

She spat and wiped her mouth on her sleeve. Chills shook her. Her mind raced for what to do next. The only thought that invaded her was a desperate need to get to Zephyr.

She involuntarily dry heaved a few more times, and when her strength returned, she ran.

# CHAPTER TWENTY-FIVE

# Earth

The five mile walk to the Vida Brigade had taken Téa and Florence one and a half hours. If Téa ran the whole time, she might be able to make it back to The Sanctuary in an hour.

Thick forest slowed her progress, brambles and thorns snatching at her as she ran. She tripped over fallen logs, and branches struck her face. Yet still, she ran.

Téa slowed only when she reached the edge of the Sanctuary. In four hours, the rising sun would wake those who slept and until then, she had time to get out. Téa crept towards the hospital, careful not to be seen by anyone who might be out for a nighttime walk.

With the hospital so close and within her sights, she stopped. Zephyr would need clothes. Téa remembered, upon arriving at The Sanctuary, Florence had given Téa a pair of baggy sweatpants and loose-fitting shirt that might fit Zephyr. She would have to figure out shoes along the way. Florence wasn't home and her hut was close, so it would be safe to go there, and Téa figured it was worth the detour so that Zephyr wouldn't have to escape in a hospital gown.

Téa slipped into the house, closed the door, turned around, and froze.

Emma and Nora slept on the hideaway bed, curled into each other. A mother holding her peaceful child, also, wrongly, unethically, and heartbreakingly, sisters. A tear ran down Téa's nose. Being only minutes in their presence, they had clung to her heart. The innocent pair, taken advantage of by the one person they should have been able to trust the most, their father, Dr. Anderson. The girls had stuck to her heart as sap sticks to a tree, solidifying and becoming one with her being. The atrocity committed against them would haunt Téa forever.

Carefully, she crouched next to the bed where she kept her things and found the clothes. When she backed out of Florence's home, Téa wondered if she was doing the right thing leaving them there. Maybe she could bring them with her? But she didn't want to put the girls at even more risk being on the run. She knew the General would not accept them, that to him, Téa and Zephyr were only assets, he wouldn't care about Emma and Nora, and Téa could not guarantee the safety of their lives. Reluctantly, she walked away, determined to come back for them when she could.

When Téa reached the hospital, she floated across the ground as soundless as she could. Crouching low and hugging the dark hallways, quiet as a church mouse, she traveled to Zephyr's room.

Téa turned the handle and slipped inside, flipping the lock. She hurried to Zephyr and shook him awake. He woke, startled, and she put a hand to his mouth, raising a single index finger to her lips, her eyes wide and serious.

Zephyr nodded and Téa whispered to him when she removed her hand. "We have to go. I brought you some clothes. We'll have to find some shoes on the way."

Zephyr shook his head and asked quietly. "Téa, what's going on?"

She dropped her arms to her side, crumpling the shirt she brought for Zephyr in her hands over and over as she paced the small room. "It's not safe here!" She whispered, "It's maybe even worse than Dunamis. They are not at all what they say they are. I can explain on the way, but we have to go now."

Zephyr listened and when she got close enough, he grabbed the shirt from her and nodded. "Okay... I trust you. We don't need to worry about shoes, they put my stuff in that closet."

He swung his legs out of bed, winced, and put a hand to his side.

Mid stride, Téa stopped, realizing that he wasn't healed all the way. "Are you okay? Maybe I'm blowing this out of proportion. Maybe we could stay a while longer."

"No, no. I'm okay. Just a little tender. Whatever is going on has you in a panic in the middle of the night, so I'm thinking we gotta get out of here."

Téa smiled and her fidgeting hands calmed. Zephyr always said the right thing. He knew her heart. She ran back to him, held his face between her hands, and kissed him, hard and quick.

He smiled. "Hey, I thought we weren't doing that anymore."

Téa grinned in return and shrugged her shoulders. She grabbed the clear plastic bag that held his shoes and clothes from the closet. She opened it and was greeted with the putrid scent of rot. The clothes were stiff with dried blood and debris, and the shoes were stained. She gagged. His clothes had clearly not been washed since the accident. She grabbed the shoes and sealed the bag back up, grateful she had brought the sweatpants and shirt for him.

Téa turned off the machine that gave a constant read out of his vitals, so that it wouldn't alert the only nurse on shift currently dozing in her chair outside the room. Then she helped Zephyr get dressed. He struggled to lift his arms above his head. She took precious seconds to avoid hurting his sore, recovering body.

Ready to go, Zephyr stood next to Téa at the door. She gave his hand a quick tight squeeze. "Let's go."

Knowing the sun would not start rising for at least another two and a half hours, they could fast walk instead of run, back to the Vida Brigade. Time was luckily on their side since Téa didn't think Zephyr could handle running, and it would give them time to talk.

When they were a safe distance outside the Sanctuary, Zephyr spoke first. "Are you ready to tell me what's going on?"

*How could she explain it all?*

Her pulse quickened as she looked for the right explanation. Finally, she decided to rip the band aid off, her words spilling out in a rush. "The Sanctuary has plans to destroy space station Luna, and they want my help to do it." Zephyr started to say something, but she held up a hand. "There's more." She took a deep breath and cleared her throat. "They also have plans to destroy all Dunamis food storage. There are pockets of resistance all over the continent and it looks like it will be a synchronized attack."

Surprise spread across Zephyr's face as his skin paled even further. "Holy shit, Téa. Do you have any idea how many people would starve? That food doesn't just feed Dunamis, it feeds the civilians as well."

Téa shook her hands out trying to dispel her nerves. "Zephyr, I know. We can't let them do that. They are so focused on defeating the enemy, but at what cost?" She stopped for a minute and looked to the sky. "And they knowingly allow abuse to happen. Maybe they think it's for the greater good. I don't know."

Zephyr squinted and tilted his head, "What do you mean?"

Téa glanced at him. "You know Dr. Anderson?"

He nodded, "Yeah, my doctor who did the surgery, what about him?"

Téa took a deep breath and she continued. "He has a daughter, Emma, and a granddaughter, Nora." She paused talking as they walked to gather her strength, then said. "Dr. Anderson is... also Nora's father, and I think Florence knows, or at least she is turning a blind eye."

Zephyr stopped and put his hand against a tree, his eyes downcast and sad. "Shit."

Téa stood next to him with her arms crossed shaking her head. "Florence was being evasive when I had asked about Emma and Nora. She said Emma has never mentioned who the father of Nora is, so I think Florence uses it as an excuse for herself to not intervene. The Sanctuary military, they call themselves the Vida Brigade, they know too, at least two of them do anyway. They steal the drugs for him, which could be used for surgeries, but they were joking about it being for something else. I'm sure they know he's using the drugs on his daughter." Téa laughed a cruel ironic sound, "At least he had the decency to drug her, maybe she fought back too much."

Téa hid behind her hands, and finally allowed deep, heavy sobs for Emma and Nora to leave her body. Zephyr held her.

She hiccupped before continuing. "I think the Sanctuary, well at least the few who know, turn a blind eye because Dr. Anderson is their only surgeon, and they can't afford to lose him. I don't think it's possible the whole community knows, there's too much good here. Her thoughts drifted to Gabriela and how tenderly she held Miles. But the ones who do know, are in positions of control here. It's not safe, it's not right what they're doing."

Zephyr held her close until her breathing steadied. After a few minutes, he said, "Come on. Let's get out of here."

When they reached the boundary of the Vida Brigade, Zephyr whispered, "So, what's the plan?"

Téa looked at him. "Do you know how to start a car without a key?"

He grinned. "You mean hotwire it? Yeah, I can do that."

Téa sighed in relief. "Good. The whole plan kinda relied on that." She let out a nervous laugh. "I know where their vehicles are. Luckily, they're parked uphill from here. I'm thinking we push one as far as we can so that they don't hear us, you get in and what did you call it? Hotwire? Then we get the hell out of here."

He smiled and squeezed her hand. "Sounds easy enough to me."

Téa stared deep into his beautiful gray eyes. "Zephyr, I think we have to go back. To Sandstone. I think we need to warn your father. He's a cruel man, but he does keep the people alive, and I don't think he'll kill us. He said himself that we were his greatest assets. He must still think that we can activate our Connex genes together, and I think he's our only chance at stopping all this destruction."

Zephyr shook his head. "Téa, he'll keep us captive, and he will obliterate the Sanctuary. Obviously, there's evil here, but there has to be good too."

Téa's voice came out in a tense whisper. "I know we'll be walking into a prison, but we'll be saving thousands.

We won't tell him where the Sanctuary is at. We'll make a condition for exchange of information."

Zephyr dropped his head, staring at the ground. "I'm not sure that will work with him."

Téa gently gripped Zephyr's arm. "It's all we have Zephyr. We can't stop these attacks on our own, we need help. We have to try."

He brushed the side of her face, pulled her closer to him, and kissed her softly. "Okay, Love. Lead the way."

Warmth flooded her cheeks. Smiling, Téa held Zephyr's hand tight, finally taking charge for the first time in her life. She knew the plan would work. Her plan. Not Zephyr's or someone else's. Hers. She could end the killing. The destruction, the hate. The years of who is more powerful than who. If she could just get them to stop and look at what they were doing, if only she could help them see the pain, and the havoc that their demolitions of control were causing.

The sound of beetles clicking around them, and the dew in the grass around their ankles, alerted Téa to the coming rise of dawn. They had to hurry.

Stealing a truck was easy and they were fortunate that none of the vehicles were locked. Breaking a window would've made too much noise. Zephyr said it was lucky that they were older models, it would make it easier to bypass the ignition switch.

Zephyr, weakened from his injuries, struggled to push the truck after engaging neutral gear. So, it fell to Téa, who was in top physical shape from working the gardens every day and eating real food on a regular basis. Zephyr climbed inside to steer and use the brakes. Once they were far enough away down the hill to avoid being heard, Zephyr got the truck running.  They were at least ten miles away from the Vida Brigade when they saw the first streaks of light in the sky. They had made their escape.

Téa's elation of successfully evading the Vida Brigade without notice fell away, replaced with a heavy stone in her gut. They were on their way into the devil's den. Zephyr said it didn't matter if they did not know the way back to Sandstone from where they were at. As soon as they got to any check point, the General would be alerted. All they had to do was keep driving on major roads and wait until they came to any town.

Zephyr began the escape from The Sanctuary in the driver's seat, but after exhaustion took hold of him he moved over to let Téa drive. She figured out how to control the vehicle once Zephyr showed her the basics. Gas, steer, brake.

Zephyr laughed and said, "You're a natural, Téa." He chuckled some more. "But you're lucky it's not a stick shift."

Téa playfully glared at him, but didn't ask what he meant by that.

# Chapter Twenty-Six

# Earth

The sun was high in the sky by the time they made it to a town in the more sparsely populated North. It was as though everything moved slowly but fast at the same time. Téa was numb to everything happening around her. As though she watched from under water. It only took moments for a soldier to recognize them, seconds for that soldier to radio the General, minutes to have them restrained, and hours for General Thomas Strauss to arrive.

The General did not say a single word. He walked up to them both, stopped in front of Zephyr, raised his leg and kicked him hard in the gut. Zephyr fell to the ground.

Téa, shocked back to her senses, screamed, "Please, he's injured already. You'll kill him!" pleading with him to stop when he pulled back his boot for a second hit.

"Missy, he's lucky he's not already dead. Shut up before I beat you, too." The hate oozing out of this man was palpable.

Téa, scared of causing more harm, remained quiet. The General ordered his men to shove black coarse fabric bags over their heads and shove them into a helicopter. They stopped once to refill. When they landed, soldiers removed their hoods, and as if no time had passed at all, Téa was back inside the tall brick walls topped with barbed wire. Steppe Two.

Terror filled Zephyr's face. He whispered to Téa. "I thought he would take us back to Sandstone. This is not a good sign, Téa."

"I hear you boy! You best shut your trap!" The General growled.

They walked in silence through the cold cement labyrinth of Téa's childhood, the General leading them through places below ground that Téa had never seen during her time growing up on the base. A soldier opened a plain metal door and shoved Zephyr in.

Zephyr turned around in the dark cell trying to run back out as the soldier slammed the door in his face and locked him inside.

That action awakened Téa's adrenaline. Her pulse raced as she grappled with the rough arms holding her. She knew she would never be able to break free but fought anyway.

"That's enough!" The General vibrated with anger; his calloused hands shoved her roughly forward. "If you want to keep breathing, you will stop struggling now!"

The General pushed Téa into a stark white room filled with lab equipment. Microscopes, Bunsen burners, petri dishes, glass beakers, and so much more that Téa could not name littered every corner. The soldiers that accompanied them, stopped at the threshold, and shut the door.

Téa was alone with the General.

He shoved her roughly into a chair, her hands still bound behind her, she cried out in pain and the General growled in anger. "You know, Missy, you've created quite a mess for me. Really, I should just kill you now."

Fear coursed through her veins, desperation in her voice. "No! You don't want to do that. I have information you'll want, and I'm willing to trade!"

The General laughed at her. "I doubt there is anything of value. I know everything, or haven't you heard?"

Defeat began to erode away at Téa's resolve, she had imagined this all happening so much differently. Her only card to play was giving up some information. She growled out at him. "Your food supply is at risk. Are you willing to starve? It sure looks like you've never missed a meal."

The General slapped Téa hard across the cheek, her whole body was thrown to the side from the impact. The hot sting covered her entire face.

"Watch. Your. Mouth. Bitch," the General hissed.

Téa did not say anything else. Her whole body trembled as the General walked away from her.

He talked with his back turned. "Hue Hillside was stronger than I thought."

Surprise at hearing Hue's name again shot through Téa as the General moved to face her. He was so close she could smell the stench of his breath. He spoke with a low menacing tone that chilled Téa to terrified silence. "We pulled the skin from his flesh. After three days, his right forearm was bare. Ripped out his fingernails one at a time. He begged us to stop. We had to re-start his heart twice after we submerged him in water. We started cutting off toes before he finally talked, spilled his secrets like a rotten can of beans. Guts all over the place when we were through with him. We already know of the impending attacks on our food supply."

Téa leaned over the side of her chair and retched, nothing left inside of her but bile.

"Oh, Darlin, now don't go making a mess of my floor. I just had it waxed." His grin was so wicked she could not look at him.

"Luna." The words came out of Téa as a whisper, struggling to stay coherent through her dread.

"What was that? You're going to have to speak up, Missy."

He forcefully yanked her chin towards him, and she spit in his face. The General grabbed two of her fingers and bent them backwards so fast, Téa did not register the breaks until seconds after. She screamed out in agony, wailing until the General covered her mouth with a hand that stunk of decay. She bit him, and he pushed away from her, howling in anger.

He pulled his hand back for another blow when she started yelling. "Space station Luna will be destroyed! Did Hue tell you that? I bet not!" She used all her willpower to not look away from his dead eyes.

"You better talk, girl," he growled.

"I will... I will tell you everything. But you have to let me, and Zephyr go."

The General laughed. "You really think you're in a position to make demands?"

Téa shrieked at him. "You don't know where the Northern Resistance is! I do."

He stopped laughing at that. "You best start talking now. I don't think you'll make it through, *this little piggy went to the market.*"

The image of the General cutting her appendages off one at a time made her toes curl and her stomach clench. "I will tell you everything, but you have to let us go."

The General paced. He had his hands clasped behind his back. He opened the door and ordered one of the soldiers to retrieve Zephyr.

Moments later one of the soldiers dragged a limp Zephyr in by his armpits, hands still tied together behind his back. The soldier dropped him to the floor. Zephyr groaned and coughed up blood, Téa's heart dropped at the sight.

The General kicked him in the back and screamed. "Get up, boy! I didn't raise a pussy!"

Zephyr spit blood on the Generals shoes. Just as the General was going to kick him again, Zephyr rolled away and sat on his haunches. He leaned forward on his lower legs and struggled to raise himself to standing.

The General grabbed him by the throat, Zephyr was dangling.

Zephyr's skin turned from pink to blue before Téa cried and screamed at him. "Please, stop! They are smuggling themselves into your next supply run to the space station.

They plan to blow it up. To destroy your back up Earth and make you focus on healing this planet." Snot ran down Téa's nose. She hiccupped and tried to catch her breath.

The General's mouth twitched at the corners in a sickly grin. "Now see, was that so hard?" He pulled a knife from behind his waist, brought it to Zephyr's throat, and sliced.

Red ran down Zephyr's chest, his eyes huge, mouth gasping for air, a fish out of water. His body convulsed as the General kept hold of him.

Then... Zephyr was still.

# Chapter Twenty-Seven

# Earth

T he sound that came out of Téa was inhuman. Electricity soared through her veins, blue lightning igniting
her nerves, hypodermis on fire. Every electron in the air,
down to the nucleus pressed up against her. She knew then,
her Connex-B gene was active.

She remembered what she had read. '*Superhuman
strength, accelerated healing, manipulation of metal.*'

She focused, pulled her hands apart, and broke the bind-
ing, freeing herself. Felt the sting on her face and the breaks
in her fingers, healed. Her muscles got tighter, stronger,
she felt it all.

The General looked satisfied. A fat cat licking the cream
from his lips, as though her Connex gene awakened was

what he wanted all along, "There it is. You and I are going to do great things together."

"*Never*," she growled the word out through her clenched teeth with determined eyes. She swung an arm forward and the chair she was sitting in moments before, flew at the General. He ducked, but Téa manipulated the metal chair with her mind. It twisted and snaked around the General's body, holding him, slowly squeezing tighter and tighter.

Téa raised a fist and as she envisioned smashing his skull open with her newfound strength, he yelled at her. "Wait! You have a sister!"

Téa stopped. *Impossible.* Yet her whole body tingled with hope. She narrowed her eyes at him. "*You're lying.*"

"She's aboard Space Station Luna. Release me or you'll never meet her."

Doubt crept on the edge of her mind, but powerful rage overruled. "I'm stronger than you. I'll fight my way to her. I don't need you."

"Oh, but you do." He said through a wicked grin. "I have a kill switch." He snarled. "If I don't enter a code that only I know every three days, the space station will blow up." The General said with an evil smirk.

"Bullshit!" Téa shouted, her body tense with vengeance waiting to be released.

The General's voice was low but clear, too controlled, too unphased. "I can prove it. Release me."

Her mind raced for a solution, but none came. Reluctantly, Téa unbent the metal holding the General with her powers.

"There. See. Civilized." The General rubbed his neck and wrists and straightened his shirt and tie. "Follow me."

Téa never hated another thing more – obeying the General – but the desire, the possibility to know family was stronger. She followed him to the other side of the room, to one of the desks. He booted up one of the monitors, placed his thumb on a fingerprint pad hooked to the computer, and the display awakened. He selected one of the secure documents and there it was. A countdown screen. Seven boxes for numbers, Operation Luna command key, and a single button.

Execute.

The General looked over his shoulder and grinned, knowing already that he had won. As if to put salt in the wound, he opened another screen. It was surveillance of the space station. Dozens of rooms.

The General selected one with a girl a little younger than Téa, but not by much, maybe sixteen or eighteen, stretched out on a pink yoga mat performing a stretch. Oblivious or immune to the watchful eye on her. Moving slowly, her long, dark, straight hair fell over her shoulder as she leaned to one side, pushed herself up on one palm, and raised her other hand above her. Téa couldn't see the girl's face through her curtain of hair, but she had all the proof she needed that there was someone, multiple someone's, worth saving.

Téa's knees went weak.

The General stood from the desk, arms crossed, smirking. "Perhaps we can chat over dinner."

A volcano of frustration and hate bubbled up within Téa. "Or perhaps I can torture you the same way you tortured Hue."

The General had a venomous gleam in his eye. "I'd like to see you try. I think you know, Missy, that torture would not work on me. I always get what I want."

Téa felt he was telling the truth, but even if he was fibbing, she didn't have the time or the resolve to torture him. She would be forced to hear him out if she wanted to save this person who could be her sister. But would the price be worth it?

The General spoke. "I hear lamb chops are on the menu tonight. I do love a good mornay sauce. It would be a shame to let it go to waste."

"Not a single soul will touch me, yourself included." Téa stalked off, not waiting to see if he would follow, careful not to look at Zephyr's body, afraid she would collapse.

The General barked orders at the one guard that had remained stationed outside in the hallway. "Take his body to the incinerator."

The guard saluted and disappeared behind the lab doors.

Téa's stomach rolled with nausea, "You're a monster." She said, in barely a defiant whisper, trying to keep her tears from falling.

They walked on, and when they approached the corridor that led to the kitchens, the General stopped her. "Oh Téa. You know the mess hall food is shit. We're going back to Sandstone."

The journey with the General was like a whole new form of punishment, being trapped in such close quarters with him for the hours long journey. Téa counted the seconds in her head, trying to keep a brave face, attempting to stay the tears that wanted to overtake her. She would not let the General see her as weak.

Finally, Téa was grateful for the trip to be over, but Sandstone was not as welcoming as she remembered. A great dead thing. It was dark and cold, and much too big. All she wanted to do was go to her old room and let her tears wash her memories away.

Inside the front foyer, the General directed his solid gaze at her. "You smell ripe. Clean yourself. Be in the dining hall at nineteen hundred. Sharp."

As the General walked away from her, she resisted the strong urge not to snap his neck right there.

As she moved through the corridors to her room, she could see Zephyr's gray eyes in every gray stone. Opening her door, she sat on her bed. It was still unmade from the morning they made their escape, as if time had frozen inside Sandstone, the place where they had shared their first kiss, she could almost catch his scent in her sheets at the memory of it. Feel his arms around her as she entered the bathroom for a shower. Feel his caress with every piece of clothing she removed.

How could he be gone? In an instant he was just...gone. Her heart ached. A hole carved out that could never be filled.

The possibility of a sister she never met was the only thing keeping her from drowning. She struggled to keep her head above water as the waves of grief crashed straight through her.

Téa practiced using her new abilities, controlling metal. She turned the shower knobs on without touching them, moving them back and forth until the water was comfortable. Testing her strength, she stood next to the tub, she placed a hand on the edge and squeezed. The porcelain disintegrated to dust in her hand where she grabbed it. Finding a pair of hair scissors in the drawer after getting out of the shower, she cut open her skin on one hand. It healed almost instantly.

She knew she could kill the General easily, but everyone aboard the space station would die. Was her sister an innocent? Were the others up there ignorant to the happenings down here on Earth? How many lived in the stars? She could not have their deaths on her conscience. She would have to hear the General out. Learn what he had in store for her.

After her shower, she dressed in layers and a new pair of running shoes. Leaving her room, she paused and looked down the hall to Zephyr's door.

Inside his room, guilt threatened to devour her. She never should have talked Zephyr into coming back here. She should have known the General couldn't be trusted. Her tears silently fell as she dragged her finger lightly over the furniture, taking in Zephyr's ghost. She went to his closet, pulled down a navy button up jacket and hugged it tight. She rubbed the material against her face, breathed him in, then shook the jacket out, and put it on. It was baggy, and she had to roll up the sleeves a couple inches. Téa left it unbuttoned, and pretended the sleeves were Zephyrs arms holding her, giving her strength.

She took her time making her way to the dining hall, knowing the gallows awaited her there. The General was seated at the head table as though it were just another Sunday morning.

"You're late."

"And you're the wart on a hippo's ass." She sneered.

The General's eyes widened with surprise. "Don't test me, Téa. I will let the space station vaporize."

Téa wasn't great at lying, so she did her best to keep her voice steady. "I have never met this supposed sister, and I've been alone my whole life. Let it explode. I'm simply curious about what you have to offer me, besides allowing your own precious space station to stay in existence."

She finished her statement with a glare and the General for once seemed unsettled. She was winning.

Or so she thought, until he said, "You forget, Missy, I have watched you your entire life!" He yelled out. "I know you. You would do anything to save her. Besides, if you meant what you said, you would have killed me by now."

Defeated, Téa tried to sit at the opposite end of the table, but he stopped her with a gesture and pointed to the place next to him. She shivered as she walked to her assigned spot and sank in her seat. "What do you want me to do?"

A gleam of victory shone in his eyes. "I want to see if my other son can activate your Connex-A gene. Obviously, Zephyr couldn't. I realized he never would be able to as soon as you and he ran off together. Of course, I cannot control you here, but on the space station…"

He didn't need to say it, she would be a rat in a lab. She knew what he meant. Téa sneered at him. "Why do you need me? Don't you have plenty of men in cages with the Connex-B gene to study?"

"As a matter of fact, I do. We have created many unstable homes for Connex-B carriers to force their genes to activate. It's the only way. Of course we tried creating serums to force it out. Unfortunately, the serums never worked. Gross mutations and death after a few hours were some–" He paused for the right words. "of the minor complications.

"For years we have studied them, of course, with safety precautions. I, personally, am a fan of kill switches." He flashed his evil grin. "Every one of them, once they are tested for the marker, have a little implant put in at the base of their skulls. If I find them to be a threat, snap, just like that, out like a light. Unfortunately, my idiot son," he laughed, "deactivated yours at some point during your initial stay at Sandstone. It went offline a couple days after your arrival. I almost killed him then."

Téa remembered when she had fainted, she had woken up with a tender neck. She thought it was from the fall, but Zephyr must have injected her with something.

The General demanded more wine from one of the staff then kept talking. "You know, it's surprising. We have tried various different *scenarios* to activate Connex-B genes."

He took a full glass of wine from the woman that Téa recognized as Eleanor. Téa thought it was odd that Eleanor, being the house manager, would be doing such simple tasks as fetching wine. Téa pulled her gaze away from the woman and tried to focus on the heaping excuse for a man seated at the table next to her.

The General took another swig of wine and began rattling off the different ways he had found to torture his subjects as if he was reading off a shopping list. "Families who beat the subject, families who beat a friend or relative in front of the subject, drug addict parents, parents who take advantage of them, or allow *others* to take advantage of the subject, sometimes even while the parents watch." He said with that sickly evil grin of his. "But, the most successful cases of the Connex-B gene activation were neglect. Homes where the child was left alone for long periods of time, never fed on a regular basis, isolated from others, never given love or affection. Does any of that sound familiar, *Téa*?" he growled.

"Fuck you." Téa forced back tears, her heart breaking as he pointed out the childhood she had endured.

He laughed again and continued. "Now... you can choose to kill me here, handle the affairs of the entire continent by yourself. *Or*. You could have a soulmate, your sister, a family of your own, and live your life out in peace. Far, far, away from me." He grinned wide like a lion preparing to eat its prey. Lamb blood dribbled down his chin as he talked.

"You're disgusting."

He stopped chewing, spit his mouthful out in a napkin, wiped his face, and leaned over her, venom in his words. "Tell me. Is the old hag still alive?"

Téa's blood ran cold. "How do you know about Florence?"

The General laughed and leaned away. "Ah, so she is. When I met her years ago, it was the same night I met my wife, Victoria. I caught Florence and two others stealing from me. I killed the man first. The hag got away, but I kept the younger girl, Victoria, for myself. Tell me, did Florence never tell you she had a daughter?"

A chill ran through Téa, numbing the tips of her fingers and toes. Florence had not told her. Téa didn't say anything.

The General leaned back in his chair, pleased with himself. "With so few people left on earth, I thought my son would have figured it out. Apparently, he was even more of an idiot than I realized. Florence was Victoria's mother."

Téa's mind buzzed, she was fitting the puzzle pieces together, slowly locking all the parts into place. Her voice shook. "Florence is Zephyr's grandmother?"

His voice dripped with glee. "Why do you think the woman is so set on her vendetta at the expense of so many lives?" He shouted at her. "My wife was already pregnant with the twins when I took her for myself. Her useless husband should not have allowed her on supply runs with them to begin with. They were all ignorant."

Téa struggled to keep up, her mind racing and cataloging all this new information.

The General kept talking. "Tell me, why does the resistance need so much Rohypnol? I see what inventory goes missing from our supply facilities. Surely, they are not performing *that* many surgeries. My guess, Téa, is that the resistance is not as guilt-less as they seem."

Téa's stomach turned at the truth in his words.

The General continued, "Humans are corrupt. Always have been. Why not start new? You can be in control of the space station. Let me study you. In return, you get to start a new world. Someday Earth will expire, and you will be left with everything you need to start again. The way I see it, you are saving the human race."

Téa hated that just maybe, the General was right. She could get away from all the bloodshed, the sadness. Meet her sister, meet Zephyr's brother and start a family. What other choice did she have? "One condition," Téa said. "I can't trust that you won't blow up Space Station Luna. If you deactivate the kill switch for the space station permanently, I'll go."

"This is not a negotiation, Missy. That kill switch is all I have to keep you in line. Take my offer or leave it."

Hopelessness and resignation settled within Téa. "What's your son-" she stopped herself. The General didn't deserve to call them his sons. "Zephyr's brother, what's his name?"

He grinned. "Ian."

"When do I get to meet him?"

The General smiled, "Tonight. You leave tonight."

# CHAPTER TWENTY-EIGHT

## Earth

Téa sat in the back of the General's SUV. The launch pad with the spacecraft headed to Operation Luna was several miles south from Sandstone.

The General cranked the air conditioning on full blast to chill his boulder-like body. The tips of her toes, fingers, and nose were ice. She tried to fold into the corner of the car to disappear, trying not to breathe the same air as the horrible excuse for a human sitting next to her.

She stared out the window watching the departed world pass them by, the large expanse of forgotten things. She wondered if she was doing the right thing, going round and round in circles, it all came back to one deciding factor. She could not live with herself if all the inhabitants of the space station were killed because of her. She also held onto the hope of family, of love. Perhaps she would have another chance to kill the General. Maybe she could sneak onto a spacecraft of cargo, like the Resistance was planning. Or maybe she would live out her days in peace, away from all the monsters.

Téas' thoughts continued to whirl around in her head like a hamster in its cage. But soon her thoughts faded away and an overwhelming despair took their place. It didn't feel like much mattered anymore after Zephyr's death. She did love him. She doubted her feelings for him after learning of his betrayal, but soulmate or not, she had loved him. She had given him her whole heart, and now that heart was returned to her broken. She didn't know if she would ever be able to give it to another in hopes of that person healing it, or maybe she could heal it herself someday.

She knew only one thing for sure, the General must die. She didn't know how, but when the time came, she would not hesitate. He would pay for the pain he had caused, the lives he had taken and destroyed, and the torment done at his hands.

The ungodly excuse for a man spoke to her. "Miss Garcia, you understand our arrangement. I will allow you and your sister to live. I will allow Ian to live, and I will not eviscerate the space station. In return, when you meet Ian and your Connex-A gene is activated, you will allow me to study you. The doctors aboard the space station will take regular blood samples, and evaluations. I am in constant communication with them here on Earth. I see everything. *You will not fight them.*" The General looked at her, she didn't say anything. "One last thing. You will find the traitor, the spy, whoever it was that Hue was communicating with, and you will eliminate them."

Téa swiveled her head towards him, mouth agape. "What! That was *not* part of the deal. I'm not your assassin!"

"You will do as you are told." He barked at her.

What could she say? She didn't have any other hold over him. He had the kill switch.

They finished the journey in silence.

When they arrived at the launch pad, everything was too loud. The roar of the massive engine, stories high, shook their surroundings, and she couldn't imagine how it would feel when they actually took off and the enormous thing would be working at full power.

The General pulled one of his soldiers aside and shouted at him over the noise. "She is to be strapped in, and do not let her out of your sight!" Then he spoke to Téa. "You understand our arrangement, Miss Garcia? You will be a good little girl and get yourself on that spacecraft. Then you follow *every* order that I give. Or..." He made the puff boom sound of a bomb going off and imitated an explosion with his hands. Then he laughed as he walked away.

The soldier grabbed Téa's arm and jerked on her to drag her away. She yanked free, clutched his arm, and squeezed; his arm, easy to manipulate now that she was stronger than she'd ever been before. He shouted in pain as he tried to pull his arm free. "Fucking bitch!"

She released him and narrowed her eyes as she hissed at him. "Do. Not. Touch. Me," and gestured her hand out for him to lead the way.

He looked like he wanted to hit her but thought better of it and stormed off. Téa followed. They rode in an elevator, more cage-like than box, up ten stories then it stopped. The doors slid apart, and in front of them hung an open-air walkway headed to the rocket. The wind rattled, and the beams under her feet threatened to topple her over as they crossed.

At the entrance to the rocket, she had to crawl through a white padded narrow tube on hands and knees, and before he followed, the soldier swung the long rifle he was carrying behind his back. Her nerves tightened with him behind her, grateful she could protect herself with her newfound power.

Tons of metal on every surface made up the interior of the spacecraft. Metal seats, bars, harnesses, knobs and buttons. All made of metal. The volume of noise increased so loud it turned into a constant buzz and hum. Impossible to hear each other. The soldier pointed to a seat, and she sat down. He pulled a metal padded harness down from above her head and clipped it into place, then shoved a full face oxygen mask roughly onto her, and walked away. When he pulled the round door closed as he left, a large lock slid into place, leaving Téa alone again.

Her heart pounded, her breath fogging up the mask, and fear seized her limbs. She couldn't even hear the sound of her own breathing. The engine ramped up. Her bones rattled, her teeth vibrated, her whole body shook. A digital board across from her with illuminated red numbers started a countdown.

10..

9..
8..
7..
6..
5..
4..
3..
2..
Darkness.

# CHAPTER TWENTY-NINE

# Space Station Luna

S he was here. Annabelle's mystery woman from Earth was *actually* on Luna. The news had spread quickly, and Annabelle had rushed to sneak a peek of her as she was wheeled to medical. The next few days the space station was abuzz with a flurry of guesses as to who she was and why the General had sent *her*. The only people to ever come to the space station were the Generals' soldiers. This woman, from the looks of her and the way she arrived, was not a soldier. That could only mean one of two things, he had sent them a spy, or a new resident.

Annabelle's stomach was in knots. Professor Trombol had changed the passcode to her apartment and the surveillance room and had refused to speak with Annabelle. The first generation stalked around Luna; the tension clear on their faces.

No one from Earth had been sent to live on space station Luna in fifteen years. Not since Annabelle and Ian– they were the last two orphans sent up, and Annabelle was convinced of that being the reason they were so close. They must have known each other and bonded as young children even though Annabelle could not remember that far back.

Then there was Sawyer. They had gotten so close lately after finally taking that last physical step with each other, Annabelle even had a few things at Sawyer's place like a toothbrush and a spare change of clothes. But Sawyer was on such a constant watch of the mystery woman, waiting for her to regain consciousness, that they hadn't seen each other in days.

Annabelle hovered around medical a little too frequently and had started to worry that Sawyer suspected Annabelle's obsession, and Annabelle wanted nothing more than to explain to Sawyer that she didn't have *those* kinds of feelings for *her*. That it was simply an admiration. This woman had survived as the only female on that cruel military base for years. That kind of strength was hard not to be impressed by.

Even Ian was difficult to nail down for company. He had volunteered himself to be Sawyer's right-hand man the moment the woman from Earth had arrived. Annabelles' loneliness bore at her so deeply that she had even stooped to hanging out with *John from accounting* on her off-hours. Annabelle had to keep reminding herself that the two people who loved her most would tell her if there was anything to tell. Still, it was hard to think of anything else.

So, Annabelle waited. She went about her work in the greenhouse. The peace lilies were flourishing from Annabelle's combination of nervous and excited energy. She had never seen them so healthy and bountiful, as if they were getting a fresh start. She could feel the shift in the air. Something big was happening.

Annabelle knew it in her gut.

Change was happening.

# CHAPTER THIRTY

# Space Station Luna

Téa lay naked in an entirely white room, with only a thin piece of paper covering her body. Her whole being ached, her mouth was dry, and she felt fuzzy, as though her ears were stuffed with cotton. She sat up and her head swam. She put a hand to the side of her skull, trying to stop the spinning and quickly realized the paper slid down too far. She grasped at it, and it crinkled as she held it closer to her body, attempting to keep herself decent.

Someone spoke to her from a smooth sounding speaker system, the voice pleasant and gender neutral, "Miss Garcia, welcome. You are on board spacecraft Luna. Please remain calm, I am going to enter the room to speak with you further. Nod if you understand."

Téa nodded.

The door to her room was flush with the walls. It made a long beep noise followed by a loud click, then cracked open. A person of average height stepped inside. The soft lines of their face made them appear young and kind. They kept their red hair in a pixie cut, were slender and fit and wore loose fitting medical scrubs. Téa watched them approach and realized that they couldn't be much older than her.

"Téa, my name is Sawyer, I'm the physician here for Operation Luna."

"Where are my clothes? Why am I naked?" She said in a panic.

"My apologies." They said calmly. "You arrived covered in sweat, vomit, and you had soiled yourself."

Téa's eyes widened in horror, and she clutched the paper tighter, curving in on herself.

"Please do not be ashamed. The General is a cruel man. He should never have put you on a spacecraft without any training, or preparations. It is a wonder you survived the journey."

"How long have I been here?"

"Three days."

She tensed in surprise and worry. The last time she passed out, something was injected into her to eliminate her personal kill switch. What if they had done something else to her while she was unconscious?

"Téa, please slow your breathing. I promise you are safe here."

A desperate, incredulous laugh tumbled from Téa's mouth, and she almost screamed. "Safe? Safe? Is that a joke? Nowhere is safe. Haven't you figured it out yet? It never ends!"

"Téa, please, I do understand. The General may have us under surveillance, but we see even more than him. We did not violate you in any way. Here, I brought you some clean clothes."

They handed her a bundle of simple clothing.

"I will step out and allow you to dress."

They left her. Téa put the clothes on swiftly then paced. She was not sure if she should stay in the room, then remembered. She was powerful now. She peeked her head out, and they were waiting for her.

Embarrassment flooded through Téa from being caught trying to sneak away. Sawyer smiled at her quietly.

Téa's cheeks flushed. "I'm sorry."

Sawyer laughed, "It's quite alright." They smiled, "You don't need worry here, Téa. I promise."

Téa scoffed, "You'll understand that I need to figure that out for myself."

Sawyer raised their hands in surrender, "Fair enough." They said and smiled. Then they said, "If you'll follow me, I'll show you around."

As they walked Téa couldn't help but stare at Sawyer, trying to figure them out.

Sawyer had their hands clasped behind them and laughed, "Do you have something you'd like to ask me?"

Téa hesitated, then said. "Forgive me, but, um..." She trailed off, unsure if she should ask.

Sawyer chuckled, "How do I identify?" They tilted their head, and smiled.

Téa quietly nodded with a sheepish grin.

Sawyer took a deep breath. "I was assigned male at birth, but my heart and my head were born female. Thankfully there were doctors here on Luna that helped me align my body with my heart. Of course, with the General's laws, that would not have been possible on Earth." She smiled.

"Can I call you 'she'?"

Sawyer laughed, "Yes. I prefer the pronoun she, but you may also call me by my name."

"Right, of course, I'm sorry."

"No need to apologize. This generation is just now becoming open and free, at one with who they're meant to be. People have found themselves in my situation for centuries, but it is only recently that we have been able to speak our truths."

The impossibility of freedom twisted Téa's face into one of denial.

*Free? Nothing in my world has ever been free. I've felt like a prisoner my whole life.*

Téa's heart sunk, she pressed her hand to her face, willing herself not to cry. When she raised her eyes she saw, Zephyr. The air left her lungs and her heart pounded in her chest. He was walking straight to her. She whispered so only she could hear. "Zephyr?"

The man smiled and introduced himself. "Hello, Téa. I've been looking forward to meeting you. I'm Ian and I'll be your co-tour guide!" He radiated joy.

Téa sank to her knees, heart breaking all over again. Sawyer and Ian rushed to her side and helped her to stand back up.

Sawyer asked, "Are you okay?" Téa couldn't answer. Sawyer said kindly, "Let's get you some water, and maybe some food. Ian, help me get her to the kitchens."

Téa had trouble focusing, the few surroundings she took in all seemed the same. White. Hallways, doors, large open rooms. When they got to the kitchen, she finally saw some color. Green, red, and yellow. There were miniature gardens in every corner of the kitchen. There were fresh herbs she guessed, and saw a basket of apples, and another of bananas.

"Ian. Grab her some water, will you? Here, Téa, eat this." Sawyer handed her a banana. "Potassium will help."

Téa peeled the yellow flesh from the fruit, its aroma filled the air. Téa gratefully devoured it, suddenly feeling the intense hunger of a body that had gone days without eating.

"There. Better, right?" Sawyer smiled. Téa nodded gratefully.

Ian filled a cup with water, and Sawyer guided her to a table where they sat together. Sawyer handed Téa a second banana and Ian passed her the glass of water. They waited until she had finished her last bite.

Ian patted her knee gently just like Zephyr would have done. It was all too much. Fresh, hot and salty tears streamed down her face and throat. Sawyer and Ian sat with her, letting her work through her emotions and Sawyer wiped Téa's tears, nose and face, loving and tender.

With a full belly and another drink of water, Téa welcomed a semblance of calm. For a reason she didn't fully understand, she felt that the pair of them would listen to her without them needing to say a thing. "Ian, I don't know if you are aware, but you had an identical twin brother. Same gray eyes, same hair somewhere in between blonde and brown, same angular and strong face, same smile, same body language."

Téa had to stop to take a breath to hold back more tears that wanted to overflow. "He was the only human who ever genuinely cared for me, and I for him. The man who called himself your father, the General, murdered him." Téa clenched her teeth and shuddered before continuing. It was hard to get the words out. "Without an ounce of hesitation. The General thought Zephyr was no longer needed, and he just sliced the life right out of him, in front of me."

They sat in the silence of emotion until Sawyer and Ian both had misted eyes. Ian stood up and turned away, his body heaving with silent sobs. Sawyer pulled Téa into a side hug and cleared her throat. "Well, you're here now and we're going to take the General down together. He will never be able to hurt you again."

Ian turned back around and spoke softly, "I had a brother?" His voice had a catch in it as he asked, "Did Zephyr... know about me?"

Téa's lip trembled; her chin quivered. She wished she had told Zephyr when they had walked through the forest after leaving the Sanctuary. She shook her head. "No".

Ian nodded his head. "Will you tell me about him, someday, when you're ready?"

"Yes." She knew the words wouldn't come out now, but the thought of talking about him, of keeping his memory alive, filled her with hope and the possibility of being healed someday.

The three gravitated back towards one another, embracing in a group hug. Sawyer broke apart first, "Shall we show you around?"

Téa only wanted to huddle in a ball and hide, but she knew the General was still looming in the distance back on Earth, waiting. A realization struck her. She had just touched Ian, hugged him, cried with him, and nothing. No connection or feeling like when her Connex-B gene had activated.

He was not her soulmate.

Fear gripped her by the jugular. What would the General do when he figured it out? Would he let them all blow up?

Sawyer and Ian were walking away to finish their tour. Téa panicked, she grabbed Ian by the hand, pulled him to her lips, and kissed him as passionately as she could. He did not shove her away, but he also did not respond to her.

Téa pulled away, faked a smile, and whispered to him, "The General is watching, he needs to think we are in love or this whole place will blow."

Ian laughed. He actually laughed. "Téa, we know of the kill switch. We bypassed it years ago. Of course, the General doesn't know that, but now if he forgets to enter his passcode every three days, or simply chooses not to, the only thing that will blow up is an old-fashioned alarm clock. Also, you can speak freely. He can't hear us, only watch. I'm sure he makes up his own words with whatever he hopes we are saying."

"No...No, no, no, no!" Téa stood stiff with shock. "It was all for NOTHING!" She shrieked in anger, pounding her fists on the counter. "The only reason I came here was to save all of YOU! To keep him from *blowing you all up*. I had a chance to kill him and didn't. He could be *dead* right now. Rotting in the ground for all the things he has done!"

Ian cautiously stepped close to her and patted her back, his voice so kind, so much like Zephyrs'. "I'm so sorry. Even if we had known, there would have been no way to intervene quickly enough. Perhaps with more time, the first Generation could have delivered a message to you. But Téa, you did the right thing, you chose good over evil. Life over death. That is all that matters anymore, that we all as one people start making right choices."

Téa was not in the mood to hear 'how right' she was. The General needed to die, and she had her chance.

She stormed out of the kitchen past Ian and Sawyer. Not knowing where to go, she went down hallways, turning one way, and then the next.

That is when she saw it. A silver strand with a glittering band around the neck of a stranger. She followed it around a corner. Her necklace. Her one and only possession, her only constant. She was furious, betrayed by these people. She reached for the woman's arm, and forced her around to look at her.

# Chapter Thirty-One

# Space Station Luna

The reaction was instantaneous. This was not a sexual reaction, not a passionate reaction, there was no desire. This was more, something pure, and unconditional. Something that could never be broken by a lover's quarrel. This was absolute love. This was Téa's soulmate. She felt it in her whole being.

They saw each other with more than their eyes. It was as though they could see each other with their hearts. Sad when the other was sad. Happy when the other was happy. Unsettled when the other had a nightmare. Every long-forgotten memory that they had of one another came flooding back.

*Téa sitting on her mother's lap, two years old, as her mother sat in a rocking chair, nursing and singing baby Annabelle to sleep.*

*Three-year-old Téa holding one-year-old Annabelle's hand as she learned how to walk, their father cheering them on in the background.*

*Four-year-old Téa and two-year-old Annabelle standing on step stools watching their mother heat olive oil in a pan. "See girls. This is the best way to make toast. Just slice the bread, wait until the oil is hot and popping, place your bread in the pan, count to thirty, then flip, and count to thirty again."*

*Four-year-old Téa and two-year-old Annabelle on bicycles with training wheels, helmets too large for their little heads, peddling and shrieking with joy, and their parents running behind them laughing and beaming with pride. "Go! Go! Go! You got it girls!"*

*Five-year-old Téa, and three-year-old Annabelle, seated at a long grand table, Sandstone dining hall. "Téa dear, you dip your roast in the Au Gus. Just like this, darling. Yes, well done."*

*Téa and Annabelle, in the backseat of a fine car, their mother and father on the seat next to them, smiling at one another, holding hands. A blinding light. A loud horn. Crunching metal. Glass shards flying as the vehicle rolled again and again. The General's boots walking up to the destruction, their parents screaming, pleading. Two gunshots. "Gather the children, one comes back to base, one gets sent to Luna." The General walking away. Hands reaching in, grabbing, child screams. Hue Hillside. "No need to be so rough, soldier.*

Let me take it from here." Hue gently removing layered silver necklaces from their deceased mother. Removing their parents' wedding bands, placing each one on a chain, and putting one necklace around each girl. Hue whispering, "he only truly needs one of you right? Maybe I can save one. Soldier! This one here goes to the space station. Send the other to Jefferson home for girls."

That was the last memory they shared together. The visions stopped.

Hue had tried to save Téa her whole life.

The girls finally looked at each other with clear eyes. Understanding, love, family. They held one another and cried tears of joy, never wanting to let go of her sister, her soulmate, ever again.

# Chapter Thirty-Two

# Space Station Luna

Téa and Annabelle sat next to each other on an examination table. Sawyer gently tucked a strand of Annabelle's long dark hair behind her ear. Annabelle blushed.

Sawyer looked at them both. "Your Connex-A genes are confirmed active, ladies. Abilities can be unpredictable with the soulmate gene, so do try not to blow us all up." Sawyer winked at Annabelle and then talked to Téa. "And, of course, you, being the first and only person ever to have both Connex-A and Connex-B, we especially do not know how your abilities will develop."

Sawyer grasped Téa's hands and looked at her intently. "Please, be careful with your emotions." Sawyer stepped back, removing her blue medical gloves, and dropped them in a bin. "Téa, I'll let you get reacquainted with your sister. Annabelle, I'll see you at home." Sawyer kissed Annabelle on the lips, smiled then left the room.

It was quiet for a minute before Téa said, "Wow, so you and Sawyer... I'm happy for you. She has a kind energy."

Annabelle blushed again. "It's pretty new. She knows I'm not ready for anything serious. I'm only eighteen and she's a solid three years older, and we don't actually live together, she just says, 'Mi Casa es su Casa' and I guess I do have a few things at her place. Toothbrush, hair comb..." She paused and looked at Téa. "I'm rambling."

Téa smiled at her sisters' happiness, but tilted her head and asked, "Isn't twenty-one a little young to be a doctor?"

Annabelle grinned and looked down, "Not really. We start our apprenticeships at fifteen up here." She looked back up excitedly, "I'm a gardener!" Annabelle beamed with pride. "What about you? Anyone special back on Earth?" Annabelle immediately regretted the question. She knew what Téa had endured on base, and it hadn't been too long since she had disappeared from Steppe Two, there was no way she had 'met someone special' so quickly.

But Annabelle was still surprised when Téa stiffened and she shook her head. Then Annabelle felt the wave of grief and heartbreak travel from Téa to Annabelle. Annabelle doubled over. "Oh sister, I'm so sorry. Oh my God. This hurts." Quiet tears streamed down her cheeks for her sisters' pain, and she held Téa close, smoothing her hair.

After a few minutes, Annabelle stood and pulled Téa up. "I want to show you something."

They walked along the white corridors with clear floors. Téa had never seen such a thing. Watching the machinery work below their feet, keeping the space station working smoothly, was fascinating to Téa. Annabelle had her arm around Téa's waist, leaning her head against Téa's shoulder as they walked.

"You know, I thought you stole my necklace." Téa laughed. "I didn't even stop to check if I still had mine on. I was overwhelmed with... everything. I was ready to pulverize you."

"Geez. Thanks, sis." Annabelle rolled her eyes playfully and gave Téa a soft shove. "We're here."

Annabelle spun Téa around to face the stars. Téa's jaw dropped. In front of them was an immense expanse of glass wall twice their height, and it curved outward, so that a person could walk out onto the glass as though they were floating in space. Téa walked towards the un-ending un-known. Completely surrounded in blackness, the scattered stars as far as her eyes could see, twinkled. She looked to the right and gasped. From their position, the moon and the earth looked to be the same size. It was a splendor Téa could never have imagined in a million years.

"Beautiful, isn't it?" Annabelle joined Téa on the glass and reveled in the moment with her. "It's my favorite spot on the whole ship."

They stayed for a while longer, admiring the beauty and secrets of the universe. Then Annabelle pulled on Téa. "Come on, let me show you around."

The girls walked arm in arm, and Annabelle did most of the talking. It turns out, all things considered, she had a good life. The space station had their own food supply. Everyone had designated responsibilities. They played board games, and did other ordinary things, like date and raise families. The community thrived, but Téa sensed that Annabelle was holding something back, that Luna wasn't as perfect as it seemed.

Annabelle told Téa everything. "When Operation Luna first started," she said. "Dunamis recruited the best and the brightest of their time. The best and brightest then outsmarted Dunamis. When the General took over and he demanded constant surveillance, the scientists and engineers came together and built pieces of the ship that would not be under constant watch.

"When they learned of his kill switch, they easily bypassed it. The General sends his goonies every few months to search the place and threaten to rough us up, but they're all dumber than a box of rocks." Annabelle laughed at her own joke. "I heard that in a movie once. We have a pretty good selection of old movies up here." She smiled.

"The tech geeks even managed to hack into the surveillance at Steppe Two." Annabelle continued. "It has a one-week delay, but still, we see his every move, mostly. And the best part... we discovered his deepest fear." Téa's head jerked toward Annabelle, who had a gleam in her eye and spring in her step. "He's scared of traveling through space. That's why he has never come here himself."

Téa doubted that there was anything the General was afraid of. "He's never set foot on Space Station Luna?" Téa asked. "How long have your scientists watched the General? Do they know why the General killed Zephyr's and Ian's mother?"

Annabelle shifted uncomfortably and her sister's unease bubbled in Téa's belly. "Wait, what do you mean, Zephyr and Ian's mother?" Annabelle asked.

"Did you not know?" Téa turned to look at Annabelle, concern creasing her sisters' brow.

Annabelle shook her head.

"Yeah," Téa said. "The General abducted their mother when she was trying to steal supplies from a Dunamis facility. She was already pregnant with the twins–"

"Wait, twins? Ian has a *twin* brother?" Annabelle asked.

"Had. Ian had a twin brother. Zephyr, he was the man I fell in love with after leaving Steppe Two. The General killed him–" Téa gulped, "and sent me here."

Téa felt Annabelle's heartache. "Does Ian know?" Annabelle asked.

Téa nodded. "Yes, he just found out. Well, about the brother and General part, it was a pretty short conversation. I'm sorry, Annabelle. Are you and Ian close?"

Annabelle nodded, but Téa didn't need to hear her answer. When Téa talked about Ian, she could feel Annabelle's bond with him.

"I'm sorry for his loss." Téa gently squeezed Annabelle's shoulder. "He's lucky to have you." Téa said.

Annabelle stopped in her tracks, sending waves of guilt and grief into Téa. "No. I'm the one who's sorry. I watched you all the time. I would sneak into the surveillance room. I could never do anything to help you, and you were so alone.

When you left Sandstone, we also lost communication from the resistance. I was worried sick. I had no idea where the General would send you, but here you are! And I am so happy you're here."

Téa froze in fear. "The Sanctuary didn't tell you I was gone? You haven't had any contact from them?"

Annabelle hesitated. "No. I don't think so anyway. I'm not exactly *allowed* in surveillance and the first generation hasn't filled me in on recent happenings. Why, does it matter?"

Téa stared at her with wide eyes. "We can't trust them. The General knows the Resistance was planning to sneak onto a cargo ship headed here. But if the General manages to kill them when they try to come here, the Resistance will send another wave, I'm sure of it, there's no lengths they will not go to in order to win the war."

Annabelle seemed surprised. "Wait, what do you mean the Resistance was planning on coming here?"

Téa's anger tried to bubble to the surface again but she pushed it back down. "They were planning a giant synchronized attack to blow up Dunamis food storage all around the North American continent, while a second group was going to blow up Luna. They hope it'll force Dunamis to work on healing the planet."

Annabelle paled. "They're going to sabotage the space station?"

Annabelle's fear, her betrayal, and her disgust, which morphed back to fear, touched Téa and she asked, "Annabelle what's going on? Did you all not know?"

"No."

Téa's protectiveness over Annabelle had her rattling with rage against the Resistance. The Space Station shook slightly from the effect of Téa's power.

Then an overwhelming calm came when Annabelle placed a hand on Téa's chest. "Téa, you need to relax. You can't lose control up here. Your powers. We don't know enough yet."

Téa took deep breaths, clenched her fists, and forced herself to calm down. Then Téa felt Annabelle's urge to run and asked. "Where do we need to go?"

Annabelle looked to Téa, determined. "We need to call a meeting. Promises be damned. Professor Trombol will understand."

Téa was thoroughly confused but followed Annabelle. Téa kept expecting someone in charge to step up, for Annabelle to search out a person of authority, but she never did. They came upon a speaker box attached to a wall where four different pathways intersected. Annabelle pressed a red button, and a speaker crackled to life overhead, Annabelle's voice boomed all around them. "Urgent meeting. Ten minutes. Community rec room. I repeat, urgent meeting, ten minutes."

Téa found Annabelle's spirit and fearlessness liberating.

The whole community, at least three hundred people, gathered in a large recreation room. Annabelle explained to Téa as people filed into the room, that this space was one of the places the General didn't have eyes. Although, he was probably suspicious at the sudden disappearance of all the inhabitants from his screens, if he was watching. They usually reserved community meetings for when it would be middle of the night in the General's time zone.

Annabelle addressed the crowd, projecting a calm and gentle presence. She did not stand at the head of the room, but rather, she sat on the floor in the middle of everyone. She kept her voice steady and soft, but loud enough for everyone to hear.

"I'm sure you have all heard by now, this is Téa from Earth. She has told me some disturbing information."

An older woman with short white hair hurried into the room and gave Annabelle a warning glance. But Annabelle continued. "Before I say what I'm going to say, I want you all to know that I trust you to maintain your emotions. I trust you all to be able to handle the information I am about to share with you. It is imperative that you all remain calm."

Téa saw that there was definite confusion around the room, but also curiosity and nodding and Annabelle seemed to have everyone's full attention as she spoke.

"The General has not been implementing our research. The poison seeping into the Earth is still spreading."

There was a quiet murmur that traveled through the room as Annabelle said. "I know this is a shock, but please remember to remain calm, I have more to say."

"There is a resistance on Earth that is determined to fight back against the General. However, I have just learned that they also have plans to infiltrate the space station and sabotage it."

The older woman in the back who had looked at Annabelle warningly, suddenly sat in a chair heavily, shock spread across her face.

Annabelle continued, "I know this is a lot to take in, but please, remember how important it is to maintain control of our emotions, now more than ever."

Annabelle was quiet and suddenly so many voices spoke at once, talking over one another. No, not over. With. Everyone spoke with each other, and never escalated from a peaceful discussion. Not a single person lost their temper. Not a single one pulled rank or doubted whether the other was 'sound' enough to have an opinion. No one doubted Annabelle or where she got her information from. No one accused her of being emotionally unstable because she was a woman. Not a single person shrugged her away as if they were just tolerating her presence or doubted her intelligence because she was young or because her skin was not white.

When everyone had their say, the overall consensus was that they would be ready for any resistance arrival. They all spoke and listened to each other. No one voted or suggested one human voice did not count. They all communicated until everyone was comfortable enough with a resolution.

When all dispersed after the meeting, and went back to performing their individual responsibilities, the older woman with white hair approached Annabelle and said, "That was a bold move, Annabelle. You realize the risk you just took?"

"I do, Professor Trombol." Annabelle said. "But I was right. I told you, the truth is always the right answer. Sometimes you have to trust that people will do the right thing."

Professor Trombol nodded, "Careful, Annabelle. Being lucky one time does not equal a sound hypothesis."

"Yes, Professor." Annabelle responded.

When the Professor walked away, Annabelle looped her arm through Téa's again and grinned as though it were any ordinary day. "We have a few hours to kill," she said, "let's get you set up in a room. You can bunk with me!" Annabelle smiled like the sun, she radiated joy and warmth. "I'll tell Sawyer after dinner that I'm staying in my room tonight. She'll understand. I want to spend time with my sister."

# Chapter Thirty-Three

## Space Station Luna

W hen they arrived inside her room Annabelle said, "So before we get you settled, I have something I need to do."

Téa nodded, she felt Annabelle's need to go. "Is it Ian? He's important to you?"

Annabelle replied, "He's been like my only family all these years, I need to check on him."

Téa nodded, "I understand, I'll rest awhile. I'm pretty drained anyway. Being unconscious for a few days really sucks the energy out of a person." She said wryly.

Annabelle laughed, "Thanks sis, I'll be back soon."

After one last smile at her sister, hesitant to leave, Annabelle shut the door, and then hurried towards Ian's room.

Her mind raced. Ian just found out that he had a brother, and that the General is his father. She couldn't even imagine how he must be feeling. She had to get to him. Annabelle's fast walk increased to a full-blown run. But after a few concerned looks on other people's faces, she realized she might be creating a panic and forced herself to slow down. Finally, she arrived at his door.

Annabelle knocked and Ian immediately opened the door. His eyes were bloodshot and snot rimmed his nose. "Belle." He said.

Without sparing another second Annabelle wrapped herself around his torso. He dropped his head onto hers and she held on tight while his sobs rocked their bodies.

When his breathing finally slowed, Annabelle said. "Ian, I'm so sorry."

He pulled away and wiped his nose on his sleeve. Annabelle found a clean washcloth on his nightstand and handed it to him. He took it and blew his nose as they both sat down on his bed.

After a few minutes of silence, Ian finally talked. "So, I heard about the rec room meeting. Bold move, Annabelle. Smart not to mention the Connex genes though, ya know, one revelation at a time."

He let out a soft chuckle, and Annabelle's relief at hearing that small sound from him was overwhelming. *He's going to be okay.*

"You have a sister." He smiled, then said, "I'm happy for you, Belle. Really."

Annabelle leaned against him, "Thanks, Ian." She sat back up and asked, "So what are your plans for tomorrow?"

"Yes, Annabelle, I'll cover for you, bond with your sister."

Annabelle tilted her head at him and widened her eyes as a smile played on the corner of her lips. "Actually, Ian, I was going to ask, if you would be the one to spend the day with her tomorrow?"

Ian sat in stunned silence as Annabelle smiled, then said. "I think it would make me especially happy if my siblings got to know each other."

Annabelle watched as Ian grinned and his wet eyes lit up, "I'd be honored, Belle."

They wrapped their arms around each other and sat in quiet laughter together before Ian finally said, "What would I do without you, Belle?"

"Surely, you'd perish!" She said playfully and nudged his shoulder. "Are you going to be okay?"

"Yeah, I'm good. Go. Get to know your sister, she seems really great, a little heartbroken, but great."

"Thanks, Ian. See you later?"

"Yeah, later." He smiled.

As Annabelle headed towards the door, she paused before leaving and turned back around. "Hey, Ian?"

"Yeah, Belle?"

"I love you."

She had never seen such happiness crease his eyes, it warmed her heart more than ever.

"I love you too, Belle. Good night."

"Night, Ian."

Annabelle practically skipped back to her room. Sure, there were big things to deal with, but for tonight, and at least one day, the big problems could wait. For now, she was going to have a family, and enjoy every moment of it.

# Chapter Thirty-Four

# Space Station Luna

Annabelle and Téa struggled to pull in a second twin size mattress to her room, which they had snagged from an oversized supply closet, huffing and puffing and giggling the whole way. Another shove and it finally burst through Annabelle's doorway. They fell onto it, laughing and breathing heavily. Annabelle's smile was so radiant Téa could swear pure sunshine poured straight through her.

After she caught her breath, Téa asked, "Hey Anna? How is everyone so peaceful? The community meeting, I mean, there was no yelling. It didn't seem real."

Annabelle was pensive before she replied. "Do you know about the poison killing Earth?"

"I know that Earth is dying, that people debate about the cause, but what does that have to do with what just happened?"

Annabelle leaned up onto her side, held Téa's hands, and looked her in the eyes. "Everything." Téa was quiet as her sister took a deep breath and continued. "The destruction of Earth has been centuries in the making. Nation after nation failed to come together and put their selfish desires for power and control aside for the benefit of the world."

Téa noticed that as Annabelle spoke, her words sounded memorized. As though it were something all Luna civilians are taught as standard history. It surprised Téa that such transparency would be taught anywhere.

Annabelle continued. "Inflated egos of Men, convinced they knew best, forced policies and practices that further depleted natural resources. They refused to listen to those who knew how to stop the ruination of Mother Earth. Unnecessary wars were an ugly constant to maintain supremacy."

Annabelle's eyes glistened and her breath shuddered, "The scientists up here discovered early on that humans can literally poison the Earth through negative emotions. Anger, fear, sadness. It was not only the people poisoning their own food, or only Dunamis either. It was everyone. Their evil hate, disgust, terror, and disappointments. Everything negative seeps out of our pores like an invisible gas and pollutes the world."

Annabelle gripped Téa's hands tighter as they lay next to each other, and she smiled through her tears. "But, we can also heal it. We can love each other, accept each other, give way to our stubborn ideals, and just allow everyone to be how they want to be, feel how they want to feel. We can literally make things grow through positivity. Everyone has the ability; it is ingrained in us. The Connex genes may be rare, and they may give us superhuman powers, but no one needs a Connex gene to effect the world around them."

Téa sat up and looked at Annabelle. "I made a yellow tulip grow once, I thought I was crazy. Zephyr and I were in his garden back at Sandstone. It was the first time that I realized I might have feelings for him. I felt so content at that moment, and then I saw it. The tulip was actively growing, I watched it out of the corner of my eye but shrugged it off."

A realization dawned on Téa. "Annabelle, so we know that the General is aware of the natural poisoning. I think I understand now, he never went into the gardens, and he refuses to come here, and Steppe Two, it's on the edge of a desert sector. That man is only made of poison. He doesn't have an ounce of kindness in him. He's not scared of space; he's scared of destroying the lifeboat for mankind."

Annabelle's tension touched Téa. Her sister sat up straighter, a tremble in her voice. "That's not good Téa. What if the General decides he no longer sees the space station as an asset? What if he decides he'll just let the world die with him?"

Téa stood, her fists clenching at her sides. "Belle, I have to get back to Earth. I have to kill him."

Téa could feel Annabelle sending calming waves as she scooted closer to her sister and reached for Téa's hand.

"Killing is never the answer, Téa. Haven't you been listening? We have to love each other. Everyone."

Téa yanked her hand away. "I could never love that man. You weren't there. You haven't seen what he can do."

Annabelle crossed her arms. "Oh, haven't I? You have no idea what I've seen." Her voice shook, "I've been watching him for years, Téa, and I had the same memory you did of him killing our parents." A sob escaped her lips, "I had to watch the way you had to live back on base."

Téa had a moment of guilt and sadness for her sister. But her hatred for the General built back up and she raised her arms and shouted. "It's not the same, Belle! You haven't seen someone you love get brutally killed right in front of you." She glared, "And the abuse! What about all those boys with the Connex-B gene that he experimented on. That he's *still* experimenting on?"

Annabelle sent more calming waves. "Téa, you can't lower yourself to his level. The actual fate of the planet, of this space station, depends on it."

Téa finally loosened her tension. "And what if he decides to send his troops here? Or worse, comes himself?"

Annabelle embraced Téa and said gently. "We'll just have to hope that doesn't happen. All we have to do is wait. Live our lives up here in the stars, away from all the hate. When the time is right, go back to Earth, and start healing the planet."

Téa pulled back to look at Annabelle. "So that's the plan? Do nothing? Let the resistance and the General destroy each other, then swoop in to pick up the pieces?"

Annabelle rubbed Téa's arms. "Yes sister. Sometimes the hardest thing to do is nothing. Come on," Annabelle jumped up as gracefully as a ballerina, shining her radiant smile, "getting that mattress in here took forever, I think it's dinner time already."

Téa was resigned to her sister's will, if only for now. She could not let go that easily.

The entire community ate together. Everyone shared and laughed, taking turns serving each other a smorgasbord of various fruits, veggies, and pastas. Lovers fed each other. Children ran under foot having mini food fights. The happiness seeped into Téa's bones.

Téa watched from afar as Anabelle caressed Sawyer's cheek. They held each other close, whispering sweet nothings, fingers intertwined, and then they shared a kiss goodnight. Annabelle practically danced back to her seat next to

Téa, and it warmed her heart almost more than she could bear.

Afterwards, the sisters stayed up all night chatting like schoolgirls, catching up on lost time. Annabelle had so many wonderful memories to share of her time growing up in space. The whole community had helped to raise her. Taking turns sleeping in her room as she worked through her toddler nightmares. Teaching and supporting her. Showing her how to grow the crops with more than just her gleeful goodness.

Téa, in return did not have many happy memories to share, unless she counted the times on Steppe Two that she didn't get caught stealing, and her moments with Zephyr, which were still too painful to talk about. So instead, she and Annabelle created fantasy stories of a healed world where they grew up together with their parents. First dates, prom, high school graduation, their parents twentieth wedding anniversary, bringing home new pets, and sneaking out for parties.

Before they were too tired to keep their eyes open, they took one last walk together down to the observation deck, blankets wrapped around their shoulders, stepping into the glass, hovering through space as they tried to name the stars.

The next morning after breakfast, Annabelle told her that she had a lot to catch up on in the gardens, and that Sawyer was meeting her for lunch for a little afternoon delight–'If ya know what I mean, wink wink'–but not to worry, Ian was going to spend the day with her.

Téa forced a smile as Annabelle left and tried to control her unease. The idea of seeing Ian again, the stranger who had Zephyr's face, was not how she wanted to spend her morning. She shook off her nerves and headed to the recreation room where Annabelle told her Ian would be meeting her.

He sat at a table, putting together a puzzle. The box was old and frayed, and said it had 1,000 pieces, with a picture of a river full of pink salmon with beautiful cliffs in the background on the front cover.

"Hey, need some help with that?" Téa tried to hide the quiver in her voice.

He turned to smile at her. "Yes, please, it's a doozy."

They sat together quietly, putting together the pieces. When the puzzle was over halfway done, Ian asked, "How are you doing, Téa?"

"Honestly, trying not to look at you."

He looked at her with hurt in his eyes and scooted an inch further away.

She realized how harsh that sounded and rephrased. "I'm sorry, I didn't mean it like that. It's just, looking at you, it's so much like looking at Zephyr. You even wear your hair the same, long up top faded to a buzz around the neck." Téa gazed into the distance. "It's funny. We hadn't even been in each other's lives for a full month. Not even a full lunar cycle, but he felt like everything. Like my life hadn't even started before I met him. He deserved so much more time than what he got."

"I'm so sorry. Truly. I wish I could have met him." Ian dropped his head. Téa, knowing now how important her own sister was, imagined that Ian hurt for the brother he would never know.

"I'm sorry, too," Téa said. "He would have been thrilled to know about you. The thought never crossed either of our minds, of having a sibling somewhere out there. Down on Earth, the people are still only allowed one child, but he craved family. We talked about it, about starting a family together."

Ian smiled at her. "Thank you for sitting with me."

"Anytime. So, tell me, what do you usually do around here?"

Ian shrugged and said, "I'm kind of like a 'Jack of all trades'. I assist Sawyer when she needs an extra hand. I help out in the nursery when someone needs a day off or comes down with sickness. I help to jar the extra produce. Basically, whatever extra help is needed," He paused and pointed at himself with his thumbs, "I'm your guy." He said proudly with a grin across his face.

Téa laughed and they continued to work on the puzzle together, Ian doing most of the talking until Téa asked him. "So, is there anyone *special* in your life?" She smiled and nudged him.

He laughed, "No, I don't have a significant other. I haven't found that special someone yet."

Téa nodded, "I see. So do you usually spend your time alone putting together puzzles?"

Ian chuckled again. "No, I *don't usually sit and put together puzzles*," he said sarcastically with a laugh. "I actually prefer working out in the gym."

Téa looked away and said quietly, "Well, that's another thing you had in common with your brother."

Ian's smile dropped and they sat quietly together until the puzzle was done. After a while Téa's stomach grumbled audibly.

She laughed in embarrassment and Ian looked at the clock. "Wow, I guess it is time for lunch already." He smiled. "Shall we?" He asked.

Téa returned the grin and said, "Absolutely."

They were close to the kitchens when someone ran towards them. "I've been sent to find you!" The young man was out of breath, he grabbed his knees and shouted. "They're here! The General's men. They came back for her! They're searching the living quarters."

# CHAPTER THIRTY-FIVE

# Space Station Luna

Annabelle had her spark back. Meeting her sister, finding her soulmate, spreading the truth to the rest of Luna, everything had come together. The weight on her shoulders vanished. Yes, the General still loomed in the background, and *maybe* they needed to find a way back to Earth, but she was no longer alone. She had everyone behind her, supporting her.

They had hope.

She literally skipped through her day as if her feet couldn't help but dance. Singing to her plants, she noticed an instant improvement in their color. The realization hit her, she controlled their growth, *that* was her ability.

She could make things grow. Joy blossomed in her chest and she twirled around the greenhouse, sprouting colorful flowers as she went.

Out of breath and cheeks hurting from smiling she lay down on the floor, laughing to herself. She couldn't wait to tell Sawyer, and counted down the minutes until her watch finally landed on the right numbers.

Annabelle stretched out her naked body against Sawyer's soft bedspread and sighed contently. "Ah, a girl could get used to this." She giggled and turned to snuggle against Sawyer.

Sawyer grinned and nuzzled her nose, "You and me both."

Suddenly alert, a commotion from the hallway drifted to their ears.

Sawyer's eyes went wide and her face pale, "Annabelle, that doesn't sound right, get dressed, hurry." She said urgently.

Annabelle hopped off the bed and tugged her white t-shirt on. She grabbed her pants next and just as she was buttoning the last button on her jeans, Sawyers door exploded open.

Debris scattered across the room and they were slammed against the back wall from the impact. Annabelle's head rang and her vision blurred. She placed a palm against her temple and tried to stop the ringing, trying to focus.

A man.

A gun.

Sawyer's split lip. Blood.

The man raised his weapon and aimed it at Sawyer.

NO.

Annabelle screamed, eyes focused on the man, a thick green vine shot from her hand. It wrapped around the man's gun, and his arm. She pulled hard, with all her new strength, and flung the man sideways, cracking his head on the ground.

A second man charged into the room, and Annabelle shrieked again.

She focused on the man, willing things to grow and squirm inside him. Within seconds, plant leaves sprouted from his mouth, choking him, he dropped his gun and clawed fruitlessly at his neck until tiny stems sprouted from his eyeballs and he collapsed.

Annabelle was having a hard time staying upright. Her breathing came in ragged and the pounding in her head intensified. Her vision blurred again, she heard Sawyer whimper and when Annabelle spun to look at her, she heard, but wasn't able to see the third soldier when he entered the room.

A flash.

A bang.

A cry.

# Chapter Thirty-Six

## Space Station Luna

Ian and Téa sprinted through the halls. Téa's mouth had gone dry.

Suddenly an invisible force hit her. So strong that she fell to her knees. *Sister.* The waves of Annabelle's fear, her pain, slammed into Téa and her heart beat so fast that she thought it might shatter.

The emotions faded and Téa picked herself up and kept running, following Ian to Sawyer's apartment, there was no longer a door and she ran inside. When she rounded the corner to the bedroom, she broke apart into a million little pieces.

Before her, were half a dozen soldiers tearing up the room. Téa's whole body tensed when one of them slapped Sawyer so hard across the cheek that the force flung her against the wall and brought blood to her mouth. Sawyer didn't fight back, she crumpled to the floor as though she had lost the will to live. That's when Téa's eyes were drawn to the other corner. Another soldier was being congratulated for a job well done, and taking pictures with his smartwatch of Annabelle's dead body.

They hadn't noticed Téa yet, when another guard said, "Fucking women. Breaking the law like this, got what she deserved."

Téa did shatter then. She shattered everything. She unleashed her powers, felt every atom, reached for every living thing on the space station. She knew, in this moment, she was close to becoming a God.

Locating each civilian on Space Station Luna simultaneously with her mind, not herself, not Annabelles body, and not the soldiers, only the innocent's. She transported them, in an instant back to Earth. Just a blink was all it took. She envisioned them on Luna, then on Earth, and made it happen.

Left with only the soldiers and the body of her sister, Téa, with electricity surging through her veins, power, and adrenaline in every cell. Arms stiff, she swung her hands out and forward with a thunderous clap, she sent a shock wave all around her, knocking the soldiers off their feet. An ear-splitting scream, guttural with force, came from somewhere deep within her, ringing off every surface.

The men on the floor screamed, tearing at their heads with useless claws, blood poured out of every orifice, their eyes, nose, mouth, ears. Some had started to cry.

Just as suddenly as it started, it stopped. Quiet echoed through the room. Lifeless bodies unmoving, a metallic scent hung heavy in the air. In a span of seconds, she killed them all with the sheer force of her mind. She looked at her hands and was not afraid. She was strong, drunk on the power of it all.

Téa trembled and shook as she slowly walked to her sisters' lifeless form. She closed her sisters' eyes and carefully lifted her silver necklace with the wedding band, and put it around her own neck where the matching one lay.

She raised her head and closed her own eyes, then focused on the body. It hovered a few inches off the ground, and she enclosed Annabelle in a luminescent bubble. A complete, earth-like supply of gasses, nutrients, and water filled the bubble. Green plants and colorful flowers grew around her body, covering her from head to toe until only her once warm face was visible. Then she preserved her. The bubble transformed into a clear shell. She would remain exactly as she looked now. Peaceful, beautiful, covered in perfect tulips, daisies, roses, and carnations. She teleported Annabelle to Earth in the blink of an eye, her final resting place would be on a cliff overlooking the ocean, Cape Perpetua in Oregon, just as Zephyr had described it.

Téa enclosed herself inside a similar luminescent bubble, made of things yet to be discovered by Man, able to withstand the ravages of Space. She brought her fists together pressing one against the other. Slowly, she pulled her fists apart, straining with effort, a deep groan awoke in the belly of the ship. Metal crunched, plastic splintered, glass shattered. She was destroying Space Station Luna. Piece by piece, the great thing came apart and flung away, speeding into the darkness. In less than a half hour, it was annihilated.

Next, she hovered just outside of Earth. She crushed satellites, taking only moments to send her adversaries on Earth into the dark ages, canceling out the drone navigation and controls for nuclear bombs.

Téa, suspended in grief, took in the astounding wonder of space. Breathing deep inside her bubble, she welcomed the nothingness, her body draining with the immense effort of staying alive inside the luminescent ball. She closed her eyes and focused on traveling to the inhabitants of the space station that she had sent to Earth.

When she opened her eyes, she was back on the surface of Earth. Soil beneath her feet. She saw the fear and terror in the civilians eyes. Most hadn't even known the General's men were on board, then suddenly they were surrounded by the wasteland of the inhabitable midland of North America. The one place left on the planet no one traveled.

She focused her energy and kneeled, then placed her hand on the dirt. She could feel the crust, mantle, and magma flowing beneath them. She pulled. Found water where there should be none. Found the seeds of life and brought them forth. She grew a forest, trees that had fruit, and created waterfalls. She encased ten square miles in a camouflaged dome. Even if she had not destroyed the satellites, no one would be able to find them.

For the first time ever, the people from the space station breathed in real air. Oxygen that had not been recycled, felt the spring of the grass under their feet. Téa had created an entire sustainable ecosystem under a giant clear dome.

Depleted and heartbroken, she collapsed.

# Chapter Thirty-Seven

## Earth

**Two Days Later**

The days after Luna passed her by in fog. Téa hardly moved. She'd slept, would get up to empty her bowels, drink the water from coconut cups that Ian would force into her hands, then sleep some more. She didn't eat and tried desperately not to think. To force Annabelle's face away from the back of her eyelids. It hurt too much to look at. Yet her sister's image insisted on making itself present in her mind. Her laugh, her smile, her joy.

Téa curled in on herself, laying on her side on the forest floor beneath a grouping of trees. Ian tried to talk to her, but she shut him out, squeezing her head between her arms to block the sound of his words from reaching her ears.

Time no longer had any meaning.

*Life* no longer had meaning.

She slept again.

"Téa!"

"Téa!"

"Téa!"

Ian shook her awake.

Téa groaned, angry, and swatted at the air. "Ugh...whaa aat do you *want*?"

Ian backed away, terror eating his whole face.

Téa felt bad for scaring him. But she also felt nothing, and everything. It was as though she had a million-degree sunburn, yet still there was ice in her veins. Then there was her heart. Oh God, her heart. Someone was tearing at it, cracking it in half with a knife.

"I'm sorry Téa, but we're all a little out of sorts here." He stopped and swallowed hard, as if he were fighting back his own tears of grief. Téa remembered how strong Annabelle's emotions were for him.

"Ian-" She didn't know what to say. She watched the muscles in his jaw jump as though he was clenching his teeth.

He didn't wait for the words she didn't have. Instead, he said, "You gave us a beautiful little oasis... but there is no shelter, no tools to build a shelter. No medical equipment. I explained to the community that the General's men had come. I saw..." He swallowed hard again, and this time Téa saw the mist in his eyes before he continued. "I saw what they did to Annabelle. I told them you were only saving us, but Téa, everyone is scared, and we can't stay here. Especially Sawyer, she needs a hospital."

Téa's pain begged her to pull Ian down with her and cry together. But the unfairness of it all, of such a beautiful soul being taken from them brought her anger back in full force.

She laughed in disbelief. "Out of sorts? You all are a little out of sorts?" Her voice rose steadily to a shout. "I'm out of my goddamn mind! I can feel it, Ian." She stood and paced as she continued to yell. "Annabelle's dead. She wasn't just my *sister*; she was my *soulmate*. I can feel my power ebbing away. I still have work to do."

The thought struck her then, so clear, so obvious. "I need to kill the General. Florence, too."

It was apparent that Ian was trying to remain calm as he spoke softly. "Téa, do you really think that is what Annabelle would have wanted?"

Téa turned her furious face to him. "No. I think Annabelle would have wanted to be *alive*."

Her words seemed to have shocked him silent. She could not feel remorse in this moment, her heart was turning black from pain and the cruelty of life, Téa would not collapse in defeat again.

Ian took a breath, then pleaded with her, "Téa, sit with me."

She crossed her arms, but seeing the hurt in his eyes, she relented and sat. He leaned over Téa where she had landed on the ground. He scooted closer to her, pulled his legs up, crossed them at the ankles, then rested his arms on his knees.

"I know you are in an impossible situation," he said. "I can't begin to imagine what you are feeling. But if what you say is true, about your powers fading. We need to get out of here. Somewhere safe, with the necessities the community needs. Please, Téa. Will you help us?"

The anger in her chest bubbled and guided her thinking. Téa knew the Sanctuary had everything they would need. She could start her revenge there. She centered herself, cleared her mind of everything around her, only focused on the living breathing souls inside her self-made forest, then... blink.

They were there.

Every space station civilian was now standing within the Sanctuary boundary, grouped together... and chaos surrounded them.

They had entered into an active war zone.

The General's soldiers tore apart the Sanctuary burrows, the walkways overhead blazed. Debris fell from the sky, knocking Phillip and his wife Mia, the jam and jelly maker, to the ground. Torrence, the blacksmith, jumped on the back of a soldier who was kicking his husband Seth, who was curled up on the ground, crying. Louis screamed when a bullet tore through his wife as they ran away. Children cried, the sound wafted through thick black smoke.

Acting on instinct, Téa enclosed the Luna civilians inside a protective dome before any of them could get hurt. Outside the dome, Téa radiated strength and stood firm, feet planted on the ground, arms straight out to her sides, and focused.

*All the destruction must stop.* She thought it over, and over, and over again. *Stop the killing.*

Dirt, rocks, and planks on fire all around her shook, then levitated around her. She willed all her strength into a single focal point.

Time froze.

Everyone not in the protective dome was frozen in time.

Bullets stopped in midair, licks of flame paused, humans stilled as if statues. Everyone and everything stopped.

Téa began to strategize in her head. If she removed the soldiers loyal to the General, they would simply return. Again, and again, they would come back. The civilians would never be safe. Annabelle had wanted Téa to choose love, to choose goodness. But she couldn't do that. No matter how badly she wanted to honor her sister's beliefs, she couldn't let evil go unpunished.

She would be their reaper.

Téa glanced down at her hands. The veins beneath her skin had turned black. Her gaze shifted to a piece of shattered glass on the ground, and she saw her eyes staring back at her. Only they weren't the familiar brown, they were filled in black, as though ink had spilled and settled there.

At the height of her power Téa's cells burned with effort, and she knew what must be done.

Téa walked through the Sanctuary, cremating every soldier, willing them into ash, into chunks of bone, and gray powder.

The man kicking Seth.

Poof.

The soldier who shot Tess.

Gone.

Inch by inch, foot by foot, she walked the boundary of the Sanctuary, eviscerating every evil being.

She found Dr. Anderson frozen and cowering behind a female nurse with a gun pointed to her head. She hesitated only a moment, thinking of Sawyer and her need for a doctor. But when Téa sensed Jessops' presence somewhere nearby, she hoped that Jessops' skills would be enough, that Dr. Anderson would no longer be needed.

Téa took her time with Anderson, tearing chunks off his body first before she turned each piece to ash. She hoped he could feel it in his preserved state, and then got rid of the soldier holding the gun.

Téa kept moving.

Florence, frozen like the others, was protecting Emma and Nora, her body covering them as best she could while the soldiers, frozen, with their weapons aimed at them. Téa destroyed the soldiers and spared the old hag.

Almost spent from the effort, she walked back to where the Luna civilians were watching from safely within their dome. Téa dropped the barrier and released time, then used the last bit of her energy to bring forth rain from the sky. She stretched her senses for every bit of precipitation in the air and doused the fire within the Sanctuary, washing away the dead.

Téa knelt on the ground, unfeeling, unmoving, shoulders hunched as the water pounded her back. No tears left to cry, so full of sorrow and loss it was hard to see a reason to keep living. She could feel her heartbeat slow, and Téa realized... she could, if she wanted to, just stop living.

She slowed her heart.

Slow, slow, slower...

Then hands, so many warm gentle hands touching her, sharing their warmth, their kindness, their gratitude and strength. Not a single one scared of her, only in awe and admiration. She had saved them all and they recognized it.

The rain stopped.

Little Nora wiggled from her mother's arms, plopped down, put her hands on the ground, raised her butt to the sky, and slowly, shakily, she took her first steps. She stumbled the two feet to Téa and put her arms out for a hug. Téa gasped, pulling oxygen back into her lungs as she forced her heart to beat back to a normal rhythm. Fresh tears found their way out of Téa, and she held onto the small girl, breathing in her innocence, her hope, her future. Within little Nora, the Luna civilians, and The Sanctuary, Téa found a reason to keep on living. She couldn't abandon them.

Téa stood, holding Nora, and passed her back to Emma, then looked to the crowd. "I don't know what we can salvage here. My powers are still active but depleted, and I won't be able to teleport us all to a new place. We will have to start over here, but I think I can send myself somewhere and bring back some camping gear to get us by."

Without waiting for an answer from them, Téa envisioned the garage at Sandstone, the place where she and Zephyr first began their escape from the iron grip of his not father.

Téa blinked, and she was there. She wobbled from the effort and put her arms out to steady herself. Staring at her arms, she noticed they had returned to normal. She looked around and found the biggest truck she could, she didn't want to leave them without transportation, assuming that the Vida Brigade had been destroyed as well. Téa began loading it with all the tents and sleeping bags that lined the far wall. It was not enough for everyone, but it would have to do.

Pausing before she was about to leave, Téa wondered if the General was at Steppe Two, or inside Sandstone? She needed more than this. Food and fresh water. She wondered if it might be safe to go inside. She imagined a majority of the General's subordinates had been sent to the Sanctuary. There could not be much security left, so if she did search through the estate, she'd probably get away with it.

She decided to risk it for the sake of all the people counting on her, and so Téa peeked out the front garage door. The sun had set and without the warmth, the desert was cold. Dark shadows crept across the sand. The wind whistling sounded like ghosts calling to her, begging her to join them on the other side of the veil.

She did not see anyone, but of course knew there wouldn't be much to see until she was closer to the castle. Moving as stealthily as she could, she made her way to the great stone structure. She didn't see any guard presence around the exterior. Inside the servant entrance it was quiet. Not a single noise. Not even the clinking and clanging of pots and pans from Angie and William who were typically moving around in the hot kitchen, could be heard.

Téa entered the oversized pantry and realized she would not be able to carry much. She thought about teleporting it all to the truck, but she was so tired, she had to save her strength to get back to the Sanctuary. She thought she might be able to find a dolly, or something else to help transport some supplies back and forth from the house to the garage. Turning around to leave, there he was.

The General.

"Fancy meeting you here." The General said as he swung an iron pan at her head and nailed her across the temple. Blood poured down into her eye blurring her vision.

Téa stumbled backward, but when she reached up to touch the wound, it closed underneath her fingertips. She had been so focused on the loss of her sister, and the slow depletion of her Connex-A abilities, she hadn't noticed that her Connex-B powers were at full strength. A smile played across her lips.

*You're dead*, she thought.

Just as the General was coming at her for another hit, she used her mind and yanked the metal pan from his hand. It hovered mid-air. Téa reveled in the look of terror that filled the General's eyes. She turned the pan so that the handle was aimed directly at his left eyeball. Faster than a bullet it impaled him, blood ran from below the pan handle, dripping down his front. He fell with a heavy thud.

General Thomas Strauss was dead.

# Chapter Thirty-Eight

# Earth

Téa sank to the ground, her back against the wall. She was exhausted, and his death was not as satisfying as she had hoped it would be. The hole in her heart was still there. Forever to be void of warmth and joy. Footsteps sounded from the kitchen.

Angie appeared and stopped in front of the pantry. She did not scream at the sight of the dead body, but calmly said, "Well, that son of bitch deserved that." She reached over the General's body for Téa's arm, "Come on honey, let me help you up."

Angie shut the pantry door, closing the body from view. She sat Téa down at the kitchen island and served her a cup of warm tea. Angie sat down next to her and blew on her own hot beverage.

After a moment of silence, Angie spoke. "We have a lot to talk about darling, do you think you're up for it?"

Téa stared at her without emotion, unable to say anything.

Angie nodded to herself; her hands wrapped around her warm cup. "Right, maybe now is not a good time. I assume killing a man takes a lot out of a person, forgive me, but you look absolutely exhausted sweetheart. How about we get you up to bed?"

Angie's words finally registered in Téa's mind. She turned to look at the older woman. "No. I mean, I can't there's people waiting for me. They need me."

"Who needs you sweetheart?" Angie asked as she placed a palm on Téa's arm.

Téa took a deep breath. "The General sent his men to a place called the Sanctuary, where the resistance lives. They destroyed it. The survivors are waiting for me to come back with supplies."

Angie nodded in understanding. "Ah, I see. And you think you can make that journey in your state?"

"I have to." Téa focused on Angie before saying, "I'm kind of a superhero now." She said letting out a soft mirthless laugh. "I can teleport what they need to them, and then come back."

Angie's eyes widened in surprise. "Woah."

"Yeah. Woah." Téa took a sip of her tea, letting it warm up her insides, and reality slowly came back to her. Then she asked, "Do you think you can help me load up some supplies? What you said, about me looking tired, it's truer than you know."

"Of course, darling, whatever you need."

The two women spent the next hour loading up as much as one truck could hold. Then when they were done, and without the looming threat of the General, Téa paused for a moment and realized she felt connected to Sandstone. Perhaps, because she had so few pleasant memories and most were made here, with Zephyr. So, she asked. "Do you think it's okay if I come back here after I bring this to the Sanctuary?"

"Absolutely, sweetheart. Afterall, Sandstone is yours now." Angie said with a kind smile.

Téa paused next to the truck, her hand hovered next to the door. "What do you mean by that?"

Angie had a twinkle in her eye, "We'll talk about that when you get back. Go on now, they're waiting for you."

Téa hesitated but opened the door and climbed into the truck, focused her energy, and blinked back to the Sanctuary.

With everyone helping, they quickly unloaded the supplies. All the while she could see the mixed reactions among the people surrounding her. Some appeared grateful, especially Emma who went out of her way to thank Téa, but most still seemed fearful of her. She did not feel like she belonged here.

Téa thought about her promise earlier to share everything she knew about Zephyr with Ian someday. She wondered if he might want to come with her, and if she was truthful, she didn't want to be alone in the giant castle. Bringing Ian felt a little bit like bringing Annabelle.

It didn't take long to find him. She grabbed his attention and said. "I'm headed back to Sandstone. That's where all these supplies came from, it's where your brother lived." She paused waiting for his reaction. When he didn't say anything, she continued. "Would you like to come back with me?"

Ian quietly stared at her. Finally, he said. "Yeah, I think that would be a good idea. Let me just talk to the others from Luna. Make sure they're good here."

When they got back to Sandstone, Angie was waiting for them in the kitchen. The space had a warm glow, safe from the cold night looking in at them from the window across the room.

"I see you've brought company." The older woman did not seem surprised to see Zephyr's twin. She wiped her hands on the apron around her waist and held her hand out for Ian to shake. "I'm Angie, and you must be Ian." She smiled.

Ian cleared his throat, "Um, yeah, yes, I'm Ian, nice to meet you."

Angie walked away towards the stove, steam rising, where she was cooking something that smelled divine. "Well, don't just stand there." She said, "Come grab a bowl. It's potato soup with bacon, chives, and cheese of course, and fresh homemade rolls."

Téa and Ian filled a bowl and sat next to each other at the kitchen island to eat. The soup was hearty and warm. It filled her belly in a way that she hadn't experienced for weeks. For the first time in a long time, she felt content, if only momentarily. It would take a lot more than a bowl of soup to warm the cracks of her heart. Téa's eyelids grew heavy in the hush of the night. Her arms tingled with fatigue. She teetered on the edge of the stool and Ian gently caught her.

The exertion she had put out finally caught up to her. She didn't think she could even stand on her own. Angie and Ian's voices were muffled around her. Suddenly, she was lifted. Ian carried her in his arms with Angie guiding him through the castle to Téa's room. He carefully placed her in bed, quietly backed out of the room, and Téa could scarcely hear the click of her door as it closed before she fell into a deep sleep.

Ever reliable, the sun called to Téa with its morning light, caressing her with its rays through the open curtains of her room. She resented the sun, that it tried so readily to invigorate her back to life. Téa's eyes cracked open, heavy, and crusty with dried tears. She slowly sat up and the room spun. She shuffled to the curtains and yanked them shut, then fell back into her bed clutching a pillow over her head. She retreated back into the warmth of her comforter, closed her eyes, wanting only to sleep away whatever years she had left to live.

She had fallen back asleep when a knock at the door woke Téa, and when she opened her eyes the light of day had already dimmed.

"Téa, honey, it's Angie. Can I come in?"

Téa tried to respond, but her voice came out hoarse and weak. Angie opened the door even though Téa had not answered, and gently placed a tray of food on her bedside table. Téa felt the bed dip from the weight of Angie sitting down next to her. Téa's muscles ached as she slowly sat up. She eyed the glass of water on the tray and greedily grabbed it.

Her throat was soothed as she gulped the cool liquid down. She wiped her mouth on her sleeve and set the empty glass back down. "Thanks."

Angie looked at her quietly before saying, "Sweetheart, Ian filled me in on some things. Take all the time you need, we'll talk later, okay?"

Words would not come, a single involuntary tear slipped down her cheek. Angie patted Téa's back, got up to leave, then closed the door behind her.

Téa forced herself to eat. After, her feet were heavy and dragged along the floor as she made her way to the bathroom. When she looked in the mirror it was a stranger staring back at her. Deep bruises under her eyes and curly hair frizzed and in knots. She pulled a twig from a stray lock and then the trembling started. Her legs shook and she collapsed to the floor, allowing the grief to consume her as she whimpered on the cool tile.

When her last sob left her, Téa picked herself up off the floor and drew herself a hot bath. As she washed away the dirt and the hurt, the thought crossed her mind that she'd like to stay locked in her room forever. But then, she remembered. There were people counting on her. The boys in the Connex experiments deserved their freedom, just as she deserved hers.

Once she was dressed, Téa looked again in the mirror. The sadness still hung heavy on her shoulders, but her determination to make what she could right in the world, drove her to keep moving forward.

Outside of her room, Téa glanced down the hall to Zephyr's door.

Cold.

Emptiness.

There were nothing but ghosts waiting for her that way. She brushed off a chill and headed towards the kitchen looking for Angie. When she arrived, she found not only the older woman, but also Ian, and Eleanor. The room quieted as though moments ago they were all speaking about her.

Téa tried to ease the tension by smiling and saying, "Hey, everyone. How's it going?"

When no one answered her, she asked. "What happened to the General's body?"

Angie spoke, "Ian and I drove him a few miles out, and buried him in a shallow unmarked grave. The wild will slowly eat him."

Téa nodded, "Probably better than he deserved." She hugged herself, and after another minute of silence, said. "What's going on?"

Angie walked over to Téa and gently put her hand on the small of her back to guide Téa to a stool at the kitchen island next to Ian. "Here, honey. Why don't you sit down? We have a lot to talk about."

Angie was about to sit down next to Téa when Eleanor placed a hand on the older woman's shoulder. "It's okay, Angie. I've got it."

Perplexity creased Téa's brow as Eleanor sat next to her.

Eleanor gently took hold of Téa's hand and looked her in the eyes. "Téa, how much do you remember of your childhood?"

Thinking of the unpleasantness of her upbringing at Steppe Two caused Téa to shy away. She slowly pulled her hands away from Eleanor's and clasped them together between her legs. "I don't remember much before Steppe Two. I have flashes from the orphanage, and when..." Her voice caught in her throat at the memory of the first soul-mate connection with Annabelle. "When I met Annabelle on the space station, I had a few memories of her and I together. One was our car accident. I think that's why I have such a hard time remembering. Looking back now, I'm pretty sure I had a really bad concussion that was never cared for at the orphanage."

Eleanor quietly listened on one side, and Ian gently patted her back from the other.

After a moment Eleanor said, "Téa. I am your paternal aunt, your father's sister."

Téa's eyes widened in surprise.

Eleanor's next words came out in a rush. "I wanted so badly to tell you before. But the General threatened your life if I ever let slip who I was." She took a deep breath before continuing. "You see, Sandstone estate belonged to your parents. Angie and William even worked for them before the General."

Angie's neck flushed from across the room and Téa wondered why. Perhaps a flame of emotion for Téa's parents?

Eleanor continued. "Your mother and father were both high up in Dunamis politics, your mother the highest, and they opposed the funding for Operation Luna. Hue Hillside…" Téa heard the catch in Eleanor's words and saw the glistening on the rims of her eyes. Eleanor cleared her throat and spoke again, "Hue was your father's best friend, and your godfather. After your mom vetoed funding, General Thomas Strauss had your parents killed, took over Sandstone estate, and your mother's position in Dunamis. Over time, General Strauss killed anyone who opposed him."

Eleanor's unshed tears finally fell, and her head drooped. But Téa was not mad at Eleanor's secret. Where there should be frustration at all the lies, there was only hope. A chance for family after everything she had been through. Téa smiled, fell into Eleanor's chest, and wrapped her arms around her aunt.

Eleanor laughed in surprise and squeezed her back.

# Chapter Thirty-Nine

## Earth

Téa teleported them just outside of Steppe Two. She flexed her fingers, feeling the power course through her body. The hot sand from the dead landscape around them shifted under her feet with each step. Tumbleweeds rolled around their ankles pushed by a hot breeze.

"Are you sure about this, Téa?" Ian asked from beside her. "We could give them a chance to do the right thing first?"

A mischievous smile curled her lips. "Where's the fun in that?" She paused, "Don't worry, brother. I won't kill anyone." She hesitated. "*Unnecessarily.*" She winked at him, then looked at the tall cement wall before her topped with barbed wire.

Téa reached with her powers, searching for the metal rebar within. She found it in her mind's eye and grabbed hold, then yanked forward. A thundering crack echoed through the air as the solid wall exploded sending debris flying all around them. Téa shielded Ian, who did not have healing powers like herself, from injury. When the dust settled Téa stalked forward, clothes torn and hair wild, a lioness ready to hunt down her prey.

Three soldiers rushed out screaming orders to open fire. Téa held up a hand and stopped the metal bullets in midair as though they were hitting an invisible wall and they dropped like dead flies to the dirt. The soldiers froze in shock as they watched their ammunition, their only sources of power, die.

Téa shouted, "Drop your weapons! I want to speak with the man in charge!"

One of the soldiers lifted a trembling hand to the radio strapped to his shoulder and made Téa's request. It only took minutes for a man in a suit to arrive. He was surrounded by a dozen armed guards that he cowardly hid behind.

Téa yelled at him. "I am Téa Garcia, daughter of former president of the United States, Isabel Garcia!" She stood tall and proud. "General Thomas Strauss is dead. I am here to demand that all Connex experiments cease, and the subjects are to be released *immediately*."

The man in the suit scoffed. "What makes you think you can start giving orders? Just because of who your mom was?"

Téa grinned, she hoped he would say that. Nearby in a row were five tanks. Téa turned to face them and focused. She looked for every metal bit, down to the nuts and bolts. It only took moments for her to grab hold of each and every one of the massive artilleries. She lifted the tanks with her mind five feet into the air, and in a flash, metal loudly groaned, and glass smashed as she squished the tanks like tin cans. She dropped the flattened armored combat vehicles with a sickening crash, and clouds of dirt puffed out around them.

She then turned back to the men and spoke loud and firm. "Drop your weapons, *now*."

All the soldiers, including the ones surrounding the man in the suit, trembled as they knelt down to drop their guns, and when they did so, Téa caught a full view of the man in the suit, the front of his pants was wet.

Téa strode up to him, menace in her voice. "Where are the Connex boys?"

The man whimpered and shook in his dress shoes, "They aren't here. They're all housed at Raven's Glade."

It took Téa a second to remember. She thought back to that first day with Zephyr, where their helicopter had landed just outside of the community with the fake gardens, where Zephyr had told her the principal members of society lived with their families. *How far did the General's lies spread? So many falsities. Where did the truth in this world disappear to?* It was no wonder that humans were poisoning the Earth. *We're all corrupt.*

The sadness in Téa that always lived on the edge, following her everywhere, threatened to bubble back up. She held her resolve to free the boys and glared at the man before her. "Very well. I'll need a team and helicopter to transport us there. But first I have a personal matter to attend to.

Where is the body of Zephyr Strauss buried? I'd like to bring him home for a proper burial."

The man stammered as his knees quaked. Téa glared at him, and finally he said. "I'm sorry ma'am. He was incinerated and his ashes were taken to the dump."

A flame of indignation ignited within her. She felt the burn start in her toes and travel up her body. She could no longer contain the frustration, and sadness fueled by hate. She screamed out an ear-splitting cry, and when there was no more air in her lungs, she took a deep breath and felt it. The man had a metal hip. She reached for it in her mind, grabbed hold, and flung him backwards as hard as she dared, remembering her promise to Ian, not to kill anyone.

Téa hunched down and wrapped her arms around her legs, allowing the sobs to take her. She felt Ian rubbing her back with soothing shushes. "Come on Téa, let's go."

She wiped the tears from her face and stood, allowing Ian to wrap her into a quick strong hug.

Raven's Glade was even more eerie than she remembered. Her skin crawled with unease as she, Ian, and the team of soldiers stealthily moved around the outside of the seemingly perfect row of residential houses.

Téa's hand hesitated as she reached to open the front door of the first house. She slowly and quietly turned the knob and pushed the door open. A pungent smell of body odor assaulted her nose. She walked inside the dark house and the day disappeared behind her. Slight streams of sunlight filtered in through partially open curtained windows, enough to see around the room.

A musty scent emanated from wet moldy towels strewn about the living room floor. To her left was the kitchen where the fridge door was left ajar and empty. Depleted plastic bottles and empty cans littered the countertops.

Room by room they searched, finding no one living inside, until only the basement remained. The door to downstairs was padlocked. Téa easily manipulated it off, and it clattered to the floor. Each bare wooden step creaked as they made their way down. At the bottom stair Téa stepped off and heard a splash. There was a half inch of water stretching from wall to darkened wall. It seemed as though the house flooded on a regular basis, and no one bothered to repair it. The stench of sewage made her gag and hold her sleeve over her mouth and nose.

Something moved in the corner sending small ripples across the water. "Who's there?" Téa said.

No one answered but Téa heard a small whimper coming from the far corner. Ian clicked on a flashlight behind her and aimed it into the corner of the room. There sat a small boy, wearing nothing but an oversized stained white t-shirt, sitting on a soiled mattress. His collarbone jutted out, his cheeks were sunken, and there were heavy metal shackles around his neck. He shied away from the light shining in his eyes, and tried to hide his face behind his thin arm.

Nausea rolled in Téa's stomach and tears sprang to her eyes, but she pushed back her own emotion to be strong for the boy. She moved slowly and spoke softly, "Hey there, we're not going to hurt you. I'm Téa, what's your name?"

The boy did not answer and tried harder to hide into the corner of the brick wall. Téa, as carefully as she could, released the metal chain holding him. The boy jumped in shock when the heavy metal clanked as it fell. His eyes were squeezed shut tight and his little body trembled.

Téa moved closer to him inch by inch. She slowly removed the jacket she was wearing and said softly, "I'd like to help you. Here." She reached her jacket out towards the boy, but he did not move. Téa cautiously and gently touched the boy's shoulder, and he went slack against her touch as he kept his eyes shut. *He's used to obeying.*

Téa sucked in air, swallowed the lump in her throat, and ground her teeth to force back her tears. The boy did not fight as Téa wrapped him in her jacket and scooped him up into her arms.

Outside she carefully sat him inside one of the black SUV's and checked in with the rest of the teams. They found a dozen boys total, varying in age from five to seventeen years old, but not a single adult.

*Someone must have tipped them off.*

When Téa learned that Raven's Glade was only one of many Connex residences, her heart shattered again and again. She didn't know if she had anything left in her chest to break. Téa vowed to do everything in her power to hunt down the offenders and make them pay for their horrendous crimes. She raised her head to the sky and took a deep breath, wishing more than anything that Zephyr was by her side.

"Come on, sis. Let's get these boys home." Ian said.

She fired all of the previous staff at the Jefferson Home for Girls and Boys. They removed all the bars from the windows and rooms. They filled the place with creature comforts like books, art, and music supplies. All of the people who were locked up due to the Worldwide Re-population Act were released without stipulation, but many offered to help out at the orphanages. They were quite possibly the best people for the job, knowing themselves what a life of imprisonment felt like. They could help the boys begin to heal.

Many of the older boys offered to join Téa and Ian on their expedition across the continent to teach the population how to grow their own food. There was healing in creating life. It was the next step in freeing the people from the control of Dunamis.

There were occasional, but minimal, outbursts from people loyal to Dunamis. But a majority of the soldiers only enlisted because they had no other options. Most were happy to follow Téa.

Without satellites for efficient communication, Ian traveled with Téa from town to town, liberating the people by informing them of Dunamis's demise. It was slow progress, but the boys from the Connex-B experiments, especially, found it beneficial. Téa could see the boys' hearts being stitched back together through the happiness that shone out through their eyes as they taught people how to garden. They also took groups of soldiers with them to each town, but instead of weapons, they now carried seeds, and shovels, showing the many communities how to grow their own food.

Ian had originally estimated it would take close to a year to reach every place within the North American continent. Towns that were close to one another could pass on word, saving them some time, but they were pleasantly surprised when they reached the Western Resistance, where California had once been.

The Western Resistance had radio transceivers to communicate with other resistance groups. Florence had told them that long distance communication without the use of satellites still existed, and that the Sanctuary had some, but theirs were destroyed in the battle with the General's men. The Western Resistance had extra to share, so they would be able to bring communication back to Sandstone and the Northern Resistance.

After that, only two months into their mission, Téa and Ian sent out groups of soldiers in their stead with supplies to all the major hubs, and instructions on what to do. Their mission was complete. They could finally go home.

# Chapter Forty

## Earth

"So, what now, sis?" Ian asked her as they sat together eating breakfast in the grand Sandstone dining hall.

Téa swallowed her drink of orange juice and wiped her mouth on a napkin. "I think I just want to do nothing for a while."

Ian was quiet and Téa knew from his body language that he wanted to say something. "Ian, come on. Just spit it out. What's up?"

He pushed back from the table leaning in his chair and tapping a foot on the floor. "I feel like I need to go back to the Sanctuary. I'm not sure why. I just feel like it's where I'm supposed to be." He relaxed and shrugged his shoulders, "Besides, Florence is my grandmother and Ted is my uncle, and I wouldn't mind getting to know his kids and his wife. It wouldn't be the worst thing to get to know my family."

Téa's heart ached at the idea of Ian leaving. She had let a majority of the staff go back to their own lives, and the idea of her, Eleanor, Angie, and William, rattling around the giant castle seemed lonely. But she did not want to hold Ian back. If he felt like he needed to leave, then she would let him go without guilt.

She smiled and reached for his arm, giving it a gentle pat. "If that's what you feel like you want to do, then I support your decision." Téa shot him a serious look, "But I don't trust Florence, and you shouldn't either. Be careful. And I insist on regular visits. I'll miss you."

Ian stood up and wrapped her in a big bear hug, swaying her side to side. "I'll miss you too."

Téa heard knocking on the bathroom door, Eleanor's voice drifted through. "Téa, darling, are you okay?"

She tried to answer her aunt, but another wave of nausea threatened to rise within her. She moaned in discomfort and Eleanor opened the door.

"Sweetheart, this is the fifth day in a row that you've spent your mornings on the bathroom floor. All you can eat is saltines, and you don't have a fever." She paused, tapped a foot and crossed her arms. "You need to go see a doctor. The closest one is at Steppe Two."

Téa shouted in alarm. "No! I will never step foot back in that place. Dunamis is mostly doing fine on their own now, and I can handle anything they need by radio." Téa dragged a hand down her face and shook her head, "I'm not going back there, Auntie."

Eleanor took a deep breath, relaxed her arms, and crouched down next to Téa. "Well then, I'm having a doctor brought here. End of discussion."

With that, Eleanor left Téa cradling the porcelain god.

Sawyer was a welcome surprise. She walked with a cane, a slight limp to her step. The soldiers had broken her right leg so badly that it was mostly held together by screws now. Otherwise, she was just as Téa remembered. Pretty, her red pixie-cut hair was a little longer now, and her clothes were a little looser than before, but overall a familiar and comforting sight.

"Sawyer..." Téa was at a loss for words. She hadn't seen her since the battle, and she suddenly felt guilty for not reaching out sooner, for not checking in on her. A wave of emotion struck Téa right in the heart and suddenly her words were trapped behind a lump in her throat. She swallowed multiple times then tried to speak again.

"Sawyer, I'm sorry, I should have..." Her throat closed tight and her jaw clenched with the effort of fighting back tears.

Sawyer took a step forward, carefully leaned her cane against the wall, and slowly sat on the bed next to her. "I'm sorry too."

Téa heard a hiccup next to her and looked over to see Sawyer's face glistening from the sun reflecting off her tears. "I should have protected her."

That did it. Those words opened the flood gates and Téa's tears were flowing. "No. I should have. It's not your fault, Sawyer. There's nothing you could have done to stop what happened."

Sawyer shuddered, her breath came out shakily. "It's not your fault either, I hope you know that."

Téa could only nod and bite at her cheeks. She finally after a few moments of silence said. "I'm so sorry I didn't reach out to you. I just didn't know what to say."

Sawyer flashed her a small grin, tilting her head to the side. "What would there have been to say?"

Téa was quiet. Sawyer patted Téa's knee, then said. "Well, enough tears, hmm? Let's figure out what's going on with you."

Téa smiled gratefully and nodded her head.

"Why don't you tell me what's going on?" Sawyer said.

Téa replied, "I'm sick all the time. I mean nauseous. I can't keep food down in the morning and barely anything throughout the day. I have terrible headaches, so intense I'm in bed most days." Téa hesitated, a flush of embarrassment flooded her cheeks. "My boobs are tender too." She said quietly.

Sawyer narrowed her eyes and glanced at Téa. She cleared her throat and then asked. "When was your last period?"

Surprised by the question, Téa didn't know. The doctors at Steppe Two controlled everything about her body for as long as she could remember. Her periods were random and spotty, it wasn't something she had a lot of time to worry about when she was always on edge, protecting herself from the men on base.

"Um, I really don't know," Téa replied.

Sawyer took a deep breath before asking, "How many sexual partners have you had."

A pinch of sadness and longing clipped at Téa's heart at the memory of Zephyr inside her. Of his soft and warm caress that she would never feel again. She looked away and said, "Only one, and only one time."

Sawyer spoke quietly, "And how long ago was that?"

Téa had to think hard. So much had happened in such a short amount of time. "Um, I'm not sure exactly about three, maybe four months ago, I think."

"Do you think you can give me a urine sample?"

Téa nodded in reply. Sawyer got up and lifted a large black bag onto the bed. She rummaged around inside until she found what she was looking for and handed Téa a clear plastic cup.

Téa was sixteen weeks pregnant.

After the intense shock wore off, Téa cried tears of joy, so overwhelmed with the knowledge that a little piece of Zephyr would go on living. She marveled at everything she had survived in the span of only less than a year. Now she was being rewarded. She would have a family after all. She did not feel worthy of this blessing, the little piece of sunshine, a gift to begin healing her heart.

Eleanor was as doting as any mother. Waiting on Téa all hours of the day, drawing warm baths, and giving her niece foot rubs. Finding ways to make every food craving happen.

Téa's mood swings were intense. She still craved her sister's presence and wished for just one more moment with Zephyr. But the growing force in her belly was powerful, too. It kept her wanting to live. The pain in her heart eased just a little each day. Téa felt herself more in tune with her body then she had ever been before. She caressed her growing bump, smiled, and cried at every flutter, every swirl, punch, kick, and jab.

As her due date approached, Téa knew the baby inside her would be born with powers of its own. The strength and the electric hum within her increased every month. The birth sucked almost every ounce of Connex-A power Téa had left, but she would have given her life for this beautiful child, her and Zephyr's daughter, Celia.

Celia was indeed born with powers, the next stage of the human race. She did not have a Connex gene that needed to be activated. The power was in her, a steady force of will. Celia's birth was not only a gift to Téa, but to the whole world, forever to be cherished. The infant was able to draw out poison from the Earth and vaporize it to nothingness, just by being nearby. It happened naturally, and at birth extended to a ten-mile radius, with the possibility for growth as she got older.

When Celia was born, Sandstone Estate returned to its former glory. Beautiful gardens surrounded the luxurious castle. Téa planted a weeping willow next to Zephyr's empty resting place, as a memorial for him.

Ian sent word that he would be coming to Sandstone to visit his new niece, and he would be bringing the rest of his new family. Ian had found his soulmate after all, in Emma, and loved little Nora as if she were his own.

When the beautiful little family arrived, they all went out back. Téa cradled Celia. Emma glowed with happiness, her face and body filled out, and she caressed her own growing belly. This baby, Nora's soon to be half-sister, was completely made from the consensual love between Emma and Ian.

The women left Ian alone for a moment, Téa glancing back for a second to see Ian kneeling beside the marble headstone and heard him ask for just one moment with his brother, and one last chat with Annabelle. Téa vowed that Annabelle and Zephyr's legacy, and memory would continue; their daughter would know that her aunt and her father loved her.

And they would have. Téa felt it in the stars.

Without Dunamis control, people started loving who they wanted to love; soulmates who had not been eliminated gravitated towards each other. With less anger, hate, and violence, the Earth began to heal, one layer at a time. Celia's birth sucked a majority of the toxic decay away, giving humanity a fresh start, but the people would have to choose goodness in order to keep healing the planet.

There was just one question that remained... How far would we let the poison spread this time?

# Epilogue Earth

Forty-six weeks ago, when commander Hue Hillside had tasked Scott with placing the book, 'Supernatural Abilities in an Evolving Generation', in Sandstone Estate library, it was the first task he had ever been assigned by The Resistance. His nerves were a wreck as he thought about the task at hand. *What if the General found out? What would happen to him? How would he make sure that Téa found the book?*

Shortly after being assigned his task, Téa approached him in the kitchen. Scott took it as a sign from God. He put on his best acting face and suggested she explore the library. He even offered to take her there himself. He smiled, pleased with the thought that his first mission would be a success, and his confidence to fight Dunamis stealthily from the inside grew.

"Hey, Scott, did you hear?" Scott's bunkmate charged in the room full of adrenaline, a sick smile on his face. "They caught one of those bastard traitors! Hue Hillside, they're interrogating him now."

Scott's stomach turned at the thought of Hillside enduring the full wrath of the General. He snuck down to the lower level where prisoners were kept, but there were double the number of guards. Scott could hear Hillside's painful scream echo down the hall, and guilt tore at him as he backed away. News traveled quickly of Hillside's death, and fear gripped at Scott's insides. He was terrified that it was only a matter of time until he was found out to be a traitor to Dunamis as well.

Scott's anxiety tumbled out of control; his thoughts raced. Commander Hillside was his contact within the resistance, he didn't know what to do now. Who else inside of Steppe Two knew he was a spy for the resistance? Telecommunication had gone down, and even if he could contact someone inside the resistance, he wouldn't know how, or who to talk to anyway. So, he bided his time. Did his duties at Steppe Two and kept his head down.

Scott walked with his shoulders hunched towards the mess hall when he was suddenly stopped by a loud and powerful voice.

"You there!"

Scott looked up. It was the General addressing him. Scott's blood ran cold.

"Come with me. My pathetic traitor of a Son has finally come to his senses and turned himself in, you will accompany me to retrieve him." The General shouted.

Panic flooded through Scott, but he did as he was told.

When they arrived on the scene Téa was there with Zephyr. The General had Scott and another guard place black bags over their heads and handcuff them before getting on the helicopter. Their flight arrived back at Steppe two and when they landed, the General ordered Scott and the other guard to follow him. The other guard had hold of Zephyr and shoved him in a closed room. Then the General posted Scott outside the door of the labs, while the General interrogated Téa.

Scott debated on blowing cover and charging in to stop the General. The waiting was brutal and just when Scott decided to burst in and save Téa, the door opened and he was ordered to retrieve Zephyr.

When Scott opened Zephyr's cell door, the other soldier was in there beating him. Scott wanted to run at the other guard, but he wasn't sure it was the time to fight back, there was so much he didn't know, so Scott cleared his throat and said. "The General ordered me to bring Zephyr to him." Acting on instinct, he added. "He also said you're dismissed." Scott wasn't sure why he added that last bit in, maybe he wanted to be alone in the long corridor, or maybe it was the way the other guard disgusted him. The way so many of the soldiers enjoyed the torture of innocent people made his skin crawl. His heart raced at the lie, wondering if this was the thing that would get him caught.

The other guard shrugged. "Probably won't have anything left to guard when the General is through with him." He said through a wicked grin, wiping blood off his hands as he said. "I'm gonna get some chow, bout dinner time."

Scott breathed a sigh of relief when the other guard walked away. Guilt tore at him when Zephyr let out a moan of pain, he wanted to get Zephyr out of Steppe Two, but there was no way they'd make it. Reluctantly, he heaved Zephyr to the General. Scott was as careful as he could be, but Zephyr was heavy, thick with muscle and Scott was what some would consider scrawny. He didn't mean to, but he lost his hold and dropped Zephyr at the General's feet. Guilt spread through him like a fire as he closed the door and waited in the hallway. Minutes passed, then a scream so loud and inhuman, the sound of metal crunching and the General demanding to be released, which Scott realized meant the General was the one in danger, no longer Téa. His heart pumped rapidly, protocol would be to rush in and protect the General, but he hated that man, so he held steadfastly outside the door.

It was seconds when Téa exited the labs ahead of the General, Scott stood to attention and held his place at the door as the General ordered him to take Zephyr's body to the incinerator. Scott saluted as the General and Téa walked away, and then went into the lab. He saw Zephyr's body on the ground, unmoving and throat bloody. He raced to Zephyr's side hopeful for a chance that he was still alive.

Scott held two fingers against Zephyr's limp wrist and found a pulse, faint, but there.

Hope and urgency surged through him as Scott grabbed under Zephyr's arms and heaved his body to the medical wing. When he arrived, he shoved the doors open and shouted, "This soldier has been injured, we need help now!"

The solitary doctor in medical jumped in surprise. "Oh my lord, is that the General's son?

Scott shouted, "Yes, now help me!"

The doctor shook his head, "No. Zephyr is a traitor. I will not go against the General, I won't risk my family."

Scott, breathing heavily from the effort of still holding onto Zephyr's body with one arm, used his other to raise his handgun and aim it at the doctor, "I said, we need help now." His voice was more solid and intimidating than he could have ever guessed he had the strength to project.

The doctor froze, eyes wide, "Okay, don't shoot, help me get him on the table, grab two bags of O negative blood from that fridge over there!"

The doctor worked on Zephyr for hours. He said it was a shallow cut that had not hit any major veins, the blood loss was messy but minimal, Zephyr was lucky; maybe the General was hesitant as he cut his Son's throat. The biggest problem was that it appeared he had been suffocated. They would not know the extent of any possible brain damage until Zephyr was awake.

When the doctor finished helping Zephyr as best he could, his voice shook in terror as he said, "I cannot be found defying the General. You have to move him to a town hospital outside of the military base. Now. And do not mention my name."

Scott's mind raced. He knew the doctor was right, it wasn't safe to keep Zephyr here.

*How am I going to do this?*

He didn't have his own vehicle; gas was hard to come by for people who were not in places of power. Excitement took hold when he thought of the perfect solution.

He talked a fellow soldier into letting him onto a supply truck headed to a local town. From there Scott lied about who he was and got Zephyr admitted in the town hospital under a fake name. The nurse who helped him said the patient's outcome was unpredictable considering how long he had been unconscious, but they would do everything they could for him.

When Scott got back to Steppe Two, he had to cover his tracks. His first stop was having the doctor write a death certificate and a crematory order. When the General arrived back at base and asked Scott about the whereabouts of Zephyr's cremains, Scott handed over the records and informed the General that he had been thrown in the dump.

The General seemed pleased. "Well-done soldier, glad I don't have to deal with that ungrateful little brat anymore, dismissed." The General walked away, and Scott breathed a sigh of relief.

*He had gotten away with it.*

When news of the General's defeat reached Steppe Two, Scott celebrated the downfall of such an evil dictator. But there were still handfuls of Soldiers who were loyal to Dunamis, and when Scott cheered and clinked glasses of beer with his comrades, one of the Dunamis loyalists shot Scott in the head, killing him instantly.

The secret of Zephyr died with him.